ABANDONED AND UNSEEN

TWO BRANDED PACKS ROMANCES

CARRIE ANN RYAN

ALEXANDRA IVY

Abandoned and Unseen
A Branded Packs Novel
By: Alexandra Ivy and Carrie Ann Ryan
ISBN: 978-1-943123-04-9
© 2015 Alexandra Ivy and Carrie Ann Ryan

For more information from Alexandra Ivy, join her MAILING LIST.
For more information, please join Carrie Ann Ryan's MAILING LIST.
To interact with Carrie Ann Ryan, you can join her FAN CLUB.

ABANDONED AND UNSEEN

Abandoned

When bear shifter, Anya Tucker fell in love with the wrong man, the only thing she left with was a broken heart—and her two bear cubs. Now she's mended her wounds and learned that in order to raise her babies she can only trust herself. When her sons meet the lazy cat next door and fall heads over tails for him, she'll do whatever she takes to protect them—even from a past she'd thought she'd left behind.

Cole McDermott is a jaguar on a mission. Long naps, a willing woman, and a full stomach is usually all he needs when it comes to relaxing after a long day of protecting his Pack. Then he meets Anya and the burn of temptation is silky and tantalizing indeed. When a horror from Anya's past threatens everything she loves, Cole will put everything aside and fight for her family—as well as his own.

Unseen

Nicole Bradley had no reason to live after the humans murdered her son. Not until she learns to hunt down those responsible for his death. Shifting into her wolf form at night, she slips out of the compound, determined to do as much damage as possible. The last thing she expected was to discover secrets that could destroy the SAU.

Polar shifter, Tucker Stone, lives off the grid. It's the only way the Unseen can avoid being rounded up by the humans and tossed into a compound. Besides, he's a loner by nature. But he can't walk away when he sees the pretty female wolf in danger. Risking exposure, he takes her to his hidden den and tries to heal her wounds.

Can a reclusive polar bear and a wolf with a death wish find happiness together?

ABANDONED

A branch cracked under the soft pad of a paw, but Cole McDermott didn't twitch his ears at the sound. The wind brushed his fur, the scent of predator and home wrapping around him. He kept perfectly still from his perch in the tree beside his house. He didn't want those tracking him to know he'd heard their loud trek through the forest. In fact, he'd heard them long before they'd mistakenly stepped on a fallen branch. These two needed lessons on how to properly hunt their prey.

That, however, was not Cole's job.

Normally, as a Tracker, he would have been the one hunting. Today, however, he was the prey. And as the prey, he'd do his best to stay still so the hunters wouldn't know he'd caught on to them. To lie in wait would allow those who hunted him to fall into a false sense of security. His father had taught him that long ago.

He was currently sprawled out on a low branch, close enough to the ground that he'd be able to land easily if he fell. Of course, he was a cat, so he always landed on his feet. And since he was in his jaguar form, he'd be in even better shape if he fell. Of course, he hadn't fallen out of a tree since he was a cub, so the point was moot anyway.

The hunters came closer, their steps becoming tentative even as they grew louder. He flicked his tail, once, twice. The hunters froze, their bodies pressing closer to the ground. Cole may have had his eyes closed, but he could still hear the underbrush pressed close to the hunters' tender bellies.

Cole yawned, his mouth stretching wide, his fangs gleaming in the sunlight that filtered through the trees.

See? Harmless cat here. Just sleeping the day away. Easy prey.

If only these hunters knew the truth. But again, he wouldn't be the one to teach them such darkness. They didn't need to know that behind the yawn, the stretch, was a predator in its own right. They would soon find out.

But not today.

The two hunters came closer, and Cole forced himself not to move. It wouldn't do to alert them that their prey was well and truly awake.

When one of them batted at his tail, Cole held back his smile. Well, as much of a smile as he could, considering he was in his jaguar form at the moment. The other one went to his twins' side and batted as well, each of them letting out a tiny growl when Cole curled his tail up, making it harder for the two bear cubs to attack.

Cole swished his tail back and forth, enjoying the way the two cubs rolled around in their bear form, chasing each other when they weren't jumping at him. These two hunters needed to learn a few things about tracking, but they'd learn it from their family eventually. He just enjoyed hearing them sound happy, innocent. If they'd been in human form, he was sure the two would have been laughing.

There wasn't much to laugh at these days in the compound.

He let the two play for a bit longer, not even bothering to open his eyes. They weren't climbing the tree to get him so they'd be safe. Bear cubs could climb for sure, but they were still in the learning stages at their age. He thought they were about four, but he wasn't sure. He hadn't actually spoken to them. Instead, he'd stayed in cat form each time they'd snuck their way to his tree over the past two weeks.

Cole didn't bother worrying or getting angry about two bear cubs encroaching on his territory. He had other things to worry about, and something like this was minimal. In fact, he'd rather just lie in the tree and conserve his energy for the cage and ritual fighting he'd be partaking in a bit later. That always got his adrenaline up. It also kept the Packs happy since all three species were now forced to live in one compound thanks to the humans who thought they could control what they didn't understand.

Plus, as Tracker, he could be called upon to protect his Pack at any moment. He had the best sense of smell of the entire Feline section, and he was pretty sure he could out-track even the bears and wolves he was forced to live with. So, if someone were coming at them within the compound —or, even outside the den walls since he could jump pretty darn high—he'd be able to find out who it was and take care of it before someone got hurt. That was his duty to his Alpha, and he was damn glad to do it.

Other than that and the fighting, he'd rather just lie in this tree and soak in the minimal sunrays that hit his fur. If a willing woman showed up and wanted to scratch an itch, he wouldn't be opposed. But two cubs who just wanted to play, after having their caged-in life be rocked from the boundaries up, wasn't worth Cole bolstering the energy to stop them. As long as they weren't using their claws on him, he was fine.

Of course, on that note, perhaps he should have cared a little bit more.

After all, where there were bear cubs, there was probably a momma bear just around the corner. And *she* didn't hold back with her claws.

"Owen! Lucas!"

And that would be momma bear right then. He let his claws come out slightly, only to dig into the branch he rested on. He'd heard that Anya Dare had a wicked right hook, and he wasn't in the mood to go flying when she found out her cubs had been playing with him without her supervision. That woman had no sense of fun when it came to her kids. It wasn't as if he'd ever hurt the cubs.

She didn't know that, however.

She only saw a lazy cat, who didn't bother to shoo her kids back to their prison—aka their new home. Of course, it probably wasn't like that. She just didn't like her cubs hanging out with *him*. Anya hated him for some reason, and he could never quite figure out why. It wasn't as if he'd known her for long. The Ursines had only been living with the Felines and Canines for two weeks. In fact, the Felines hadn't been living in the Canine compound for that long either. Everything was still new, but Anya had seemed to take a firm disliking to him the moment she'd seen him.

And now it sounded as if he cared. Well he didn't. He only cared about sleeping, sexy shifter females who wanted in his bed, and protecting his Pack. And not necessarily in that order.

Cole finally opened his eyes to see Anya glaring at him. Damn she had pretty eyes—bright blue, flashing with a hint of fire and anger. He wasn't that far up from the ground, and the grizzly momma had to be close to six-feet tall; she could have easily jumped and taken him down with one paw.

The cubs let out tiny growls from behind his tree. Cole risked his life, considering Anya still glared at him, and turned to watch the two little boys in bear form peek out from either side of the large trunk.

Anya let out a small growl, and Cole shot his gaze to her. She curled her lip at him then stalked toward her sons. Cole stayed where he was, not wanting to anger her further. He wasn't in the mood to go up against a momma grizzly in a rage. He wasn't sure if he'd win.

"What did I say, boys? What did I say about leaving the house without telling me?" She folded her arms under her ample breasts, and Cole did his best not to stare. He couldn't help it. She was fucking gorgeous—not that he'd tell her that. Ever.

He valued his life, after all.

Owen and Lucas lowered their heads and padded at the dirt. They were adorable. Seriously. Cole loved kids, and one day hoped to have a few of his own with a nice cat who was adventurous in bed and would meet him stride for stride when it came to protecting his Pack. Or maybe he'd mate with a nice little submissive who would pamper his cat while taking care of the other side of the Pack that most never knew existed.

What Cole *wouldn't* be doing, was dealing with Anya for longer than he needed to. He might like Owen and Lucas, but he did not want to be on the receiving end of an angry female protecting her cubs. No one in their right mind did.

"Don't think looking cute will get you out of this, boys," she said firmly, but Cole still heard the smile in her voice. She wasn't a bad mother, a little overprotective, but he couldn't blame her for that. Not with what was going on around them. "You guys snuck out of the house. I was *scared*. Don't you get that? You can't just sneak out of our home like that and not tell me where you're going. You *know* you can't come out to another's territory without permission. Especially *his*."

What did she mean by that? *Especially his*. What was so wrong with *him*?

Cole kept his gaze on the boys as they made their way out from behind the tree, their heads down and their little paws dragging along the dirt. They didn't look scared, more resigned that they'd gotten caught breaking the rules. Cole held back a wince. He should have done something about them coming out to him, but he hadn't thought they were hurting anyone. Despite the fact that he'd been around cubs all his life within the compound walls, he wasn't that used to children.

The cubs went to her legs, rubbing their necks and bodies along her. She reached down and rubbed their heads, her mouth a thin line. "Don't do it again, boys. I'm not going to lose you. Got me?"

The two made little growls then sat on their rumps, blinking up at their mother. Seriously. Adorable.

Anya probably wouldn't appreciate him saying so, however.

"You found them?" a deep voice said from the direction of Anya's home.

Cole flicked his ear toward the intruder, his body tense. "Yes, Oliver," Anya answered. "They're right where you thought they'd be. With *him*."

He was starting to hate the way she said *him* like that. Cole searched his mental file for who Oliver was within the

Ursine Pack—yes, bears, cats, and wolves were each called Packs. That's what happened when the damn wolves named things centuries ago and Cole's ancestors had gone with it. Oliver was the Foreseer of the Ursines. Meaning he could tell the future—or at least make some predictions about immediate changes or danger based on premonitions. Cole wasn't quite sure what it all entailed since Felines and Canines didn't have a Foreseer counterpart. Instead, the wolves had an Omega, and the cats had a Shaman—or at least they would once they found him or her. It was hard to find each of their hierarchy within the walls of their confinement, but that was another story altogether.

Oliver was not only the Foreseer but Anya's brother, as well. For some reason, that relieved some of the tension in Cole's joints. He wasn't quite sure how he felt about the fact that he'd not only gone tense, but had lost that tension when he figured out who the other male was.

"Go with your uncle, boys," Anya ordered, her voice firm but not angry anymore. "I need to talk with Mr. Feline over here."

Cole held back a wince. She wouldn't even say his name. Well, this couldn't end well; though he hadn't thought it would once she'd stepped toward him all angry-like.

The boys gave him one last look then started the walk back to their place. Oliver raised a brow at him then followed. Cole wasn't quite sure what to think of that brow, but at the moment, he had other, more pressing matters to deal with. Namely, the momma bear glaring daggers at him.

"You need to stop encouraging them," she snapped. "They're babies. And they are curious. I get that. But we don't know how safe it is here, and you just sit here all lazy-like and let them play with your tail. You're an adult. A Tracker. Act like it."

He opened his mouth in an exaggerated yawn. She'd yelled at him for this before, and it wasn't his fault. The cubs were, like she'd just said, curious. If they wanted to play with his tail, then he'd let them. They weren't hurting him, and Anya needed to breathe.

"You're an asshole," she snapped. "So freaking lazy you can't even turn back to human and defend yourself. Some Tracker the cats have. Leave my boys alone. If they come back here, send them back to me. Or come get me. I don't want them out on their own. I'm all they have, Tracker. I'm not going to let them get hurt because you think it's fun to break my rules."

First, he wasn't going to shift because he'd be naked. And being naked near her when he had a hard-on—because, come on, she was freaking sexy—wasn't worth risking his life after she got a look at him sporting wood because of her. Second, he wasn't lazy, he just picked his battles. As for her boys? Next time, he might just send them back. She had a point when it came to safety. He would never hurt them—they were cubs—but there were human patrols coming through the compound at all times. He wouldn't see those boys hurt because the humans were in the wrong. However, he wasn't going to shift and tell her this. She didn't want to hear it. She had her own reasons for being angry, he suspected, and him defending himself wouldn't help. Instead, he swished his tail, his eyes on hers.

She lifted her lip in another snarl then threw up her hands. "I can't with you." She turned on her heel and stomped back toward her home. He couldn't help but watch the way her jeans hugged her ass as she did so. She was one sexy blonde Amazon of a woman. Not for him, but it didn't hurt to look.

"I see you're making all kinds of friends," Gibson drawled as he slid through the trees.

Cole had scented the wolf come up a few moments before but hadn't let on to Anya. He wasn't sure she'd noticed the man there since she'd been so focused on Cole. Plus, with all the new smells around her, he knew it would take a bit longer than a couple of weeks for her to get her bearings when it came to the different scents of the compound. He didn't want to see her embarrassed for her outburst in public. And he didn't know how he felt about that last thought. Instead of dwelling on it, he stretched, lifting his back in a curl before jumping down to the forest floor. With a shake, he shifted back to human. It was fast, a painful reminder that his body held two forms that didn't quite mesh when one thought of the physics behind it.

"Get some pants on," Gibson said smoothly. He ran a hand through his dark black hair that always ended up in his face. The damn man had one of those emo rocker hair-cuts that looked like it took an hour to get perfect each morning. Though Cole knew it just came naturally to the wolf. "You're late for your appointment, and I don't need to see your bare ass."

"It's a cat ass," Cole said with a grin and shook it before bending over to grab the pair of sweats he'd left in a nearby bush.

"I so didn't need to see that. I think I'm blind."

Cole smiled wide as he slid his sweats over his hips. "You know you liked it."

The wolf flipped him off, the ink on his fingers standing out against his pale skin. "I might like cock and pussy equally, but that doesn't mean I want yours, asshole."

"Like I said, you like my asshole."

Gibson let out a groan.

"See, you're groaning." Cole smacked the man on his back and started walking. "I don't know how you ever lived without me."

"It was much easier, let me tell you," Gibson muttered.

Gibson muttered a lot, but also talked Cole's ear off when he wanted to. The other man didn't speak much according to the rest of the Pack. He apparently liked Cole enough to open himself up a bit more. He was the Pack tattoo artist, in charge of not only personal ink, but also the ritual ink that came with being a mate, a Pack member, and a shifter. The three emblems blended into one full tattoo once a shifter found their mate, though most of the Pack members only held two—the brand the humans forced them to wear that Gibson tattooed over, and the tattoo that signified what Pack they were born or made into. He did that work for wolves alone, but he also did other work—like the piece he was doing for Cole—for the other shifters. There was a feline artist, the one who had done the ritual work on Cole's forearm, but he liked Gibson's work better. Not that he'd ever say that. People may be pissed about him and Gibson's friendship, and that he let the other man work on his back, but the rest of the shifters would just have to get over it. The three Packs had been forced to live in one small compound—times were changing, and hating one another for being a different kind of shifter had to be pushed into the past if they were to survive.

"You're looking serious over there," Gibson said as they walked into the wolf's home. He pointed to the chair near the tattoo station and lifted his chin. "Sit. I'll get you ready. Now, tell me what's on your mind."

Cole did as he was told. He hadn't bothered to put a shirt on, so he didn't have to deal with that. "I thought you didn't like to speak while doing this. That's what Holden said." Holden was the wolf Alpha. He'd married a newly-turned human a couple of months back, and that had been the catalyst for not only the move of the Packs but so much more.

"I don't like to speak unless I have something to say. And I like talking to you because you usually just listen." Gibson worked on setting up his station and prepping Cole's back. This was the second day of work on the piece. While humans would have to wait between sessions, he healed fast enough that he only had to wait a day. He could have probably done it all in one session, but that was asking a lot of the wolf who had his own duties within the compound.

"So, you never did say anything about Anya. Why does she hate you so much?" The wolf's foot worked the pedal and he began working on Cole's back. The buzz of the needle settled Cole's cat and he relaxed, even as he thought about Anya and her apparent dislike of him.

"She called me lazy."

Gibson snorted. "Well, you kind of are, but probably not for the reasons she thinks."

"I'm not lazy." Cole scowled. "I just don't like wasting my energy on things that I won't win. Or at least things that won't be worth it if I win. The cubs wanted to play, and I didn't want to growl at them to go. At least with me there, they were safe.

"But she didn't see it that way. I'd say she shouldn't have let the cubs get out, but there's no way to stop shifter cubs sometimes. The fact that they felt safe enough to venture out tells you she raised them right. Thanks to the humans surrounding us, some shifters scare the hell out of their children to keep them safe. So much that they inherently cripple them."

And that was the crux of it. They were shifters, not human. They had the ability to become the animal they were born with and, therefore, had to assume the responsibility that came with it. When they'd come out to the humans and revealed that there was something more to them than the others understood, shifters had been forced into compounds—collared and branded, but not forgotten. He'd been three when his parents risked their lives trying to protect him. They'd lost the battle, and he'd ended up raised by a group of shifters within the den walls who had tried to heal the orphans of their generation.

His people had lost so much, and now with each new decision brought on by the Shifter Accommodation Unit—the SAU for short—he was afraid they'd be one step closer to a new war where the casualty of peace would be far greater than the wars of their past.

Gibson worked on his back, and Cole tried to settle the deep ache in his bones that told him that peace was far from being within his grasp. He may be deemed lazy by a certain momma bear, but he hadn't earned that description. He'd fight for what was his—bleed for it, die for it.

Only, a new age was upon them, and the three shifter Packs were forced to live with one another as punishments for crimes that shouldn't have been deemed offenses in the first place, Cole wasn't sure he would be able to fight an enemy he didn't understand.

His world had changed once again, and he knew he'd have to take a stand with his Pack and with the other Packs he now lived with, to protect his people. He just prayed Anya and her cubs weren't caught in the crossfire. He'd seen the pain in her eyes, the weariness that came from years of being on alert, tuned to the danger from those who would rise against them. He didn't want to see that again, didn't want to see the woman who had raised those cubs hurt because of a battle far from being won. Only he didn't know why he felt that way, nor did he feel he had the right to.

He was only a lazy cat, a Tracker, a jaguar. Only worth the blood he put on the line.

Nothing more. Nothing less.

2

Anya Dare ran her hands through her hair and refused to think about that damn lazy cat and his feline ways. She knew she probably shouldn't have been so curt with him, considering it was *her* sons that had snuck out of her home and gone to the damn tree. But she always got flustered around him.

And *that* was the cause of her attitude.

She'd barely seen Cole in his human form since she was forced to take her family and move into the new compound. In fact, it seemed the only times she saw him were when he was lying about in that tree, not caring that her two boys were playing with his tail, and completely ignoring her instructions. Well, that wasn't exactly accurate. The only times she'd spoken to him were when he was relaxing, but she'd *seen* him outside his tree area.

She'd caught glimpses of him around her new den. He

was the Tracker for the cats, so he was always on patrol—his body on alert, though the damn man somehow made himself look relaxed, as if he hadn't a care in the world. If she hadn't seen the intensity in his eyes when he was watching out for a human guard patrol, she would have thought him the worst Tracker she'd ever seen. But she'd seen into those hazel depths and knew he *cared* about his Pack, his people.

And that bugged her to no end for some reason. Though it shouldn't have because, hell, he was doing his duty to his Pack. But he just *bugged* her.

It had nothing to do with his chestnut hair that was longer on the top but cut shorter on the sides. Nor did it have to do with his beard that she knew was long enough to touch his chest if he lowered his chin ever so slightly. She was *not* attracted to a freaking cat.

Sure, she could admire his form—human and shifter. She was a woman, after all. He was taller than her—which at her height of five-ten wasn't actually as common as she'd like. And he had smooth muscle that didn't make him look bulky, just strong as hell. But admiration was all it could be. Appreciation from afar; annoyance up close. Because, darn it, she didn't have time for lazy cats and their indolent ways.

Again, it was only her attention to detail that made this matter. She was just looking out for her people in a new compound. She'd noticed many cats and wolves. Cole was *not* special.

He was annoying, conceited, and not worth a second look. Or a third. Or even a fourth.

"You done brooding over there?" Oliver asked, a smirk on his face.

She stuck out her tongue. Real mature. She was the younger sister, after all; she shouldn't have to be as grown up as her big bear of a brother. Of course, they were both in their early thirties, and that two-year difference didn't matter much. Technicalities.

Oliver ran a hand through his shoulder-length hair and grinned. She wanted to take a photo so she could remember that smile since he didn't do it often. The weight of the Pack —the world—rested on his shoulders most days, and she didn't know how to help him. But if acting as young as her sons helped her brother smile, she'd do it again in a heartbeat.

"Momma, I'm sorry," Owen whispered, his hands clasped in front of him and his head lowered. He was her quiet baby. He followed Lucas and did what his brother did, not because he had to, but because he wanted to. He was happy being a follower and doing what he could to make their day better. He was her emotional baby, and she loved him.

"Yeah, Momma, sorry for running away." Lucas bounced on his feet as he spoke, his teeth biting into his lip. Lucas was her loud and take-charge baby. He took Owen on adventures and wanted to explore everything before moving on. While Owen may stay back and study something a little longer, Lucas was ready to jump into the next thing quickly. Though he could be a little louder, he was sweet when he needed to be. He was her fiery baby, and she loved him just as much.

It was hard for Anya to stay mad at her boys for long, but sometimes, they needed to learn that boundaries were put in place for a reason. She hadn't grown up within the confines of a compound. She'd known what it was like to run free in the forest, to have to hide what she was, yet still know she was *free*. Her children had been born after the Verona Virus, and into a world where they had never tasted the freedom she craved. And because of that, they had to learn the hard way that their world wasn't one they could let their guard down in. She hated that—*hated* it—but maybe one day she'd be able to give her children something better than the tall walls that surrounded them.

Anya knelt in front of them, trying not to smile. She wasn't truly angry with them. She couldn't be when they were just being curious shifter children. But she'd been scared. And *that* was something that needed to be addressed. Because, despite the fact that they were inside a small compound with numerous shifters she didn't know or understand, it was the humans who ventured in that worried her most of all.

The humans thought they owned them. They ruled over them. Put laws on them, and branded them. She'd been forced to watch her cubs be branded just last year. The Alpha had taken the pain inside himself, using the magic of the Pack to keep her babies from agony. The humans didn't know the Alpha could do this, and she would be forever grateful that they didn't. The SAU thought they were subjugating the entire shifter population to fire at a young age. Instead, the Alpha—Andrew in her Pack's case—felt each lick of flame as his own. If the humans found out what the shifters could do, they'd use it to their advantage. Then they'd find another way to hurt the shifters' children. She'd been forced to watch her babies' flesh be burned and marked so that they were forever known as *not* human at a glance.

And because of this, because of her nightmares about the screams she'd forced them to voice, though she knew they'd felt no pain, she had to be strict when it came to their safety.

"I know you're sorry, boys." She felt Oliver's gaze on her, but her brother let her do what she had to. Her brother was unmated, and because she'd been an idiot years ago, she was, as well. She and Oliver raised her boys together because there was no way she'd be able to do it alone, but in times like these, Oliver let her lead. They were *her* children, her responsibility, the lights of her life.

"Are we in trouble?" Lucas asked. He shifted from foot to foot, looking far too cute for his own good.

"Yes, but that's because you have to learn to be careful." Lucas opened his mouth to speak, but Owen nudged his shoulder into his twin's. Lucas closed his mouth, and Anya held back a sigh. Damn it. She didn't want to be the nice and mean parent all at once. She wanted a partner, had wanted it all those years ago. But the human man who had told her he loved her when he'd visited the compound with the others had lied. He was one of the medical professionals who had come in to do health checks on the Pack. Some had been there under that guise, but had actually wanted to learn more about shifter physiology. The man who had taken her to bed had told her he wanted to help people. She'd believed him, stupidly, and had ended up pregnant.

When the thought of being labeled a shifter lover became too much, he'd left her pregnant and alone.

"Momma?"

She closed her eyes at Owen's voice and took a deep breath. She needed to keep her head out of the past and look toward the future. Her sons were her future, and they were the most important thing—not broken promises and lies.

"I know you want to go out and play, but we're still new here. We need to make sure we all understand how this new compound works."

"But I like the cats," Lucas said. "I mean, you told us there were others like us, but different, but we only saw bears before."

"Uh-huh. I like seeing the cats. And sometimes there's a wolf that sleeps under the tree when Cole sleeps in the branches. They're friends I think."

Anya thinned her lips. That wolf would be Gibson, the Pack tattoo artist. She didn't envy that job in the slightest since part of his job was to ink over brands and make them the shifters' own. He and Cole were friends it seemed, though she didn't know the wolf well. She didn't know the cat well either. Or at all.

"I think they are," she agreed, trying to keep her attention on her sons and not the cat. "But boys, please do what I say. Okay? Once we know the lay of the land, we can go out and play more, but for now, we have to be careful. I know it's not fun to be locked up inside all the time, but it won't be forever."

Her boys nodded, their little faces in frowns. She held out her arms and they went to her, wrapping their tiny little arms around her neck. She squeezed them tightly, inhaling their little boy scent. Her babies wouldn't be little forever, and she cherished these hugs, even if they came after her having to be harsh.

"Okay, now I have to go to a meeting with your uncle and the Alphas, but the maternal bears will watch you to make sure you stay out of trouble."

Owen smiled up at her, his eyes bright. "We'll stay out of trouble."

"You bet," Lucas agreed.

Anya thought they had a fifty-fifty shot at not getting put in the corner by one of the maternals, but she didn't say that. Cubs needed to push their boundaries as they found their dominance and structure, but it was the safety issues that made her worry. A momma bear always worried.

She kissed her sons quickly then led them to the maternals' camp, an older building that they were renovating. When they'd been forced to move into this compound, they'd left their homes and pasts behind. They'd been allowed to bring whatever meager possessions they'd acquired over their lives, but that was it. Now they were forced to use a third of the compound that had once been filled with all wolves. People were living two to three families to a home while they worked on building more. She and Oliver had their own place since he was the Foreseer and needed space to keep sane, for lack of a better word, but their home was half the size of the one they'd used to have, and honestly, their old place hadn't been all that large. The wolves and cats were helping with the construction since they too had to build more to accommodate their numbers. Things were in such flux that she wasn't sure what the future held, but she'd go into it with her chin held high. There wasn't another choice.

"I'm not really in the mood to deal with a meeting of the Alphas," Oliver said softly as they made their way to the center of the den. The compound had been split as evenly as possible into thirds with the addition of the bears, but the center was for *all* shifters. The forested area was also mixed, as the humans hadn't allowed them that much room to begin with. Anya had a feeling the territory, as it was, would one day blend even more. There wasn't enough space to keep just a dividing line between them. That was one of the points of the meeting that day, she knew.

Oliver was part of the meeting as the Foreseer, and since

he didn't have a mate, he was allowed to bring Anya. Visions took a lot out of him, and he needed someone there to catch him if he fell. No one would ever dare think he was weak for his need of another, but it still took a toll. It also wasn't as if he could lean on anyone else. The closer he got to someone, the less clear his or her future became to him. He couldn't read his own path, nor could he get more than a casual glimpse of hers or her sons'. She hated that he put so much distance between himself and the rest of the world, but he did so to protect them. Or so he said. She'd always thought it was a way to protect himself, as well.

"It won't be too long, I don't think. It's just the Alphas, Betas, and your counterparts, right?"

Oliver nodded. "Plus whatever mates and family members they have. The mantle isn't just on the shoulders of those with the title. Though I don't know if there *are* counterparts right now. The wolves don't have an Omega, and the cats are missing their Shaman."

It broke her heart to hear it. Before they'd been locked inside the compounds thanks to the humans' fear after the Verona Virus, bears, cats, and wolves had roamed free. While they were out there, they could venture to other Packs and meet those that could eventually join them. It was easier to find true mates, and those that would fill the roles of Alpha, Beta, and whatever their third member was —Omegas for wolves, Foreseers for bears, and Shamans for cats. Now though, they only had a small pool of shifters to work with. The bears had been blessed with finding a Foreseer, but the others were still searching amongst their own. It could still happen, she knew, an Omega or Shaman could be born to the Pack, or even born out of tragedy. It wasn't always known from birth what a shifter would be. The three species might have had their territory disputes in the past, but there had never been a true hatred between the three. She wasn't sure there was now either, beyond the teasing and close quarters.

Anya let out a breath as soon as they entered the outdoor circle where the meeting would take place. Holden, the Canine Alpha, and his mate, Ariel, were sitting on a log, leaning into one another. Holden's Beta, Soren, sat on the ground, leaning between the slightly spread legs of his mate, Cora. Cora wasn't a wolf, but rather the tiger princess. Her father, Jonah, the Alpha of the Golden Pack, sat across from them, talking with the two of them and his Beta, Max. There had to be history between Max and Soren and Cora because Anya could practically taste the tension.

Her own Alpha, Andrew, sat on another log, while his Beta, Megan, stood on her tiptoes behind him, stretching. They weren't mated, but rather best friends. And fierce protectors. Anya liked the fact that the bears had a female Beta, considering dominant females were just as tough, if not tougher than their male counterparts.

A spicy scent hit her and she turned on her heel. Cole meandered toward the circle, his hands in his pockets and a cocky grin on his face.

She barely held in the urge to snarl at him. The damn

man hadn't even bothered to put on a shirt. Rather, he'd put on an old pair of jeans that molded to his thighs far too well. He'd also forgone shoes.

He passed her with a wink, and Oliver stepped between them. Her brother raised a brow, and she let out a sigh. It wouldn't do to punch the cat in the middle of a freaking Alpha meeting. Maybe she'd do it later. He was far too cocky for his own good.

Of course, she couldn't stop thinking of the word cock when it came to him, and that angered her even more. Her bear stretched inside, waking up and wanting to shift. She pushed it back, knowing it wasn't time. She'd shift later and beat up a tree or something. That would help alleviate this pressure in her chest...and other places.

"Cole, good, you're here," Jonah said and nodded toward one of the last two empty logs. They just had to be right next to one another. She sighed and took the one closest to her own Alpha, though Oliver sat directly next to Andrew since he might need to whisper visions if they came. That left Anya sitting next to Cole.

Of course.

"Where's your shirt?" Cora asked then yelped. She rubbed her thigh and growled at her mate. "I'm allowed to notice he's not wearing a shirt. Plus, he has a bandage on his back."

Soren kissed behind her knee, and this time, it was Jonah who growled. The wolf might be mated to Cora, but daddy tiger probably didn't like seeing his precious kitten nibbled on in public.

Oh to be nibbled on. It had been far too long.

Cole leaned toward her as he turned slightly, showing off his back to the circle. She refused to move away from the heat of his body. It was just hormones. Nothing more. She wouldn't give him the satisfaction of showing him that she was uncomfortable with his presence.

"Gibson just finished up round two," Cole explained, his voice a smooth growl. "It's still sore so I didn't want to put anything on it that would rub. I'll take the bandage off soon so it can breathe."

He'd probably gotten a big-chested female cat on his back or something equally crude. Of course, the man would get more ink. Because it was damn hot. And he had to annoy her. Because, apparently, everything revolved around her.

"I can't wait to see all of it," Megan said as she sat down on the other side of Andrew. "Gibson does good work."

"That he does," Holden added. "And now that we're all done admiring Cole's naked body, can we get on to business."

Ariel elbowed her mate in the ribs. "Be nice."

"I was being nice," Holden said deadpan.

"Anyway..." Andrew said softly, a smile in his voice. "I appreciate that we're having these meetings together, but I think they should be at least weekly from now on. We have too much to lose by not sharing what we know."

Jonah rubbed his chin. "Everything?"

Holden frowned. "We are all Alphas of our Packs, our people, but as Cora and Soren showed us by mating, we are not separate entities. We will have to find a way to make this work because I will be damned if we allow the humans to kill us because we are too busy fighting with each other."

Anya wrapped her arms around her middle as the three Alphas spoke about what they needed to do in order to protect their Packs. She took everything in and tried to ignore the cat next to her, who kept leaning into her. It was as if his cat were trying to soothe her bear. She didn't need that.

She hadn't before with the boys' father, and she damn well didn't need it now.

Their Packs were changing, the rules of how they lived were forming with these meetings, these terms that meant a future for their people. Without the cooperation of the Alphas and their circle, none of the Packs within the compound walls would make it. She didn't know what the humans would do next to subjugate her people, but she'd be damned if she sat back and allowed her sons to pay the consequences of those actions.

They were her life, her everything. Her reason to keep fighting.

And if anything ever happened to them, the world would know true fear.

Because there was nothing scarier than a momma bear when her cubs were in trouble.

Nothing.

FRANK TALBOT WASN'T above begging for favors, but it killed him every time he had to ask an old acquaintance for help. He left the shady backdoor businessman's building and snuck through the alleys on his way to his own abandoned warehouse.

He sounded like some arch villain in one of the comic books of his youth before the Verona Virus had wiped out a third of the human population. He despised that he'd been forced into taking back alleys while working and living in an abandoned warehouse. But that's what happened when the SAU went batshit crazy and changed the rules right in front of him.

He was a scientist, a genius. He wasn't humble by any means. Why should he be? After all, he'd been on the ground floor for the very virus that should have been the best weapon out there if not for its deadly consequences. No matter though, all great strides in humanity had costs and sacrifice. The Verona Virus had its failures, but it had also paved the way for Frank's new endeavors.

Without the virus, the shifters wouldn't have come out of hiding. And thanks to their sacrifice in helping to find a "cure," he had been able to study the beasts. At one point, he'd even gone as far as using his own body to procreate with one of them. It had been disturbing but like he said, all strides took sacrifice.

The SAU had kicked him out when his goal for the ultimate perfections—his own brand of shifters—had crossed their lines. What a crock. The SAU was the fourth branch of the government and didn't have the checks and balances the others had. They could do whatever they wanted to the shifters in the name of saving the human race. And Frank's experiments weren't outside their norm. But those above him had lost a few shifters and needed a scapegoat.

Weak.

Now he was on his own to find a way to create shifters. Just a few months ago, one of the beasts had let it slip that it took the bite of an Alpha or a mate to create a shifter. Before that, he'd thought—along with the rest of humanity—that shifters were born and not made.

The SAU was now trying to force matings, and coerce different Alphas to make shifters. Frank had no idea if it was truly working since he'd been cut off, but he had his own plans. He didn't want to rely on adult matings or Alphas who could rip his throat out. He didn't want to deal with mature shifters at all; they were fucking animals.

Instead, he'd go younger.

He needed shifter children. If he could code their DNA at a young age, he would be able to find the bridge between humans and shifters and make an army of his own. Or rather, one he could sell to the highest bidder. He'd have the glory, and the ability to retire on a sunny island.

Of course, he knew that going younger with his experiments would take a certain...finesse. It wasn't just the idea of a younger shifter to dissect and study. No, he needed a shifter with the perfect genetic makeup to be the bridge. One that held part shifter and part human DNA.

It just so happened he knew of a child with that makeup...and that child had a twin. Frank would have a spare, in case the first didn't survive.

He grinned as he shut himself away in his warehouse. All those times of forcing himself to copulate with that female bear would now be worth it.

He'd have his live samples. And then the glory.

Perfection.

3

Anya's temples hurt, but she didn't dare rub them. Not when that damn cat kept sneaking peeks at her. Oh, the man didn't do it obviously, but she could tell when his gaze was on her. Every hair on the back of her neck stood on end, and she swore her skin broke out in goose bumps from the touch of his stare alone.

She ignored him. Or at least tried to. Her brother needed her in case he had a vision, and she couldn't be distracted by Cole. Plus, she wanted to know what these leaders were saying. They held the future of the Packs in their hands.

"We've had patrols going on for twenty-five years," Holden said. "We have our paths and what we've done in the past to protect our own. When the cats came, we included them in the routine, and even added more routes so the humans can't figure out when we will be in certain places." He met Andrew's gaze, and Anya stood up straighter. "You've only been here for two weeks. I know you're trying to settle in, and fuck, we're all trying to settle into our new homes since they uprooted us from the homes you're now living in, but are you ready to join in on the patrols?"

Andrew ran a hand over his beard and frowned. He was a big man, a huge grizzly—even bigger than Oliver. There was a reason he was her Alpha. "Why do we need to join your patrols? Why can't we have patrols of our own?"

Holden lifted his lip in a snarl, but Ariel patted his knee. He calmed at his mate's influence, and Anya felt a stab of jealousy. She'd never had that kind of connection with someone, and as time moved on, she was afraid she'd never be able to.

The wolf Alpha let out a heated breath. "Because we might be three different Packs, three different Alphas, but this is *our* fucking compound now. And bitching about the circumstances we're in, instead of trying to find a way out of captivity, isn't going to help anyone."

Andrew studied Holden for a moment then turned to Jonah. "What say you, cat? You enjoy working with the wolves?"

Jonah glanced at his daughter and her wolf mate sprawled over her lap then looked back at Andrew. "I say we adapt or perish. We all lost too much when the Verona Virus hit and we came into the public eye. It's not one against another in here. We can't afford that. So I think it's time we put aside our differences and actually work together. Things are rumbling out there, the humans are afraid. If they weren't, they wouldn't be punishing us at every turn. We need to find a way to work as one and find our freedom."

Anya let out a breath, and Andrew smiled. Her damn Alpha was too cunning for a bear. He'd probably been thinking along similar lines the entire time, but this way, he got their true opinions rather than blindly agreeing to something he wasn't quite sure of. Damn bear.

"I say we have a deal," her Alpha said smoothly. Megan snorted beside Andrew, and Anya held back a laugh of her own. "I'm not in the mood to lose another Pack member because the humans think they own us." He ran his hands along the metal collar he wore around his neck. They all wore one, a symbol to the humans that the shifters were animals, collared pets.

Only, the shifters had *allowed* the humans to put the collars on their necks. They'd done so to protect their children and legacy in a time where the future was uncertain. The humans also forced each Pack member to wear a brand that signified their species—a tribal head of their animal burned into their forearms. Each Pack took that brand one step further and tattooed their individual Pack marks on one side of the brand, while mates did the same with their marks on the other side. Fully mated couples held a full symbol, while those like Anya, those in need of a mate, wore theirs partially completed.

With each slash against them by the humans, the shifters did their best to rise above it.

"We're in tight quarters now, and as we're all still breeding and creating life, I don't see us finding more room anytime soon. We'll just have to make it work," Holden finally said after he'd studied Andrew for a bit more.

"We've won battles against them, but not the war," Jonah said softly. "Not yet."

"We're stronger as one, rather than three," Andrew added in.

Anya knew she was at the site of change, witnessing a treaty that would hopefully, one day, show her sons freedom. These three Alphas knew each other more than they let on to the humans. They'd been secretly sending runners to each of the other compounds over time, but now it was different. Now they all shared a home, and could plan face to face. The human patrols within the compound would be watching, but it was at least a step in the right direction.

They discussed the rest of the patrols for a bit longer, and Anya stretched her legs, aware Cole was staring at her. She wanted to snap at him, but this wasn't the place. Her Alpha needed her to be Oliver's support, not a mad bear with an aching paw.

Her brother let out a groan then leaned into her. She wrapped her arms around his shoulders and brought him closer. When his body shook, she pressed her lips to his hair, murmuring reassurances. Each vision took a toll on him, not just emotionally and mentally, but physically. They were killing him one premonition at a time, and there was nothing she could do about it. She just prayed that he would find a way to mate with another one day and share the burden. It was the only way Foreseers could live. Yet Oliver had put himself so far apart from others, Anya didn't see how he could last for much longer.

At that macabre thought, she let out a shudder and waited for her brother to tell them what he'd seen—that was if he could. He couldn't always relay his visions. She didn't know if he held back because he didn't want to burden others, or if he was physically unable. She didn't understand the breadth of her brother's powers and responsibilities as much as she should. That too killed her.

Heat radiated at her back, and she stiffened before forcing herself to relax. Cole put his hand on her shoulder, keeping her steady. She hadn't realized she'd started to lean off the log until he touched her. Energy flowed through his touch, sending shocks through her system. Her heart raced and she cursed shifter hearing. Hopefully, the others would think the increased beat of her heart was due to her brother's visions rather than the touch of the cat behind her. Cole's grip tightened for a moment, as if he too felt what she had, then he relaxed. Why did he relax? Did he force himself to do so? And why was she overthinking this? She didn't push him away, though she desperately wanted to. If his touch kept her steady so she could help her brother, she'd deal with it.

Oliver shook once then pulled away. She let him move

back, her hands shaking. She hated to see the grey pallor of his skin; the dark bags that formed under his eyes as the visions took further toll on his body, his soul.

Cole's hand left her shoulder, and she ignored the sense of loss she felt. Her bear must be going crazy; because that was the only reason she'd be thinking about the lack of his touch as a loss.

The others had gathered around them, silent in their worry and anticipation of what Oliver would say. However, they didn't crowd him, and for that she was grateful. Oliver hated being the center of attention even on his good days.

"Here, drink this."

Anya looked up as Cole knelt in front of Oliver with a bottle of water in his hand.

"I'd have brought the booze, but I figured you'd need water first before you drink off the effects of whatever the hell just happened."

Oliver let out a rough chuckle, and Anya relaxed. If her brother could laugh, even just a little, then he'd be okay. Her brother chugged the water after nodding at Cole. When Oliver looked a little less grey, a little more composed, he let out a sigh.

"Can you tell us what you saw?" Holden asked. He frowned and looked down at his hand clasped with Ariel's. "Or was that question insensitive?" He shrugged as everyone shot their gazes to him. He was the *Alpha*, and that was one odd statement. "What? I know what it means to hold a responsibility you aren't ready for. I was a teenager when I was forced to be the Alpha. I don't remember meeting Foreseers when we were out in the wild. Hell, I barely remember the stories of them. Us wolves and cats have been so separate from the bears, we've missed out on a lot of the shifter culture we should have grown up with." He growled again before looking directly at Oliver. "For all I know, asking what you saw was taboo, and you're going to want to claw my face off." He nodded at Ariel and grinned, even if his eyes were dark. "She likes my face the way it is."

"That's true," Ariel said softly. She tilted her head at Oliver. "I'm new to the whole shifter thing since I grew up human. I don't quite understand what just happened." Ariel was the first made shifter Anya had seen since the walls were built. It had been done to save her life, and though it was the catalyst for the change that placed them on rocky ground, Anya couldn't blame Holden for risking it all to save his mate.

Oliver let out a breath and ran a hand over his face. "I'm the Foreseer. I can see glimpses of the future if the gods allow it, but not always, and not when I want to. Hell, it's not always completely accurate because one change in how someone reacts and the future changes."

"So nothing is set in stone?" Cole asked, his voice deep.

"Nothing," Oliver said solemnly. "Though sometimes, no matter how hard you try to change the way things work out, fate has a way of fucking it up and making the worst happen anyway." Oliver closed his eyes and growled before composing himself. "You can ask what I saw, but sometimes, I can't tell you."

The others nodded as Oliver opened his eyes.

"What did you see?" Anya asked, her voice a whisper.

Oliver looked past them, his eyes seeing nothing. "I saw blood. Blood, loss, and death." His voice was hollow, a memory of what it had once been. "Change is coming, but at great cost. The world isn't ready for what is to come, but *we* must be. For if we're not...then there is no use for the hope we dug up from the trenches of agony."

Anya held back a shudder, though she felt that same shudder roll through Cole at her side. No one asked Oliver to explain what his words meant. Some things didn't need to be explained. And others were so vague, the truth behind those words so shadowed, that if they were to ask, they might get far more than they bargained for.

They ended the meeting then, their minds on what Oliver had seen and on what the coming months would entail. While she wanted to ask her brother exactly what he had seen, she knew he'd said exactly what he'd meant to. If he'd wanted to elaborate on the vague statements of blood and death, he would have.

Instead, she walked silently beside him on the way to pick up her boys before they headed home. The others had their own plans for the evening, but she wanted to let her bear out to play with her sons, then make dinner and pretend, if only for the night, that everything was okay.

She'd ignore the metal at her neck and the ink on her arm —there was nothing more she could do.

"Would you like to go for a run?" she asked, her voice devoid of emotion. She didn't know what Oliver needed, and frankly, her head hurt from dealing—or rather, *not* dealing—with Cole during the meeting.

Oliver shook his head. "Maybe not a run, I don't have that kind of energy today. But maybe we can shift with the boys and roll around. I know they already shifted today, but they are probably anxious and could use another shift to get out all that excess energy."

Anya smiled softly. "I think they could use another shift, as well. This time when I'm actually there and they aren't trying to sneak out of the house."

Oliver wrapped an arm around her shoulders, and she sank into her brother's side. "You're a good mom, Anya. Never forget that. Okay?"

She nodded, though something inside her told her that this wasn't just her brother speaking, but the Foreseer, as well. What that meant, she didn't know, but she'd hug her sons as soon as she could just in case.

Lucas and Owen bounced toward her, full of sugar and smiles as they left the maternals. Anya thanked the bears who'd watched her cubs and promised she'd help them soon. She had a shift with them later that week, but sometimes on her days off, she enjoyed watching the babies with the others. As a dominant, she'd gone on patrols in the old compound, and now she would here, as well. Plus, she did different shifts with each of the submissives, maternals, and other lower ranking sections of the Pack. Since they were not allowed to leave the den, they had to make do with what they were given by the humans. Each faction was critical to the Pack's survival as a whole and functioned on a level that ensured their survival.

Her boys ran around her legs as they made their way home, laughing and asking questions about where she and Oliver had been. They lived right on the edge of the cat's territory, hence why her boys saw so much of Cole. She figured that soon, once again, the lines of who lived where would blur. There just wasn't enough room to be picky.

"Your uncle Oliver and I want to shift and play. How does that sound?"

Lucas jumped up and down, waving his fists in the air before stripping off his clothes. Well, at least he'd bothered to do that first, instead of trying to shift before disrobing.

Owen smiled at her, so sweet and adorable. "We can shift, too?"

She ran her hand through his hair. "Of course, baby. Let's play."

Owen bounced on his feet and quickly joined his brother in bear form. Oliver rolled his shoulders and shifted as well, letting the boys jump on his back as soon as he was done. Anya rolled her eyes as Lucas tried to jump on top of Oliver's back. Since her boys knew not to use their claws while playing, the twins weren't succeeding at their goal to take Oliver down.

She quickly took off her clothes and shifted, the sharp burn and ache that came with each shift washing over her. It wasn't a burst of sparkles to shift, but it also wasn't the grotesque imagery that old movies made it out to be.

As soon as she was in her grizzly form, Owen bounded toward her, his little paws batting at her side. She yawned, pretending she didn't see him. Lucas, tired of Uncle Oliver not leaning down so he could crawl all over him, rolled toward Anya, a little bear grin on his face.

Seriously, her bear cubs were the cutest things *ever*.

She went down to her belly, knowing the boys would get frustrated soon if she didn't play along. They weren't hunters yet. One day soon they'd learn exactly what they'd need to get their prey, but for now, it was all about play.

Owen and Lucas crawled on top of her, their little padded paws digging into her fur. They didn't use claws, but she knew they wanted to. Little nicks and scrapes wouldn't necessarily hurt, but they needed to learn safety so they didn't hurt other little cubs when they weren't paying attention.

She let them play a bit longer then froze as a spicy scent hit her nose. The boys scrambled off of her, and she turned, seeing Cole in his jaguar form standing on his side of the territory by his tree. The boys bounced toward him, letting out little bear growls. Since Cole wasn't in the tree this time, they couldn't play with his tail, so they nudged into his side. He met Anya's gaze for a moment as if asking permission. She gave a nod, though it was awkward in bear form. Saying no would only hurt the fragile relationships her boys held within their new den. If she pushed them away, they might fight harder to play with the cat. While they weren't allowed to sneak out of the house to play, she was *right* there, and the boys were still under her direct supervision. It may have grated on her that Cole was there and had interrupted a family moment, but honestly, there wasn't enough space in the den to be as frustrated as she was. Cole was in *his* territory. It wasn't his fault that her babies wanted to play with him. Though she'd find a way to blame him if she could since he bothered her so much. And *that* bothered her more.

Owen ran toward her, nudged her side, and played a bit more before going back to Cole, who had rolled on his back to let the boys nuzzle into his stomach. It would have looked weird to the human population to see a jaguar playing with two bear cubs, but for shifters, this was how it had been all those years ago. It may have been done as punishment, but in reality, putting the three shifter groups together might one day lead to something significant...something great.

She let the boys play a bit longer, aware that Oliver had shifted back to human form and gone inside. From the smell of cooking meat and spices, he'd started making tacos for dinner. Her stomach growled loudly, and if she'd been in human form, she knew she'd have blushed. Thankfully, her fur hid that display of embarrassment. Cole looked as if he'd have raised a cat brow at the sound if he could have. Yes, she was a bear. A big bear. She ate a lot. Sue her.

Cole stood up and shook his body, then nudged her sons toward her. She let out a rumble of thanks and led her sons back into the house, doing her best not to look behind her at the cat that bothered her in more ways than one. She didn't know what it was about that man, but he always set her nerves on end.

By the time she shifted back, her boys were in their clothes and bouncing around Oliver as he finished cooking dinner. Anya rolled her eyes and helped them set the table. She and Oliver took turns cooking since neither of them particularly liked it. She'd be forever grateful that he'd given up so much to help her raise her boys. She could have relied on the Pack for help, and she had, but it wasn't the same as having someone move in and help change diapers and deal with midnight feedings. Others had mates and lovers to help. She'd had no one. She'd dealt with the stigma of falling for a human—an SAU led human at that—and had learned that not everyone would forgive her for having feelings for the wrong man. But none of those people judged her sons for the blood that ran in their veins. And for that, she would forever turn the other way as others judged her. They loved her sons, and that was all that mattered.

After dinner, she forced the boys to take a bath and then stuffed them in their pajamas. Three stories later, they were conked out in their aging bunk beds. Oliver had said he'd build better ones for her, but with the lack of materials, she knew they'd have to make do for a while. Oliver slept in the main bedroom, and she had the smaller office-turned-bedroom. He'd argued with her for a while over it, but since he was forced to live with two growing cubs, he was allowed to have the bigger space.

She fell asleep quickly after a long day of worrying and shifting, though that damn cat was never far from her mind. He invaded her dreams; that spicy scent overwhelming her until she woke up early the next morning, her body slick with sweat and her thighs coated with her orgasm.

Holy hell.

The damn cat had given her an actual wet dream.

She needed to go on a run for real this time. Or maybe find a willing bear, who didn't mind that she was tainted goods. On that depressing thought, she quickly got ready for the morning, showering and brushing her teeth even though her body wanted to go back to sleep and have another dream.

As she was walking out to the kitchen for coffee, she inhaled, wanting the sense of family to wash over her senses and push out the weird dreams. Only, when she took a deep breath, the scent of her boys wasn't as strong as it should have been. In fact, she could only scent the fact that they lived in the house, not that they were actually *in* the house.

Though she started to panic, she tamped down her bear and ran into the boys' room, only to find two rumpled beds and an open window.

No. No no no no. They hadn't been kidnapped or taken from her home. They could have opened the window for air and went into Oliver's room. Only that didn't account for the lack of scent.

Maybe they'd snuck out again and went to that damn cat.

Her hackles rose.

That fucking cat.

She pounded on her brother's door. "Oliver! Wake up. I can't find the boys. I'm going to Cole's to see if they went there."

Oliver opened the door as soon as she turned down the hall and grunted. "Shit. Okay, I'm right behind you."

She didn't bother to look at him, her mind on the horrors of what could happen if she were wrong about where they were. But she couldn't be wrong. Her little boys were just on their way to Cole's. That had to be the answer because she couldn't deal with the alternative.

She stomped toward his tree, following the faded scent of her little boys. Damn it. They'd gone after the cat. The fucking cat. Only when she got to the tree, she didn't see Cole or his cat self.

She huffed out a breath. With all the scents of the other shifters in the area, and the fact that they'd all been out here the previous night, she couldn't tell if her boys had been there that morning or not. She'd have a better sense of smell in her bear form, but Cole, as a Tracker, would have the best sense.

Knowing she was getting desperate, she ran to Cole's home, pounded on the door, and yelled his name.

He opened it, his hair disheveled, and a pair of jeans riding low on his hips. He hadn't bothered to button them, and she could see the trail of hair from his belly to the dark patch that should have been hidden behind his jeans. It looked as if he'd pulled the pants on in a hurry, but she couldn't care about that right then.

"Are Owen and Lucas here?" she asked, knowing she sounded frantic.

His eyes widened a fraction, and she wanted to scream. "No. I was sleeping. I don't know where they are."

"They have to be here, Cole. They aren't at home. They aren't at the tree. They *have* to be here." Her heart raced, and she knew she was screaming and probably waking up the entire den, but she didn't care.

Worry entered his gaze, and she almost broke. This wasn't the lazy cat; no, this was a man far from lazy. And that scared her more than anything.

"Where are my babies, Cole?"

He let out a breath and pushed past her, grabbing her hand along the way. "I don't know, Anya, but we're going to find them. Got me? We're going to find them."

She held on to his hand like a lifeline, her bear roaring inside. If she let the bear out, she'd rampage and not be able to think. But the fact that Cole had said they'd find them made her want to calm slightly, as well. She shouldn't rely on him and she knew it, but if she didn't, she'd miss something—miss finding her children.

The lazy cat wasn't so lazy anymore, and now she needed him more than she thought possible.

Her babies were gone.

And now this momma bear needed to find them, and that meant death for any in her way. Anyone.

4

Cole's cat scraped at his chest, but he ignored it, knowing he needed to stay calm for Anya. He'd seen the panic in her gaze, and he did *not* want to be on the receiving end of her snap if she went bear on him. He hadn't been involved in whatever the hell was going on, but he was the easiest target.

The cat wanted to hunt down anyone who dared hurt those cubs. It was such an intense reaction that he was slightly startled. He'd have fought for any of the shifters' young, but this felt different. He didn't want to think about *why* it was different, so he shoved those thoughts aside and looked down at his hand clutching Anya's.

Mistake.

Big fucking mistake.

Her eyes widened, and he had to swallow hard. He

shouldn't have grabbed her hand, shouldn't have touched her. Not when she was about ready to blow, and frankly, not ever. She hated him. Or perhaps hated everything he represented when it came to the changes in her life. Again, he pushed those thoughts from his mind, knowing he needed to focus. He was the Tracker for his Pack, and though she wasn't truly Pack being Ursine and not Feline, she was still in his den. There was no way he'd let his duties fall by the wayside because he didn't know how to take whatever feelings were going on in his mind right then.

"Let's go to where they should have been first. Then I'll shift if I have to. I have better senses in my cat form."

She nodded, her jaw setting. "I know. That's another reason I'm here. I can't make out their scents with all the new ones. I should be able to find my babies easily since they are *mine,* but with the overwhelming scents of so many other shifters we haven't been near before, my bear can't do it."

That must have killed her to admit. No shifter wanted to show weakness—especially a female with regard to her cubs. He also didn't blame her bear for the inability to sift through so many different scents. As it was, Cole was afraid he'd have to shift to his cat pretty soon to discern the boys' specific scents among so many others. It didn't help that the boys had played near his tree so often that their scent had practically embedded itself in his territory.

The fact that his cat actually *liked* that was something he'd have to explore later.

"I get it," he finally said as he led her back to her place. "We'll all get the hang of this. Of course, when we do, the humans will probably change something else." He was trying to keep her mind off the terror of what could be wrong, but he could tell it wasn't working. Her eyes were wide, but she was trying to track the boys, as well.

As far as he could tell, however, the kids hadn't been this way early that morning. He could be wrong though since they may have come another way to sneak out of the house. Only he didn't think the boys were that undisciplined to break the rules so soon after getting into trouble in the first place. *That* was what worried him. They might be little and want to explore, but they wouldn't risk the wrath of their mother the day after getting reprimanded.

The scent of an adult bear filtered through the air, and Cole looked over at Anya's brother. The man wore an old pair of sweats and a shirt he'd put on inside out, probably changing in a hurry to begin the hunt. It was early enough in the morning that most everyone would be asleep. Cole would wake them up in a heartbeat though if he needed the den on full alert.

"You find them?" Oliver asked, his brows drawn.

Cole shook his head. "I'm going to try and see if I can pick up any new scents around the house. We'll find them."

"There isn't another option," Anya said softly.

Oliver glanced between them, his gaze falling to Cole and Anya's clasped hands. Anya let go as if she'd been burned, and Cole tried not to take offense. There were more important things to think about.

Cole left the two siblings to search on their own as he lowered his head and made his way around to the back of the building. If he remembered correctly, the bedrooms were on this side, and that's where he needed to start. As soon as he found the open window, he frowned.

Something was off about it, but he wasn't sure what. He inhaled deeply, letting each and every scent around him coat his senses. He closed his eyes, trying to unweave and disregard the scents that wouldn't help him on his hunt. Not all shifters could do this so precisely, but that was why he was the Tracker. There was something...off about one of the scents. It smelled like a shifter, but he couldn't quite place it. He opened his eyes as he scented the boys. It was strong here, meaning the boys had been outside this morning and had used this window to get out. Only their scents weren't on the window itself.

Owen and Lucas hadn't opened the window on their own.

Fuck.

He lowered his head, inhaled around the wooden panes surrounding the glass and cursed.

"What is it?" Anya asked.

He'd noticed that she'd come around to the back end of the house, but he'd been focused on his scenting instead of acknowledging her.

"Someone opened this window from the outside and

carried the boys out of it." He turned to her, his cat raging at him, wanting a fight. "Whoever it was carried each boy, one at a time, then put them in a bag or something because their scent isn't directly on the ground beneath the window."

Anya growled, low, deadly. "A bag? Someone kidnapped my cubs and put them in a bag?"

He held up his hands, praying she wouldn't swipe at him. She curled her hands at her sides, and he knew she was struggling to control her bear. The bear wanted to shift and rip anyone in her way to shreds, and he didn't blame her, but that wouldn't help anyone right then.

"You good?" he asked after she took a few deep breaths.

"Nothing is *good* about this," she snapped. Her nostrils flared, but she gave him a tight nod. "But I'm not going to gut you or shift right now."

"Good to know," he said lightly. "I'm going to shift to my cat now and see if I can follow the man's scent."

"It's a man?"

"I think so," he said. "I also think the guy masked his scent somehow because I can't get a lead on exactly *what* he is. The scent is heavier here as if he just randomly popped up into existence at your window. Since that's impossible, I think he covered his trail to get here, and after a while, it wore off or something. Once I shift to my cat, I might get a better handle on it." He met her gaze. "That's also why you couldn't scent him in the room with the boys." She hadn't said as much, but she would have told him if she'd scented another in that room.

Her lips thinned and she gave him a tight nod.

He let out a breath then unzipped his pants. He hadn't bothered to button them when he'd run to the door at her knocking. He also hadn't bothered with underwear. Her gaze fell on his cock as he stripped down, but she didn't say anything. He could scent her arousal even through her pain and rage and it killed him. It wasn't the first time he'd scented it, but he pushed it aside as he had before. His dick filled and stood at attention in her presence as it usually did, but he ignored it. This wasn't the time to worry about attraction and his dick's feelings.

He quickly shifted to his cat, the familiar burn and ache not cooling his libido. He rolled his shoulders then started to track. Anya and Oliver kept a good distance between themselves and him, and he was grateful for that. They'd interfere, and he couldn't allow that to happen, not when Lucas's and Owen's lives were at stake.

In his jaguar form, each scent was intensified. The world around him felt as if each trail of forest, man, and shifter were a tactile disarray that he would now be able to unfold and unravel if he truly focused. His sight was crisper, his hearing even more sensitive. He could feel the brush between his toes, and knew the pads of his feet picked up on even the barest trace of disturbance in the ground. If he let his cat take over, he knew he'd be fully immersed in all of his senses. However, it was the man within that made him who he was. Without both halves of the whole, he wouldn't be Cole.

He followed the scent of the man—he was sure it was a man now—and the muted scents of the two boys. Since it was only scents, he couldn't tell if the boys had been struggling or not. However, he didn't taste the vivid scent of death. The boys were alive when they were taken.

That was something, at least.

He continued to follow the trail that led the boys away from the house and toward the high fence that kept the shifters in and the humans that did not work for the SAU out. Only that didn't appear to work in either case. Some shifters were still able to sneak away for Pack business, and as was evidenced by what had happened that morning, a human *could* come onto Pack land.

Cole shifted back, his body sweat-slick from shifting back and forth so quickly.

"What is it?" Anya asked. She kept a respectable distance between them, and he wasn't sure if it was because she wanted to keep the scents clean, or that she didn't want to be around him while he was naked. While most shifters didn't care about nudity, it was different when both parties were attracted to one another and fighting it. Because damn, he could tell she was fighting it as much as he was.

Oliver threw Cole's jeans at him, and Cole slid them on. It seemed the Foreseer had picked up on the undertones between Cole and Anya. He didn't know if that was good or bad, but it didn't matter right then. He'd deal with this ache later—once the boys were safe and whoever had taken them lay in a pool of his own blood.

"They scaled the fence," Cole growled. "Not well since the bastard cut himself on the way up. He's human and he's not light on his feet. Whatever kept his scent hidden from us was man-made. Science. It wasn't skill."

Humans kidnapping shifter cubs wasn't unheard of. But most who dared to try were killed instantly. And then the shifters were punished for daring to harm a human. This man, however, had used science in a way that Cole didn't understand, and that worried him. What else was out there? Why had the cubs been taken?

Cole looked over his shoulder, knowing this was far bigger than just a Tracker and a momma bear. He'd have to tell the Alphas, and *then* they could decide what to do. But they needed to get the hell out of there fast before the SAU patrols caught wind of them venturing too close to the edges of the enclosure.

Anya moved closer, her hands shaking. She leaned toward the fence and inhaled. When she froze and the scent of unadulterated fear mixed with her rage, Cole moved quickly. He cupped her face and forced her gaze to his. Oliver growled at his side, but he ignored the Foreseer. The damn man hadn't *seen* this. He hadn't known his nephews would be taken in the dead of night by a human who was able to hide from them. Foreseers might not be able to see those close to them, but damn it, this shouldn't have happened. Cole knew he shouldn't blame the bear, but fuck it, he needed to blame someone.

"Anya," Cole bit out. He ran his thumbs along her cheekbones, the skin so soft there he had to hold back a groan. *Not the time, cat.*

"I know this human," she whispered.

Cole blinked, shock smashing into him.

"No," Oliver bit out. "Fuck no."

"What do you mean?" Cole asked, his voice shaking. The only humans shifters knew were their jailers, the SAU. How could she know this particular human? Why would Oliver be speaking as if he'd heard from a ghost of their past? Dread slid down Cole's spine and he swallowed hard before speaking. "How do you know this human?"

Anya blinked up at him, agony and anger warring in her blue eyes. "Their father," she whispered. "Lucas and Owen's father."

Cole took a step back, blinking. "What the fuck?"

Anya lifted her lip in a snarl, her bear in her eyes. "It was a mistake. A long time ago. I was an idiot and too trusting, but that is *not* the issue right now. That motherfucker stole my babies, and I will be getting them back. *Now.*"

She turned toward the fence and looked ready to climb. As a cat, he could jump over it in one leap. As a bear, she'd be able to climb it just as easily. The wolves could jump pretty high as well, but he'd never seen a bear clear the fence without having to use their hands or paws first. He reached out and gripped her shoulder. She pulled away from his touch, growling.

"Don't you dare stop me, cat."

He snarled. "Think about what you're doing. You can't just leave the den with your fucking collar on without thinking it through. Have you ever been outside your den? I know damn well you haven't been outside of this one. You don't even know the interior workings of the den, let alone outside the damn thing. Take a step back. We need to talk to the Alphas and get permission before we just leave the den and risk the rest of our people."

She swiped at him, her claws out, ready to spill blood. "Those are my *sons*. They are my number one priority."

He let out a breath, trying to remain calm. "Oliver."

"Got it. Hurt her, though, and I take it out of your hide." The Foreseer ran toward the den center to get the Alphas and form an emergency meeting.

"Cole. Get out of my way."

He growled, low and deadly, his chest rumbling with the anger of his cat. "We need to make sure others know what's happening. What if your boys weren't the only ones taken? What if someone knows something that can help? Going out blind will only hurt us. It could endanger not only our lives but the boys', as well."

"Their lives are already in danger." Her bear was so close to the surface he was afraid she'd break right then if she didn't take a step back.

So he did the only thing he could to get her mind off the danger.

He kissed her.

It was a quick but brutal meeting of lips. Just to put her bear on the path of another danger, another fear that he knew she held.

She pushed at him, her claws digging into his shoulders. When she ripped her mouth from his she screamed, "What the fuck?" She looked angry, but at least she didn't look like she was on the edge of insanity as she had before. That was at least something.

"You better?" he asked.

She deliberately wiped her mouth with the back of her hand. He wouldn't let that sting.

"I won't say thank you." She let out a breath. "I need my babies."

"And we're going to get them." He held out his hand, and she stared at it for a moment before placing her smaller one in his. He squeezed once and nodded. "Let's go."

"YOU HAVE THE SCENT?" Holden asked, his brows lowered. "You can track it?"

Cole nodded. "Yeah, I can. And I will."

They'd been at the den center for five minutes with the other Alphas and various shifters who thought they could help and were already forming a plan. The entire Pack couldn't meet to discuss what was going on since the SAU was always watching. If they thought the shifters were planning a revolt out in the open, it would spell disaster for the actual revolt they kept secret.

"You're not leaving me behind," Anya snapped. "Those are my sons."

Cole nodded. He hadn't planned to leave Anya in the den at all. Though it grated on him that he'd be leading her into danger, there was no way she'd be safe back at the compound. She'd end up going feral in her worry for her sons. If he were by her side, he could hopefully keep her bear at bay while they hunted for her cubs.

"It's a human who hid his scent," Jonah said with a frown. "That worries me. What else are the humans hiding?"

"Maybe we'll find out while we're there, but my first priority is Owen and Lucas." He raised his chin but didn't meet his Alpha's eyes. There was a reason the big cat was the Alpha, after all.

"I understand," Jonah said gruffly. "But take in what information you can." He paused, looking at the others in the room. "What else do we know about this human?" He looked at Anya. "You said he's the boys' father?"

Anya's jaw clenched. "Yes, their father. He was a human scientist who led me to believe he was on our side. He lied. He left the first chance he could once other humans figured out he was a sympathizer—or at least made others believe he was. He wanted nothing to do with my pregnancy. He's never met the boys." She swallowed. "Until this morning."

Andrew, the Ursine Alpha, let out a curse. "Well, fuck it, Anya. Who is this guy and why didn't I kill him when I had the chance?"

She met her Alpha's gaze, and Cole wanted to reach out and hold her close. "If I could go back in time, I'd kill him myself. You know that."

"What's his name?" Ariel asked. She sat next to her mate Holden, her eyes glossy with tears. "What else can you tell us about him? I know you're planning to follow his scent, but is there anything else?"

"His name is Frank Talbot. That's all I know. I don't even know if he's part of the SAU anymore."

Cora sucked in a breath. "Frank Talbot?"

Soren cursed beside her and brought her close, running his hands down her back.

"What? What is it?" Cole asked, frowning.

"Frank was the one who kidnapped us," Cora said, her voice filled with the rage of a tiger princess.

Anya took a step back, her body shaking. Cole was there in an instant, not touching her, but close enough that he could catch her if she should fall. She looked over her shoulder at him, her face deathly pale. She didn't fall, but her shoulders lowered once he stood near.

"No," she whispered. "How...how is that possible?"

Andrew growled, his voice low. "It seems that Dr. Talbot has a lot of explaining to do."

Soren tilted his head and studied Cole. "We can't let too many of us leave at once. You and Anya will have to find this bastard on your own. Kill him for me, for daring to touch my mate. I will not be able to spill his blood, but you will."

Cole nodded, vowing to the wolf who loved his feline mate with all of his tortured soul. Anya leaned against Cole's chest and he put his hand on her hip, aware others were watching. He wasn't sure she even noticed, her mind had retreated into her own panic and fear. He understood that, and once they found the boys, he'd make sure they discussed what was going on between the two of them.

"Be careful," Cora said suddenly. "He got kicked out of the SAU from what I could tell. That means the SAU...and others are looking for him."

He frowned. "Others?"

Soren met his gaze. "Others. Be on the lookout."

The Unseen? Could that be what he was talking about? The shifters that had escaped being corralled by the humans lived in secret, their very existence a death sentence. What would the Unseen want with Frank Talbot? Not all shifters knew of the Unseen, but Cole did, he'd scented them before. He'd always given them a wide berth, as he hadn't wanted to alert anyone of his presence while outside the den walls...but if he could use them to find Owen and Lucas he'd break his rule in a heartbeat.

Anya pulled away from him and turned to meet his gaze. He'd find her children, then figure out the next step. Because no matter what, he wasn't letting go of this feeling, this connection.

Something had changed.

Something important.

But first, he needed to save the lives of those currently in the hands of a human who deserved something far worse than death.

Far worse.

5

Anya stood near the fence seven minutes after leaving the Alphas. The meeting itself had only taken nine minutes. It had been thirty-four minutes since she'd noticed her boys missing.

Thirty-four minutes and a lifetime of agony.

She pulled at the long sleeves of the shirt Ariel had passed to her as they'd headed out. The brand on Anya's skin would never fade away—the SAU has made sure of that—but she could at least keep it covered while they were outside the den walls.

Since she'd been forced inside at the tender age of seven, she hadn't been outside the compound except to travel from the former Ursine den to her new home. Other than that, she'd only seen the outside world via the glimpses others showed her in photographs and recounted memories. She barely remembered what the world looked like without a cage around it. She hadn't seen the effects of a badly depleted human population after the Verona Virus had almost taken them out.

Now she was about to follow a cat she didn't even like into a world that scared her more than she'd ever admit, to find her sons and bring them home. If she could kill the bastard that had broken her heart and stolen her babies in the process, she would.

Revenge would take a backseat to her children's safety, however.

Cole came up to her side, Oliver behind him. Her brother frowned, worry etched on his face. He hadn't seen this, she knew. If he had, he'd have done all in his power to stop it. She couldn't blame him for what happened, and didn't. She'd learned long ago that her fate was up to her and her alone. The others could rely on a Foreseer. She only had her brother, not the magic in his veins.

Her bear pushed at her as it had been all morning. Only it wasn't as severe as it had been when she'd been at the fence before. If Cole hadn't kissed her, knocking her for a loop, she might have gone bear and hurt herself or someone she cared about. Her bear didn't think about more than the need to make someone bleed for daring to touch Owen and Lucas. Anya had barely held in her control and almost snapped until Cole had pressed his lips to hers, keeping her sane.

She wouldn't thank him for that, though she knew she should.

She'd also ignore the way his lips had felt against hers, the way his heated body had felt pressed to hers.

There was no use thinking things like that. Her feelings were just a momentary lapse in judgment brought on by a traumatic event and the inability to cope.

Cole tilted his head then reached out, tracing the metal collar on her neck. She didn't move back from his touch, neither did she lean forward. She honestly didn't know which way her body would respond, so she stood still.

"I have the scent trail down and we need to move fast. But we can't be wearing these, Anya. It's a death sentence to take them off, but it's a beacon for anyone who sees us wearing them outside these walls. We'll have to take them off and keep them on us for when we return. We can keep the brands hidden, but we're still going to have to look as inconspicuous as possible."

She nodded, her hands going up to the clasp at the back of her neck. She'd never taken her collar off, not since she'd been forced to wear it at age seven. She slept in it, fought it in, made love in it, showered it in...everything in her life held the mark of the brand and the collar. The metal grew during a shift so she could wear it as a bear, and had grown as she'd aged. It was specially made by scientists who thought they were gods. She'd seen friends die at the hands of the SAU because those shifters had fought for their freedom. They'd lost, but Anya prayed that would not always be the case.

Cole's fingers brushed hers as he helped her with the

clasp. It wasn't easy to take off. It had been built to stay tight until the day they died. The SAU probably wanted shifters to be buried with their collars, but that didn't happen. Of the bodies the Pack was allowed to keep—the SAU sometimes took bodies to experiment on—the Alphas took the collars off so the dead could be laid to rest. As free as they could be. All would wear their brands in death, but the ink that lay on top made it their own.

The lock on the back opened with a snap and she shuddered at the sound. That wasn't the click of freedom, but confirmation of the brevity of the situation.

Cole took the collar and slid it into his hoodie pocket, his collar already off. He cupped her face, his gaze intense.

"We'll fix this," he whispered, his words a vow.

"I know." And she did. She might not have believed this cat before, but she knew from the way he tracked and the promise in his words that he would find a way to fix this. And she'd die before she gave up. There was no other option.

"Anya."

She turned at her brother's voice, pulling away from Cole in the process. She didn't know why the feline kept touching her, but he needed to stop before something happened. Something idiotic.

"Be safe," her brother said softly, his eyes on Cole and not her. She cleared her throat, and Oliver looked down at her. "I can't see what is coming."

"I know," she whispered. She patted his cheek then kissed his chin. "I'll come back with them. I promise."

He nodded. "I'll keep the house waiting for you. If the SAU patrols come near, we'll keep your absence hidden."

She closed her eyes, knowing if their escape were noticed, it would mean not only her death but likely the death of those close to her, as well. The SAU didn't take rebellion lightly.

She turned away from her brother and climbed the fence, slightly envious that Cole could jump it in one motion. She was a bear and slightly heavier than the other shifters because of her DNA. She might be able to climb as well as a cat, but she didn't have the same balance.

When she hit the ground on the other side, her knees ached, but she took the pain in stride. It helped her remember that everything she did from here on out would be dangerous. She looked behind her, but Oliver was gone. Her brother probably didn't want to stand by the fences for too long and attract attention. On that note, she raised her brow at Cole, who had a serious frown on his face.

"What?"

"Just keeping up with the scent. I'm better as a jaguar, but it's not like those are very common in the Colorado landscape. It doesn't matter that we're in a forest where seeing a bear would be common, the SAU will shoot on sight. I have to concentrate harder to track like this. It'll take more energy, meaning we can't go as far in one day."

"I know, Cole. I don't blame you for having to go slower. You're trying to save my children."

"Far cry from what you'd usually do, though."

She shrugged, following him closely and keeping an eye on their surroundings. While he kept tracking, she would watch their backs. He couldn't do it all at once, so she would do what she could to keep them safe.

"I'll berate you when we have Owen and Lucas back."

She would not think about her use of the word *we* just then.

"Good enough." He grunted. "Fuck. He got into a car here, Anya."

She froze and looked down at the tracks at their feet. "No. No. We can't lose him." For some reason, use of a vehicle hadn't occurred to her. Of course, it should have, but she'd never driven before. She didn't have the need within a den.

"I can still track him, but doing it this way is going to be a whole lot harder. If he went into the city, I might lose the trail completely since the scents will be mixed so well. We'll have to find him using other ways if that's the case."

She fisted her hands at her size. "What other ways?"

He met her gaze, his cat in his eyes. "If we can't use our sense of smell, we'll ask around, find out who knows something about shifters being hidden and taken away."

Anya took a step back. "What the hell? You can't just ask a human that? It's a dead giveaway that we're shifters. They'll kill us."

"You're right. They will. That's why we won't ask a human."

She blinked. "You're talking about the Unseen."

Cole let out a breath. "Thank God. I was worried you didn't know what they were, and I vowed to my Alpha I wouldn't speak of them to those who didn't know."

"Andrew didn't vow me to secrecy since I wouldn't tell anyone anyway. I shouldn't have blurted it out to you as I did, but you caught me by surprise. You're telling me that we're going to find the Unseen and try to find my sons that way?"

"If that's what it takes."

Anya let out a breath. "Fine, then. Let's go. We don't want to stay in one place for long."

"Got it." With that, he went back to his tracking. She'd never seen him so in his element. His face contorted as he concentrated, but then he'd relax ever so slightly, only his jaw remaining strained. The amount of energy it must take to use his ability as he did was staggering. She couldn't pinpoint the individual scents of her sons and Frank after the human piece of trash had gotten into the car. Now she only smelled exhaust fumes and her own desperation.

And the spicy scent that was all Cole.

Not that she would be thinking of that. At all.

Ever.

They moved toward the city of Denver quickly and in silence. Cole needed to focus, and she needed to keep her bear from panicking. She was far stronger than her bear, but on edge as she was, it wasn't easy to keep in control. Her gaze kept going to the mountains in the west and the plains in the east. There was nothing more beautiful than the landscape of the Denver area. Once the shifters had roamed free through these woods and peaks. They'd lived and worked within the human world, yet could shift to their other half and be free in the wilderness.

When the Verona Virus had hit over twenty-five years ago, only the humans got sick. Anya never knew exactly why the shifters were spared, but she had her suspicions. As time passed and more humans died with no cure in sight, others noticed that family groups hadn't gotten sick. Shifters were immune to the virus, and in the process of trying to find a cure, her people were revealed to the public. Shifters were not only able to help create a vaccine, but they'd also inadvertently started their own path to death.

The humans—what was left of them after the Verona Virus had decimated a third of them—were fearful of what they didn't understand. The government fast-tracked laws and stipulations, and the Shifter Accommodation Unit was born. They were the fourth branch of the government and didn't have to wait for Congress, the courts, or the President to make decisions.

Around each major city within the United States—and perhaps the world—compounds had been built for the three species. Ursines, Felines, and Canines were separated from those they loved and placed into camps where they had almost died from neglect. The SAU had eventually given them enough leeway to live and form new Packs within their cages, but it had brought them close to their extinction.

Where once, shifters would mate with different species, they were then forced to find their mates and have children with only their own kind within their respective compounds. That would have been fine for some, but not for all. When the SAU forced the cats and bears into the River Pack's Canine compound, it opened up possibilities. There were now enough shifters that perhaps people could find someone they wanted to spend the rest of their lives with, but it was still a far cry from where things had once been.

Only in recent months had a human been bitten and changed into a shifter during a mating. That had once been rare, but part of their culture. Now it was taboo. The SAU hadn't been aware that there were ways to make shifters, and now they had an idea. That idea had led to Cora and Soren's kidnapping.

By Frank.

The man who'd fathered Anya's babies.

It had all come full circle, it seemed.

As they reached the south side of the city, her legs grew weak and she knew they needed to rest.

"I can track from a moving vehicle," Cole said suddenly. "I'll get us one, steal it since no one is going to give us one. But I can still track while driving."

"I don't know how to drive," she said, taking a sip of her

water. She handed Cole the bottle and tried not to watch the way his throat worked as he drank.

"I do," he said simply. "I had to learn. We're about an hour away from downtown Denver if we drive. I have a feeling that Frank is on his way there."

She frowned. "Why? Aren't there more people there?"

Cole shook his head. "Parts of downtown are completely abandoned since there aren't as many people living here as there once was. We're about a twenty-minute hike from Colorado Springs, which lost almost all of its population when the virus hit. We'll have a better chance of getting a vehicle here and making our way up to the city." His brows rose. "Places near large military bases got hit hard. Makes you wonder, doesn't it?"

Her mind whirled, trying to process everything he was saying. "I...I don't understand."

"I don't either. All I know is that my cat is telling me to head north. And downtown has tons of old buildings that are perfect for a doctor on the run. I don't know if I'm right, but we'll find out as we go along. As for now, we've been at this for a few hours and I'd rather find a place to stay for the evening and make our next steps soon."

"But we need to keep going." Her babies needed her.

"I get that. We're going to go for a couple more hours. That will give us time to get the car and drive for a bit. But I want us to be clear-headed and ready to fight if we have to once we get closer to the city. I'm getting beat by keeping my tracking up for so long."

The fact that he would admit to such a weakness told her something—*what* she didn't know.

"Let's get going, then."

He nodded. "Frank had a car. We're on foot, so he has an advantage, but Anya, we're going to find them."

"I know," she said softly. She didn't know how she'd live if she couldn't find them.

They went for another thirty minutes until they reached an older neighborhood. She had lived in one similar to this when she'd been outside the compound. She'd played in the streets and rode her bike. She'd played tag with her brother and had laughed with her friends.

"These cars will be dead, Cole."

"Yeah, but we can find a way to jump one or something. I'm not without talents."

She frowned but followed him, careful to keep her eyes on their surroundings. If they were caught, they were dead. There would be no second chances.

They searched through a few of the garages, breaking through small windows in some cases, walking right in others. People had left their lives in a hurry all those years ago. It was a wasteland out here. What had once been privilege was now theirs for scraping by.

"I can't believe there's no one here," she said as they entered the fourth garage on their search for a vehicle they could work with.

"There's some in other neighborhoods I bet. This one's just closest to the compounds, so humans probably don't want to live out here. Denver's growing, I know that much. I bet the other cities are, as well. It's been a quarter of a century, and though the virus left a lot of the major cities without as many people, the humans are bouncing back."

"The rural areas didn't get hit as hard with the virus, if I remember right," she said, recalling memories of a time when she'd been free.

"Yep. The cities got hit the hardest. Some rural communities didn't get a single hit at all. I have no idea what the actual landscape looks like now. I just know Colorado Springs was one of the hardest hit, hence why it looks like this. I remember them saying something like ninety-six percent of the city died from the virus. A part of the percentage left living were shifters. The other hightailed it out of here."

"So many people," she whispered.

Cole's jaw clenched. "And those that survived voted to have us put in cages."

She shook her head. "They voted for a way to be safe. Or at least that's what they thought."

He blinked at her, and she raised her chin. "You're defending the humans that slaughtered us. That branded your children and put collars around our necks."

She closed her eyes, remembering Lucas's and Owen's screams as if they had happened that morning.

"No. I'm not. Not really. I'm saying they made a mistake. They thought in the moment and killed us, imprisoned us. I won't forget that, but I can't be angry all the time. If I am, then I can't raise my children." It was something she'd learned when she'd held them to her chest for the first time, their little heartbeats fast and perfect.

He studied her face for a moment then turned back to the Jeep in front of them. "I think this one will work. There's an old unit out here I can finagle to give us a jump. Plus, there are a couple of batteries on the shelf that look unused. I'll create a current and we can get on our way."

She'd angered him with her words, and she knew she should have taken them back. She hadn't said what she wanted to. Not the right way, and now he'd put distance between them. Only, perhaps they needed that distance.

She took a step toward him, ready to help, when her body gave out.

She gasped, her knees hitting the cement floor of the garage as she tried to breathe.

"Anya!" Cole knelt in front of her, his hands on her shoulders. "What's wrong?"

Her bear pushed at her again; only this time she finally understood why her bear had been acting so oddly the past couple of days. Her breasts ached, her nipples pebbling at the scent of the man in front of her.

She licked her lips, a moan escaping her. "Not right now," she groaned.

"Oh, shit."

"Yeah." She sucked in a breath and put her hands on his forearms. "Mating heat."

Cole's eyes widened, and she would have laughed at the

reaction if she weren't in so much pain. She needed sex, badly. It was part of their shifter DNA. Not all shifters dealt with it, but her family did. And it wasn't easy. It was their baser instincts coming to the forefront, their animals trying to procreate. It wasn't love, wasn't true desire.

Only when it was this hard, this...*hot,* she knew it was based on something akin to desire, to an emotion she didn't want to name. She'd been through this before and had found a nice male bear to scratch the itch. But this time, she knew it wouldn't just be an itch. This was *Cole,* and there was something different about him.

The only person who could help was the man in front of her.

The man who she didn't want to desire, even without the mating heat riding hard.

Oh shit, indeed.

6

Cole tried not to freak out. Considering his dick was hard and his hands were fisted by his sides, he wasn't sure what he was going to be able to do. He'd been around women in their mating heat before, but he'd never participated in what they needed in the end. And considering the mission he and Anya were on, this was the worst possible time for her to go into making heat. It may be a common thing among shifters, but that didn't mean it was something the two of them were ready to deal with at the moment.

He thought back to her aggression when it came to him, and the fact that she hadn't known what to do with her body when he stood too close. Or even how she'd reacted to him the past couple of days. He wanted to curse. She'd been having trouble all along but hadn't known this was coming. And if she didn't take care of herself, if he didn't help her in some way, she'd be in pain. It also didn't help that he wanted her under him like no other. He'd been lying to himself when he thought it was just anger and annoyance when it came to her presence—far from it. His cat wanted her, and damn it, so did the man. He wanted her spread out before him—naked, willing, wet, and *his*.

Only he wasn't sure that was the smartest thing to do right now. They were both running on a short supply of energy in a high rush of adrenaline. If they did this, everything would change. It wouldn't be a mating. Mating heats weren't like that. But it would be something. What, he didn't know. But he had a feeling Anya had no idea either.

She closed her eyes and groaned. "Cole. It hurts. Why does it hurt so much this time?"

"This time?" He frowned but did his best not to step forward. As soon as he stepped closer to her, all would be lost. He wouldn't be able to hold himself back anymore. As it was, he'd been keeping himself back for far too long. He hadn't even realized he was doing it until he felt the burn of unrequited need flame hot when she was near. It wasn't her fault that his cat wanted her. It wasn't her fault that the man didn't know what to do with either of them.

Anya blinked up at him, desire and pleading in her gaze. "I've been through this twice before. But it's never been as intense as this. It's always been something I could handle on my own. Or with just one man for just one time." She lowered her head and let out a soft moan. "But this time it's worse. Why is it worse?"

He watched her sway on her feet and he cursed. Stepping toward her with his arms out, he brought her closer to his chest and let out a groan of his own at the heat of her body pressed along his. He couldn't believe how fucking hot she was—and not just how she looked. Her skin was like a raging inferno, and he knew if she didn't get some form of release soon, her bear would be in trouble. He already had a momma bear on the lookout for two of her cubs on his hands; he didn't need a bear in the delirious haze that came with a mating heat denied, as well.

He cupped her face and brought his forehead to hers. He took a deep breath, inhaling her sweet scent that did nothing to help his aching cock. It only made him harder— something he didn't think was possible.

"I'll do this, I'll take care of your bear, and take care of you. But no matter what happens right here? It's something we'll have to talk about later. Because we're already pretty fucked up as it is. You get me?"

She rubbed her breasts along his chest, her nipples hard points. "I get you. We'll talk later. But I need you." She pulled back, a wince on her face. "I never thought I'd say that."

He cursed. As much as he wanted to hear that, he had a gut feeling that she didn't mean it the way he hoped—that she needed him beyond this moment, this night. But he wasn't about to think about that, not when they were outside the compound without their collars and anyone could come upon them at any moment. Like he'd said before, this was the worst possible time for something like this to happen. He just prayed that he wasn't making a giant mistake. That *they* weren't making a giant mistake.

"We'll stay here for the night," he whispered and ran his hands down her back. She shivered in his hold, and he had to rein in his cat before he took her to the garage floor and tasted every inch of her. Her mating heat had ramped up his own need, so now they were both fucked unless he helped them take care of it.

"And the boys?" She had her eyes closed, her head resting on his shoulder as she rocked back and forth. She had to be in so much pain, but she was trying to hold back. As always, her sons came first. Not that he blamed her for that, not even a little.

"We'll head up to Denver in the morning. Neither of us is in any condition to go anywhere now. We can stay here. I'll take care of you."

She narrowed her eyes at him, though he could see the mad heat in her gaze. "I don't like people taking care of me."

"Well, tonight you'll just have to let me. Because we both know you won't be able to do anything tomorrow if I don't take care of you tonight."

She rolled her eyes then groaned. "That is the worst line ever."

"It's not a line, it's a promise. It's the cards we've been dealt. So let me love you, and stop thinking you have to do everything on your own."

Her hands went to his back, her claws digging into his

shoulders. "The first time you kissed me it was to shut me up. And now, the first time we're going to have sex is because I'm in my mating heat. I don't have to take that."

"Then don't. Just take me."

He lifted her up and cupped her ass. She wrapped her legs around his waist, the heat of her pressing against his belly. He let out a small growl and turned toward the garage door that led into the house. The musty smell of a long forgotten home invaded his senses as he walked them inside, but he pushed that away, knowing he was about to do something that he might regret, but knew they both needed desperately.

He licked his way up her neck, nibbling just enough to bring them both closer to the edge.

"Cole," she breathed.

He bit down just a bit harder, not enough to break through the skin and mark her as his, but close enough that he had to pull back and get a grip on himself. This wasn't a true mating. His cat might want her, but he knew they were both riding high on adrenaline and need. He wasn't even sure what his cat wanted with Anya in the first place. It wasn't as if their kind had soul mates that created bonds with magic and all that shit. They were just flesh and blood creatures. Once his cat and he agreed on their need and love for a woman, and she wanted the same, *then* he'd have his mate. It wasn't fate, wasn't an explosion of senses that told him this one person would be his forever. It might be true that not everyone found someone their shifter half wanted in the same way—and it was even more rare now that they were trapped within compound walls—but that didn't mean it was a bond like so many thought.

He didn't know why he was even thinking about things like that right then. He had a willing and sexy woman in his arms, wrapped around his waist. He didn't need anything else. They'd deal with the consequences of their actions later.

Shit.

Consequences.

He stepped into the bedroom and set her on the floor. She nuzzled his chest, and he let out a low growl. Someone had left the sheets on the bed, and he didn't see that much dirt and dust left over. Thankfully.

The people who left this house hadn't abandoned it twenty-five years ago like some. No, considering the dust—or lack thereof—it seemed as if someone had lived here within the last year or so. Not everyone jumped ship as soon as the virus hit. Some had tried to make it—though he hadn't been around to see it. Instead, he'd been inside the Feline compound with the rest of his people.

But back to the consequences. He muttered a curse and cupped her face. His chest heaved as he fought for breath. Damn it. His cock was so damn hard; he figured he'd only last about two seconds the first time he was in her wet heat.

"Anya. I don't have any condoms." Any protection he might find inside this place would be expired by now.

She moved back, her eyes wide. "Shit," she whispered. A

sheen of sweat glossed her brow, and he knew she had to be in pain. Shifters weren't allowed to take birth control since the government regulated it. "I...I can try to take care of it myself." She ran her hand down her belly and slid her fingers behind the waistband of her jeans.

They both sucked in a breath when she found her clit. He might not be able to see what she was doing behind her zipper, but he could scent it.

He put his palm over her hand, the denim between them. He met her gaze as he pushed slightly with his fingers, angling her hand so it hit her just right.

"Is you getting yourself off going to be enough?" His voice was deep. Rough. "I can still touch you, lick you up and eat you out. But if we fuck right here, I could get you pregnant. It's your mating heat, after all." Shifters were more fertile during this time; it was why they had the damn thing in the first place.

She closed her eyes, rocking herself into her hand. It was the sexiest damn thing he'd ever seen in his life. Her cheeks were flushed, her body toned yet soft in the best places. She was damn tall, but she was a bear, so that was natural. He loved that he didn't have to bend down to kiss her. It would make things interesting in bed.

Her teeth bit into her lip as she moved her hand faster and faster. He pressed into her, helping her as much as he could. He curled his fingers and her mouth parted.

"Close?"

She shook her head. "No. Maybe? God, it's not enough."

She met his gaze, a look of pleading once again there. "I... maybe if I take a cold shower or something."

He leaned forward and took her lower lip between his teeth. She froze, her hand no longer trying to get herself off. He squeezed her once, just a tease. She licked her lips.

"I wanted you before this, Anya." Her eyes widened. "I wanted you bent over that rock beside my favorite tree. I wanted to sink my cock into your cunt and fuck you hard until we were both left panting and sated. I wanted you to ride my face as I licked up your sweet pussy, savoring every taste. I wanted that, but I ignored it. So what happens now? That's not on just the mating heat. I wanted you before. And I want you now."

"I...I wanted you, too. But I didn't want to." It looked as if the admission were ripped from her lips, but he understood. Interspecies couplings hadn't been unheard of all those years ago, but when everyone was separated, the art of seduction between the species was lost.

"Then let me make love to you, Anya. If you get pregnant, we'll deal with it together." He couldn't believe what he was saying. Maybe the mating heat had fried a few of his brain cells.

"You can't be serious."

"You need this, *I* need it. We'll take the consequences as they come. Right now it's just you and me. It's who we are. We aren't human, baby. Our animals need this. *We* need this. So listen to what your bear is telling you and ride out the heat with me. And in the morning, we'll save your sons and gut that bastard for daring to touch them. When we get home, *then* we'll deal with what happened here. But for now, just live here in the moment with me. Be here with me."

She studied his face for a moment then slid her hand out from between her thighs. He tilted his head, waiting to see what she would do. When she placed her wet fingers against his lips, he groaned. His tongue flicked out to taste her juices. So damn sweet. He gripped her wrist and brought her hand closer, licking every single fucking drop as he kept his gaze on hers. It was the most erotic thing he'd ever done, and never in his wildest dreams would he have thought he'd be doing this here with her.

When he was through, he took his hand and threaded his fingers into her hair, bringing her closer. He crushed his mouth to hers, their tongues tangling as he deepened the kiss. As their mouths fused together, he cupped one breast, pinching her nipple before sliding his hand down her belly and behind her jeans. She'd soaked her panties, and his fingers were coated at just one brush.

He pulled away slightly so he could watch her face as he pushed her panties to the side and speared her with three fingers. She threw her head back into his other hand, a shout escaping her lips as she clenched around his fingers.

"You're fucking tight, baby, but damn, you're so wet. Think you can come on my fingers? Just a little to take off the edge. Then I'll lick you up and make you come again."

Her cunt spasmed, squeezing his fingers again. "You like

when I talk dirty?" He brushed his thumb along her clit, and she shivered.

"I knew you'd be crude," she bit out, her eyes dancing. "But I'm not some pretty little virgin, Cole. So after you get me off, I'm stripping your jeans off and sucking that fat cock of yours. And I know it's fat because I've felt it against my thigh, my belly. I've *seen* you before you shifted. I know you're going to stretch me and fill me so full that I'm going to scream. And because you're a shifter, I'm going to make you come down my throat, and then fuck me hard immediately after because you can recover just that quickly."

His dick pressed hard into his zipper and he was sure he'd have a scar along the length. "Holy fuck. I love your mouth."

She licked her lips. "You're going to love it more wrapped around your cock."

He tossed back his head and laughed before pressing her clit. "I love the way you think." He pumped his fingers in and out of her pussy while his other hand held firmly to the back of her head, keeping her gaze on his. "Come for me, Anya. Take the edge off. Do it."

She arched into him, her pupils widening as she came on his hand, her cunt squeezing his fingers so hard, he almost came thinking about how it would feel around his cock.

He pulled his hand out of her pants, licked each finger, savoring her taste, then kissed her one more time. "Feel good, Anya?"

"More..." she whispered. "I need more." With that, she went to her knees and had his pants undone and his dick in her hand before he could formulate a response.

"Anya, you don't have to...oh my God, your mouth is so fucking hot." She wrapped her lips around the tip and sucked, flicking her tongue along the crease. He wrapped his hand in her hair and used his other hand to trace her chin. "Baby, this is about you. Why don't you get on the bed and let me take care of you."

She hummed along his cock, taking him deeper. When his tip reached the back of her throat and she swallowed, his eyes crossed. His knees shook, and she deep throated him before letting him go so she could lick the underside of his dick and cup his balls. He honestly never thought this would be happening, but he wasn't about to let go of the moment. He leaned over her and gripped the bottom of her shirt, pulling it up.

"Let go for a moment, baby." She held up her hands, and he slid her shirt off. As soon as she was free, her hands were back on his dick, rubbing him down to the point he had to do multiplication tables in his head so he wouldn't come on her face right then. He'd rather be inside her when he came.

"One more time." She pulled away, her eyebrows raised as he quickly undid her bra. Right as he leaned forward to cup her breasts, she had her mouth on his cock again. He swallowed hard, doing his best to make this about her, but damn it was hard when she had her sweet mouth on his dick, working him like she knew exactly how he liked it. This woman knew what she wanted, what *he* wanted, and took as much as she gave. He fucking loved that. As soon as she let him, he'd show her he could do the same.

Funny, he'd never been this...connected...to another person during sex before. But he wouldn't think about that, not right then. And maybe not ever if things turned out poorly for the both of them. He pushed those thoughts out of his head and rolled her nipples between his fingers. He loved the look of her breasts, bigger than a handful but perfect for him. He'd only gotten a glimpse of them before when they'd shifted, but now, when she pulled back from sucking on his dick, he could see her nipples were dark and hard. They were a little larger than some women's nipples, but he figured that might have to do with the fact that she'd nursed two boys. He didn't care, because damn it, she looked fucking perfect.

She dug her nails into his thighs and swallowed him down her throat again, this time growling. The vibrations went straight to the base of his cock and he cursed. His spine buzzed and he pulled away from her breasts. He wrapped one hand in her hair.

"I'm going to come. Shit. Pull back, baby."

She growled again, sucking him down deeper. When he came, his knees shook and he closed his eyes, the pressure so fucking hard he could barely breathe. He looked down halfway through, prying open his eyes, and wanted to come again at the sight of Anya on her knees in front of him, topless and so fucking strong. She met his gaze and bobbed her head, swallowing each and every drop from his cock.

"That was...that was the best fucking blow job of my life."

Anya pulled away, a satisfied grin on her face as she wiped the edges of her mouth where he'd almost spilled over. "Good. Though next time, I want to try to swallow all of you. I couldn't get all of you in my mouth."

His cat did a little prideful strut, its chest puffed out.

Her eyes widened and she gripped his thighs again.

He inhaled, the sweet scent of her arousal growing stronger. "Okay, honey, don't worry. We'll take care of you. Let's get your pants off and I'll help you. You want my mouth or my dick? You tell me. Anything you want."

"I want you in me," she said as she stood. He picked her up before she could protest. He kicked off his shoes and jeans then set her on the bed.

"Hips up, baby. Let's get you out of these pants. Then I'll fill you up and make us both feel good. I'll eat you out after."

She snorted. "Promises, promises."

He quickly stripped her bare then shucked off his clothes. He palmed his cock, still hard but wet from her mouth. "I'll make good on my promises, Anya. You can count on that."

Her skin was flushed, her curves flaring out in all the right places. She had scars on her body from fights, and stretch marks from the twins. Yet she was the most beautiful woman he'd ever seen. Those marks only showed him the depth of her true beauty.

When he told her that, she tilted her head, her gaze curious. "Really? You don't need to use lines, Cole. I know what this is. It's a mating heat."

He shook his head as he climbed on top of her. He brushed his lips along hers as he positioned himself at her entrance. "Really, Anya. I'm not using lines. I'm telling you what I'm thinking—what I've thought since I first saw you when you moved into the compound. This, right here, might be fast-tracked because of the mating heat, but we would have been here eventually. You. Me. And my dick inside you. Because you know we both want this more than you're saying. So be in the now, be with *me*. And later we'll talk more about what this means."

He wasn't the kind of cat to say these things. He was the lazy one, according to her. He liked to fight, work for his Pack, then come home and relax with a beer or lounge in his tree. If he had a woman in his bed, then he'd be great. If he didn't, then he'd do something else to pass the time. And yet right then, with Anya, it was different. It scared him more than he wanted to admit, and from the look on her face—despite the mating heat—he knew it scared her, too.

So, without dealing with any of that, he kissed her hard and slammed home.

She screamed his name, her claws digging into his back. The scent of blood hit his nose and he knew she'd broken the skin. He didn't care. He'd wear her marks with pride. As it was, he could see stars behind his eyelids. She felt so good around his cock. Wet, hot, and tight. Fucking perfect.

"Cole, for the love of God. Please move. Fuck me. I'm not weak. I'm a bear, remember? I need it rough. I need you. Now."

He grinned then bit her lip. Hard. "As you wish, Anya." He pulled his hips back and fucked her.

Hard.

She met him thrust for thrust, her legs wrapped around his waist. He slid one hand under her butt and angled her so he could go deeper. They both panted, their bodies slick with sweat. As his balls tightened, he rotated his hips so he hit her G-spot just right. As soon as he pumped into her at that angle, she shattered, her breasts arching higher. He took that as an invitation and sucked each nipple into his mouth, biting down hard enough that he'd probably leave bruises. She seemed to love it because her pussy clamped down on his cock as she came again. He followed right after, his dick filling her up to the point he was afraid he'd be drained dry.

When they both caught their breath, he remained deep inside her, his hips resting against hers. He put his weight on his forearms, up around her head, and lowered his lips to hers. He kissed her ever so softly, knowing that this couldn't be the end. He didn't know what would happen next with her or the boys, but he didn't want *this* to be it.

He'd caught a glimpse of a future he didn't know he wanted. And with a woman who had once been abandoned in the worst ways possible, he knew he'd have a fight on his hands to create it. And keep it.

She met his gaze, a war of emotions in her eyes.

Game on, he thought. *Game on.*

Because some things were worth fighting for.

FRANK TALBOT FROWNED at the two children sleeping in the cage. They'd been easily captured from the compound thanks to experimental science and friends in high places. The drugs he'd used to keep them quiet during the extraction should have worn off by now, but then again, one could never be too sure with animals. Hopefully it didn't do any lasting damage. He needed healthy specimens to continue his research.

Odd, he thought. They looked sort of like he had as a child, yet he didn't feel a connection to them. Perhaps it was nurture versus nature that made a child feel as if they were truly a person's offspring, rather than a random collection of molecules and DNA. He didn't care, though. Becoming a father to the two wasn't on his agenda. In fact, he had a few other matters to attend to before he got to work. He'd feed and wash them until it was time to begin, as he couldn't allow them to get sickly before the experiments began.

He didn't know who the boys truly were nor did he care what they thought, felt, or said.

But they would be his prize achievements.

Funny how easy it had been to take them. And their mother would never be the wiser about who had kidnapped her children. After all, he'd left her without a second glace when she was pregnant. Why would she even think of him when it came to the disappearance of her cubs? There were so many others she could blame.

This really was the perfect solution to his problem.

Perfect.

7

C ole ran a hand through his hair as they made the drive to Denver. The awkwardness level in the car had reached new heights, and he wasn't sure how to break through the tension. Anya hadn't spoken to him since they'd woken up that morning and she'd informed him that the mating heat was gone and they could go about their business. He didn't even have a chance to try and get close or kiss her. She'd put up barriers between them with a swift effectiveness he hadn't been prepared for.

Well, shit.

He wasn't sure what he was going to do now because damn it, his cat wanted her.

Wanted her for more than just a fling.

His cat had picked his mate, and the damn woman looked like she still hated him—or at least wanted nothing more to do with him. Except he'd seen a look in her eyes that told him he could be wrong. He hoped he was. But they were on their way to try and save her children from a sociopath. His needs for a mate came second to that.

His grip tightened on the steering wheel and he wanted to curse. Talk about being selfish. He was all worried about his cat and feelings while she was probably freaking out over what they had to do to save her kids. It wasn't as if this were a normal way to find a mate. They were in a stolen car on the way to a city where they'd be killed if someone caught sight of their brands. Anya had never been to the city in her life, had never truly been outside the compound. And he hadn't ventured this far north in long enough that he was afraid of what changes he would see. When he'd snuck out of the compound in the past, it had been on missions for his Pack. He didn't have time to go on joyrides and learn about the new sides of the city. As it was, keeping hold of Frank's scent was getting harder and harder. His cat needed another whiff of the bastard to keep tracking. This wasn't going to be easy. Not by far. And sitting around moping because Anya had more important things on her mind than what last night had meant was idiotic.

"I can practically hear you thinking," she muttered. "Just drop it for now. Okay? You said we'd deal with what happened later, so maybe we should actually deal with it later, hmm?"

Cole shot his gaze away and frowned. "Fine." Not the most eloquent word in the English language, but damn it, he wasn't sure what else to say.

"Fine." She inhaled deeply, closing her eyes.

He turned his attention back to the road. They'd only passed a few cars so far. No one paid them any mind, and he didn't think they would. It wasn't as if a person's first thought would be that the car they passed happened to carry two shifters that had broken out of their enclosures. To humans, that would be so far beyond the norm it wouldn't seem possible. The SAU's propaganda had shown the shifters to be nothing more than animals. Those that listened to the SAU were grateful that shifters were locked away from their children. It was safer for *them* if the shifters didn't have rights and a decent way to live.

"I don't know how you can still scent Frank and my boys." Her voice broke on that last part, and he heard her let out a shaky breath.

He grimaced. "I actually can't scent him that well anymore," he admitted.

"What?" He felt her gaze on him, but he kept his eyes on the road. The last thing they needed was to get into an accident because he couldn't keep his eyes off her.

"I told you it would be hard after awhile. I have a general direction, and I know we're going to go check those abandoned buildings near the capital. That's all we can do, Anya. I know it sucks, but without more to go on, we're going to have to find the Unseen."

He heard her hit her head against the headrest. "I was honestly hoping you wouldn't need to find another way. I thought maybe your super magic Tracker powers would get us there and get us out quickly so I could smash Frank's head in and find my babies."

He liked the sound of her vengeance, but he hated having to disappoint her. He didn't understand the depth of need within his soul when it came to her. It was like a bullet to the chest, the fractured tendons and sensations that came with what he felt for her. It wasn't as if he'd felt it right away either. It had been a slow burn at first that had built to an explosion of desires and utter helplessness when it came to her.

His cat had chosen.

The man knew it wouldn't be as easy as a call to mating.

"We'll find them, Anya," he said softly, ignoring his growing emotions. He didn't know how to deal with them anyway. He'd never felt or done anything like this before, and it damn sure wasn't the right time for it now. "I'm going to get us closer to the city and then find someone to help us if I can't get a lock on Talbot. We're not going home without Owen and Lucas. No matter what." He turned to see her studying him.

"No matter what," she vowed right back. "I know why I'm doing this, Cole. But why are you? Because you're the Tracker? Is this a duty to you?"

His jaw clenched. He wanted to save those cubs because they were *hers*. They were shifters, Pack. They might not be cats, but they were *his,* as well. He wanted them as his young, part of his mating. And it scared him more than he wanted to admit how much he wanted to see them again and watch them grow into the men they would become.

Instead of laying himself bare, he growled, "You said we'd table this discussion until later. Don't ask questions you're not prepared to hear the answer to."

Her eyes widened and she turned her attention back to the road. He did the same, his grip on the steering wheel painful.

They drove for almost an hour until they reached the center of the city. Here it looked as if part of the metropolis had moved on, as if nothing had happened. Yet other parts were abandoned, unused, unwanted. If he remembered right, many of these old buildings had been slated for renovations or reconstruction before the virus hit. In the updated parts of the city, humans hustled and bustled on their way to work or to enjoy the sites. It looked as if the only troubles on their minds were their day-to-day lives, rather than what they were clearly ignoring, what was locked up only a few hundred miles away. It never ceased to amaze him what people did to forget the cruelty in their lack of actions.

The vehicle they were in wasn't one of the older ones on the road, thankfully. Whoever had been in that house hadn't left it empty for long—meaning he and Anya blended into the world a bit better than they would have otherwise. Since the city was also situated high in the Rocky Mountains, the air temperature was a bit cooler during the season. That boded well for what they were wearing since they had to keep their sleeves down to cover their brands. Sure, humans had half sleeves and full sleeves when it came to ink, but their brands were a bit more noticeable since neither he nor Anya had any additional ink on their arms. He frowned. If he were to go on more trips like this, he'd have Gibson give him full sleeves. He'd blend in more with all of that ink instead of just the stark brand on his arm.

When they pulled into an old motel that looked like it had seen better days, he furrowed his brows.

"We'll stay here for a bit. I need to see if I can catch the scent of another shifter. Hopefully, they've heard something. If not, we can start searching for places where Frank might be holding the children. It's a long shot, but we're not giving up."

"I knew it was going to be hard, but damn it, it seems like it's an uphill battle that..." She cut herself off, her bear in her eyes. She fisted her hands on her thighs, and he reached over and placed his hand over one of hers. She didn't relax her fist, but she didn't punch him either. That had to be progress.

"It's not a lost cause. It's not insurmountable. We're just gathering what we can. But we *will* find them."

Her hand shook under his and he reached over, gently prying her fingers apart. He ran his thumb over her palm and up to her wrist. Her pulse beat hard against his thumb, its rapid pace slowing as he kept his touch gentle.

"They must be so scared. I can't even imagine what they're feeling, what they're thinking. I don't know anything." She shuddered out a breath. "This is killing me, Cole. These are my babies. They've never been alone without me before. I've never spent an evening away from them, never *not* tucked them in. Even during the forced move to the new compound, I never let them leave my sight. And now Frank comes in, using some form of cover to steal my babies. I don't know why he wants them, but knowing what he's done in the past with Cora and Soren..." She swallowed hard, her cheeks going dark. "I can't, Cole. I can't let them stay with that man much longer."

He leaned over the console and cupped her face, bringing his lips to hers. He kissed her gently, calming them both. Before they'd made love, it would have only amped their attraction and perhaps their aggression. Now, though, it proved that his cat wanted this bear for the long-term. And those cubs were in trouble, so keeping their mom safe and stopping her from turning feral was one of his top priorities.

"We'll find them." He knew it could be an empty promise and it killed him. He'd lost the scent. He'd never lost a scent before, but then again, this was the longest, most complicated hunt he'd ever been on. He might be the best at what he did, but sometimes even that wasn't enough.

"I know we will," she agreed.

Because there wasn't another option. Not when there was still air in his lungs and blood in his veins. He wouldn't quit until he'd found those boys.

He let out a breath then kissed her again. Just a quick

kiss, but one that held so much more than just a whisper of touch. "Let's get inside. They'll have rooms in here. I don't scent anyone around so we should be alone. We can regroup and then begin our journey."

She nodded, and they both got out of the vehicle, their bodies on alert. Things were so different here than in the compound. Hell, they were different than in other parts of the city, as well. They got into an old room and immediately opened the windows to clear out the stale air. As soon as they settled their home base, they'd go out again and be on the lookout. His cat *knew* Talbot was around, somewhere close to where they were. He wasn't just making up a direction and going with it. He might have lost the scent, but his cat knew something the man hadn't quite put his finger on yet. He'd learned long ago to trust his jaguar when it came to things such as this.

Something shifted near the doorway, and he turned on his heel, claws not out in case it was a human, but close. He inhaled, his eyes going wide.

"Anya. Behind me."

She didn't go behind him, but rather to his side. He didn't object, as she could fight her way through anything, but it still rankled his cat that she wouldn't stay *safely* behind him.

When the giant bear shifter revealed himself at the door opening, Cole wanted to curse. The man's bare forearms told him that this shifter was one of the Unseen— unmarked and non-collared. The man was *big*. Bigger than

Cole and Anya for sure. He could probably break them both with his pinkies.

"Cat," the man growled, his voice low, rusty.

"Bear," Cole growled back.

Anya cleared her throat and pointed to herself. "I'm a bear, but I'm sure you get that."

Cole would *not* let his mouth turn up in a grin at her words. Damn, the woman had no fear. Only, he'd seen the look in her eyes at the thought of losing her children, and knew *no fear* to be far from the truth. That sobered him quickly.

"What is it you want?" Cole asked, his voice low, but he'd lost the growl. He didn't need to antagonize this bear. "Is this your territory?" He didn't know how territories worked with the Unseen. The Alphas might know more, but as a mere Tracker, he wasn't privy to that information.

The bear tilted his head and studied him. The man had white-gold hair that brushed his shoulders and looked like he'd woken up and ran a hand through it, calling it good enough. His features were strong, like everything about him. His dark eyes weren't just dark brown, but black.

"Polar..." Anya whispered. "You're a polar bear."

Not all shifters looked like their animal counterparts while in human form, but the rare polars were in a league of their own. Or so he'd heard. Cole had never met one before. They'd been hard to come by before the roundup. He wasn't sure there was even one in the Ursine Pack.

"I am a polar. That is right, grizzly." He blinked at Anya then did the same to Cole. "You're a jaguar."

How the man knew this, he didn't know. Their scents were hard as hell to discern. Generally, only shifters of the same species could distinguish sub-species by scent.

"I'm Tucker. And though this isn't my territory, you shouldn't be here."

"Why not?" Anya asked.

"You should know that. You may have covered the brands with clothing and taken off your collars, but you are not one of the Unseen. You do not know how to live among the humans and hide yourselves like you should. I scented you a mile away. It's my duty to. Why are you here, and what will it take for you to go back to where you came from?"

Cole did not like this bear. He didn't like his attitude, and he sure as hell didn't like the way the guy eye-fucked Anya. The bastard didn't even have the grace to do it subtly. No, he fucking raked his gaze down her body, appreciation apparent.

Cole moved closer to Anya, putting his hand on her lower back. She turned to him, her brows raised. She knew what was going on, but didn't do anything about it.

Tucker snorted but didn't stop looking at Anya.

Cole wanted to scream *mine* and mark her as his. Only it sure as hell wasn't the time for that.

"I'm looking for my children," Anya said. She took two steps toward the bear, leaving Cole behind.

Cole did *not* like that. He wanted to reach for her but

held himself back, not wanting to make any sudden movements in front of this stranger.

"You let them wander too far from you, momma bear?"

Before Cole could break the bastard's neck, Anya was in Tucker's face. Cole growled and moved behind her, his hand on her hip.

"The SAU stole my babies from their beds while they slept. They've never been outside the compound except to move from one den to another. We tracked them down to this general area. If you've seen them, or heard anything that indicates they could be near, I need to know," she pleaded, and Cole wanted to tear up the world for her.

Tucker studied her face. "I'm sorry the SAU kidnapped your kids, but you need to go. It's not safe for anyone here."

Cole frowned at the man. He was hiding something, and Cole knew it. This bear had more secrets than just his identity within the human population. What would an Unseen want with this territory? Why was he so adamant that Cole and Anya leave?

"Please. I know you know something. I can see it in your eyes." Anya put her hand on Tucker's chest, and Cole growled. She moved it back slowly, but not before a lick of heat entered Tucker's eyes.

Cole had had enough. He pulled Anya to his side and wrapped an arm around her waist. "Tell us what you know. This isn't about dicking around with each other; this is about two scared bear cubs. Help us."

Tucker remained silent for so long, Cole was afraid the

big bastard was just going to walk away and leave them stranded. Fuck, he'd go and follow the bear if he had to. There was no way he'd let the polar leave without giving them information.

"Please," Anya whispered.

Tucker cursed. "Fine. But the information I tell you can't be used until after dark. You hear me? It's not safe for you to be out in the daylight. Blending in is one thing, but it's hard as fuck to blend in on this side of the tracks."

Cole opened his mouth to respond, but Tucker held up his hand.

"You don't know the area. This is my *home*. You fuck up and get caught by the SAU? They're going to come after my family. There's young here. You screw up and they die. You get me?"

"Where are they?" Anya asked, her voice calm. Too calm. Fuck, what was she planning?

Tucker raised a brow at her. "Hold yourself, momma bear. You rush out of here for what could be just a shot at finding them, rather than actually finding them, and you'll die."

Cole's arm shot out, his hand wrapping around the bear's neck before he could blink. "Threaten her again and you'll be more than just Unseen. You get *me*?"

Tucker didn't look the least bit worried about Cole's claws digging into his skin. In fact, the fucker looked relaxed.

"I'm not going to be the one to kill her. The SAU will. Stop thinking with your dick and think with your brain."

"Fuck you."

"Both of you, stop it," Anya snapped. "Where the fuck are my sons?"

"You have a mouth on you," Tucker murmured. "I like it."

Cole squeezed, a trail of blood running down this thumb. "Keep going. I dare you."

"You kill me, you don't get the information."

"Tucker," Anya pleaded.

Cole didn't like the asshole's name on her lips. Tucker slowly reached into his pocket, and Cole kept his gaze on the man for any sudden movements.

"I'm going to write down an address and a set of directions. There've been some suspicious activities going on around this one building. I think it might be the one you're looking for."

"Suspicious?" Cole asked.

"Just what I said. Odd people going in and out and sneaking around. It's not that uncommon around here, but we've been sensing shifters we haven't before."

Anya put her hand on Cole's back, her nails digging into his skin. He slowly let go of Tucker, wanting to touch Anya. If he didn't, he wasn't sure what his cat would do. He put his arm around her waist again and watched the polar write down a few notes then hand the piece of paper over to Anya.

"Thank you," she whispered.

"You're not going to come with us?" Cole asked. "If you're so worried about the other shifters, then why won't you come? Help us find the kids and kick this bastard's ass."

Tucker shook his head. "I have plans of my own." He nodded at both of them. "Good luck." With those cryptic comments, the guy walked away, leaving a nervous as hell Anya in Cole's arms.

As soon as Tucker was gone, Anya turned in Cole's arms and banged her head on his chest. "I want to go now. I want to run in there and get them. I don't want to wait until dark. We've gotten through the SAU patrols so far, why can't we try again?"

Cole tucked her hair behind her ear and rested his forehead on hers. "Anya, honey, as much as I hate to agree with that big, blond bastard, we got lucky so far." He let out a sigh and ran his hands down her back. "We don't know the area, and I won't put my trust in anyone that quickly. Plus, my cat is telling me to stay behind for darkness. It would be *smart*."

"I don't want to wait. I want my *babies*."

"I know. I want them back, too. And we're going to get them. We just have to wait until it's a bit darker. Then we'll find them."

He hugged her tighter, and she pushed at him as if realizing she'd been leaning on him in the moment. He didn't let that bother him—much.

"I don't know why that Unseen followed us, other than

the fact that we were intruders in his territory." She snorted. "It might not be *his*, but he claimed it just the same, didn't he? Still. I'm grateful he came."

Cole snorted. "Really? That asshole. He left. I'm here." He shut his mouth quickly. Why the hell had he said that? He hadn't meant to admit anything about that. Well, shit.

She rolled her eyes and threw her hands in the air. "Shut up. I don't want him, Cole. I am grateful that he took time out of his busy day of acting all broody and mysterious to find us and give us a lead. But I don't want him," she repeated. "I want you."

His cat purred, and Cole stalked toward her. "Really? Prove it."

She cupped his face and kissed him. Hard. Her teeth bit into his lip, and she pulled away, panting. He wasn't far behind her.

"I'll prove it. Later. When we're safe and not out in the open." She let out a breath.

"This isn't over," he said slowly, agreeing with her on the timing.

"Oh, don't I know it." She rolled her neck. "Now, let's get ready to go find my babies. Because I'll be damned if that asshole human who thought he could take advantage of me is allowed to breathe another day. I'm going to make him bleed and beg me for forgiveness, but I'll never give it to him."

And just like that, he fell in love with a momma bear.

Talk about timing.

8

They followed Tucker's directions, and Anya prayed they weren't heading into a trap. It had taken over an hour for them to reach the place Tucker had suggested since they hadn't wanted to park near the place and make noise. They'd left their vehicle at another location and walked to where Tucker had said the boys might be. They'd studied the building and exit strategies together before they even thought of going inside.

While she wanted to run in, claws out for her sons, she couldn't until they'd figured out what to do and had formulated a plan. Just because the Unseen were shifters, didn't make them Pack. That was something she would never forget. The secret of their existence had been drilled into her the day her brother had become the Foreseer, but she could also pray that there was a sense of good in the polar bear. She hoped that he truly wanted to help in his own way when it came to the lives of her children.

Her mind working overtime taking in her surroundings and trying to work through how they'd gotten there in the first place, she tried to focus on what was in front of her.

The cat who'd risked his life for her.

She ducked behind Cole as they stared at the seemingly abandoned warehouse. Her bear pushed at her—wanting not only the man in front of her, but also blood from whoever had dared to touch what was hers.

Cole hadn't wanted her there in the first place. Oh, he may not have told her as much, but there was no way a dominant shifter like him would like seeing her there. She could feel the pull between them—one that she was going to ignore until they were back at the compound, safe with her children. Because of that pull, she knew the immense strength of Cole's dominance. He might not want her there, but he knew she could handle herself and hadn't made light of her coming with him. He hadn't fought it or told her she didn't have enough experience. Instead, he'd simply told her the plan and asked if she had any better ideas. Then he'd gone on this mission tonight and knew she would be by his side as he would be by hers. Instead of dwelling on all of that, she ignored it, focusing on the one thing that truly mattered.

Her children.

The place looked like it was literally standing on its last leg. Dark, dreary, and so old it had to have been ready to fall down *before* the virus hit. How it was still upright—ever so slightly leaning to the side—she didn't know. The building was also the perfect place for Frank to set up shop. She hadn't seen a single SAU patrol or police cruiser since they'd begun surveillance. As soon as the cure for the virus was discovered and people started getting well, according to Cole, humans had shifted their focus to other parts of the city and their own kind. They ignored what they didn't understand, either letting it fall to neglect like this place or caging it out of sight like her people.

The government and authorities didn't care what happened in this area.

No one would care that Frank was here.

No one but her and Cole.

"Can you scent them?" she asked. She couldn't and it killed her. If Owen and Lucas had been there earlier, the rain and wind had washed away the scent. Her bear wasn't even sure they were near and it worried her. What if this was just a place where random shifters met? Just because Cole had had a feeling earlier, didn't mean it would come to pass. This could all be for nothing.

"Take a deep breath, Anya. You're freaking yourself out."

She did; annoyed she'd let herself get caught up in the vicious cycle of her doubt.

"Can you scent them?" she asked again, this time taking deep breaths to calm herself as much as possible. Controlling her bear was crucial right then.

"I can," he whispered, his voice low, sure.

She gripped his arm and forced him to look at her. "Why didn't you tell me?"

"Because I just caught the scent. We're going down there, Anya. You're not doing this without me. I'm not doing this without you. So this is what I can sense. There are shifters down there, but I can't tell if they are moving or not. The wind isn't picking that up. There's also a group of humans down there. Seventeen I think."

Anya cursed. "That could be Frank and whatever muscle he hired." They were going on the assumption it was Frank at this point, but it was all they could do. "Cora said he was good at getting people to work for his cause—even if he's on the run from the SAU." He paused. "He tricked me, didn't he?"

Cole reached for her hand and squeezed. Her bear brushed against her, wanting more of his touch. Again, she wouldn't think too hard about that. Not yet. Maybe not ever.

"He's a dead man."

His promise soothed her more than she thought possible. She took a deep breath, calming herself as much as she could. "What's the plan?"

Cole nodded toward a side door. "There's an older window on the other side of that door that looks like it's not connected to the room with the outside entrance. At least that's what I can tell from here. I don't want to use the door because I can scent humans by each of them. If we go through the window, we can take them by surprise at worst, sneak by them at best. We go in, follow the trail to the kids and get out." He met her gaze and frowned. "I know we want Frank dead right now, but..."

She nodded, knowing he was right, even if it killed her. "But if it's a choice between his death and the lives of my children, Owen and Lucas come first. Always."

"Always."

He kissed her quickly then moved down the alley toward the warehouse. She followed, her senses on alert. The hair on the back of her neck stood on end and her heart raced. She may have fought other shifters in battles for dominance and hierarchy, but she'd never been trained for this. Cole, it seemed, had. She'd follow his directions and try not to let her heart lead her. It wouldn't be smart to do anything other than that. He looked over his shoulder as he stood under the window.

"Ready?" he mouthed.

She nodded, her bear ready to shift when needed. He opened the old window that didn't have a lock and jumped through. She followed when he gave the signal, landing on her feet with a quiet thud. She wasn't as graceful as he was by far since he had the advantages of a cat and she tended to lumber like a bear. She didn't think anyone had heard her though. If the shifters Cole had scented were working for Frank or whoever was down there, it might be a problem, but she didn't know. If the shifters were caged...then it was a whole different problem.

The place was hot despite the cooler temperatures outside and smelled of mold and death. The idea chilled her skin even in the cloying heat. She moved closer to Cole and all hell broke loose. Four men came through the open doorway, masks on their faces and tranq guns in their hands. Cole lashed out, taking two down. She growled, jumping on one while using her claws to take out another. The coppery scent of blood filled the air, and her bear relished it. She took them down, not killing them, but they wouldn't be waking up anytime soon, that was for sure.

Four more men came in, drawing their tranqs. She rolled out of the way as one shot at her, the dart narrowly missing her face. She roared, loud enough to rattle the old windows in the building, but not loud enough to draw the attention of anyone on the outside. She knew better than that. She fought off two of the men, but as soon as she looked over at Cole, who had three guys fighting him, she felt the pinprick.

She looked down at the dart in her arm and licked her lips, her tongue already numb. She fell to her knees, her body going weak. Her knees ached from the impact, but she hadn't been able to move to soften the blow. Cole screamed her name, but she couldn't make out his face. Her vision grew bleary and she knew she'd failed.

She'd failed herself.

She'd failed Cole.

She'd failed her sons.

ANYA BLINKED herself awake and jolted at the feel of

shackles around her wrists. She pulled on them, the metal digging into her skin. Her body felt heavy, as if she were trying to come out of a deep sleep and couldn't quite do it.

"You're awake."

She knew that voice. She'd once let the owner of that voice into her home and into her heart. Or perhaps she wasn't truthful about the heart part. She'd fallen for pretty lies and a smile that dug deep. Well, fuck that.

She growled at Frank as he walked into her line of sight. He tilted his head as he studied her, his face drawn. He wore his precise tie and shirt, a pristine, white lab coat over his clothes. He smelled of blood, but whose, she didn't know. The fact that she didn't see spatters on his clothing worried her. What had he been doing?

"Keep growling, Anya. You're an animal, caged and useless. Well, perhaps not useless. I'll use you to further my experiments. And the brats you birthed will help me, as well."

Her bear roared, clawing at her, but she kept silent. She pulled at her shackles and felt blood seep down her skin as the metal tore her flesh. She snapped at him, knowing if she shifted right then, she'd lose her hands. The metal around her wrists wouldn't conform when she shifted, but it might be worth it.

Only she didn't know where her boys were, and she needed them safe before she killed the bastard in front of her.

"Where are my sons?" she bit out. Her teeth elongated

slightly and she sucked in a deep breath, willing them to go back to normal. No shifting. Not yet.

Frank shook his head, looking a little more haggard than he had all those years ago but still fucking smug. She wanted to rip that smile right off his face.

"You don't get to ask questions." He gestured toward the corner, and she turned.

It was only by sheer force of will that she didn't react to the sight. Cole lay on a metal table, blood pooling at his sides. He had his head turned toward her, his eyes glassy with pain. God, he looked so pale. Frank had cut him up, and Anya was damn sure it wasn't just for science. The butcher wanted to play. Rivulets of blood and who knew what else trailed down his body. Frank had sliced into his chest and sides, and perhaps even his legs from the blood on Cole's jeans. None of the cuts looked too deep, but she couldn't tell.

That must be the blood she'd scented on the man she'd once let touch her. Frank must have changed his clothes while she'd been out of it thanks to the tranq.

Her body shook at the thought of what Owen and Lucas were going through. Bile filled her mouth and her bear pressed at her. She turned toward the butcher that had once deceived her, barely holding back her rage.

"Where. Are. My. Sons?"

Frank's eyes widened at her tone, and she saw a sliver of fear slide through them. Good.

"I haven't started on their part of my work yet," Frank

said as he straightened his tie. She didn't allow herself to show her relief. Not until they were in her arms and *safe* would she breathe again fully. He could be lying for all she knew. Frank loved to lie.

She inhaled again just as someone opened a door in the hallway.

There.

She knew those scents—a brush of paper, a spear of grass, and all little boy.

Tears pricked at her eyes, but she refused to cry. Her boys were here, just down the hallway. She rolled her wrists as much as possible, trying to find a way out of her chains. Frank studied her face for a moment, probably wondering why she wasn't speaking, but fuck him. She'd find a way out of these restraints, find a way to get Cole off that table, and find a way to get her babies out of his hellhole.

Frank shook his head after a moment then walked toward Cole. She tugged at her chains again, trying to break free.

"I've studied a few feline shifters in the past, but I enjoy looking inside them to see if there is anything different between the species." Frank picked up a scalpel and studied the light glinting off the blade.

"Funny thing, when we first heard about your kind, some thought if we opened you up, we'd find your animal half inside." Frank pressed the blade along Cole's skin and tilted his head again. "I never thought that, as it didn't make sense biology-wise." He started cutting. Anya screamed.

"Only, nothing makes sense biology-wise with you filth." He cut again. This time, Cole let out a groan as Frank sliced along his stomach.

"Stop it!" she yelled. "You're not studying him. You're playing."

Frank didn't pay attention to her, his concentration on his oh-so-precise cuts. "I've studied your blood, your genetics. I've studied it all. I don't understand how to use that research to make a shifter of my own."

"Bastard." Bile filled her throat again as more blood pooled on the floor under Cole's body. Shifters were born or made by the bite of a mate or Alpha. Humans couldn't figure it out with science. Although, she knew they'd tried. The deaths of so many of her people were proof of that.

"It's going to be okay, Anya," Cole rasped, his voice weak. How long had she been out? How much blood had he lost?

"I know," she lied. Cole met her gaze, the pain in his eyes killing her slowly.

"You see, no matter how far I dig, I can't find fur. I can't find the genetic disposition that leads to shifting. It makes no sense. *You* make no sense." He dug the blade in and Anya screamed, Cole's voice mixing with hers.

The man she loved, the shifter she knew to be her mate blinked once then closed his eyes. His chest didn't move, his breaths didn't come.

She strained to hear a heartbeat but only heard the thundering of her own.

No. No. No. No. This couldn't be happening. Cole was

not *dead*. Her *mate* was not dead. She pulled at the chains once more, rage flowing through her like a river of lava. The restraints buckled at the wall, the sound of strained metal reaching her ears. So close to freedom. SO close to killing the human bastard who dared to touch what was hers.

Frank sighed. "Damn. I thought this one would last longer. I think I got too carried away." He set the scalpel down then wiped his hands on a towel at his side. "I guess it's time to start on my next project."

Fear shot through her and she pulled again, blood pouring down her arms as the shackles cut into her wrists.

"Stop! Use me! Study me!"

Frank smiled at her and her world shattered. "No, I don't think so. I'm going to study the reactions of a mother watching her children die."

With that, he walked out of the room, humming a tune under his breath.

Tears slid down her cheeks as she pulled and tugged, trying to find a way out. "Oh, Cole. I'm so sorry." She blinked, trying to see through her tears. "You shouldn't have died for me. You should be up in your tree, sleeping like you want to be. I'm so sorry I pulled you with me." She closed her eyes tightly. "I love you," she whispered, knowing he couldn't hear her.

The man she loved was dead, and she'd been too afraid of what could have been to let him know before he'd sacrificed himself for her and her children.

She scented her boys before she saw them. Her body

shook and she pulled at her restraints, her wrists practically numb at this point.

Frank walked in with a bear cub under each arm. The scent of fear wafted off each boy with such potent intensity, she knew they were practically paralyzed at this point.

Her bear clawed at her, her tendons snapping as she started to shift at the sight of her sons in the hands of a monster.

Anya did what any momma bear would do in this situation.

She lost her shit.

With strength she didn't know she possessed, she pulled at the chains one last time. Cement and plaster fell on her as the wall gave way. Her left wrist was broken for sure, but her right one was only partially mauled.

"Bite, boys! Bite him!" she roared as she stood on shaky legs.

The boys growled, and Frank's eyes widened. Owen and Lucas dug their teeth into Frank's arms and the human screamed, dropping her cubs.

Her boys let go of the butcher and landed on their feet, scrambling to her. She took two steps toward them, but before she picked them up, she wrapped the fingers of her unbroken hand around Frank's throat.

"Never again," she said quietly, her voice as deadly as a blade. "Never again." With that, she snapped his neck and walked out with Owen and Lucas, shutting the door behind them with Frank's body still in the room. She needed a moment to figure out her next step in the plan before the guards that were still left standing came storming in. The fact that they hadn't come with the roaring and screaming worried her more than she thought possible.

She fell to her knees and hugged her children close. "Shift back to human, babies. I know you're tougher in your bear forms, but we need to get out of here and I can't be seen carrying two little cubs." She kissed their little faces and pulled back as they shifted.

"Momma!" Lucas wrapped his arms around her neck, kissing her and crying.

"Oh, babies," she whispered, hugging them close.

"Momma, what's wrong with Cole?" Owen asked, his voice so low she almost didn't hear it.

She hadn't forgotten Cole, but she honestly didn't know what to do with his...body.

Anya swallowed hard and tried to compose herself. "I think there are scrubs or something in that closet over there," she said, ignoring Owen's question for the moment. Her boys were naked and still wore their collars and brands. "Get dressed and be quick. Okay?"

They nodded at her, worried looks on their little faces.

"Where's your collar, Momma?" Lucas asked.

She put her hand to her neck and cursed. The collars had been in Cole's hoodie pocket. She prayed Frank hadn't taken them or she'd be dead as soon as she made it back to the compound.

If she made it back to the compound.

No, she wouldn't think like that. She'd get her boys back to the compound and find a way to move on with what happened here. But first, she had a few things to do before the human guards came sniffing around. It was a miracle she'd been safe this long.

"Come here for a moment," she said softly. She quickly removed their little collars and put them in her hoodie pocket. Her wrists ached, and she knew she'd need a healer soon, but she'd live with the pain for now. "Now go find a long shirt to put on boys. I need...I need to see to Cole."

They scurried off quietly to the closet, and she went back in the other room and over to Cole's body. "I'm sorry," she whispered and kissed his brow. "Thank you for getting me to my boys." She reached into the pocket of his hoodie lying on the table and pulled out their collars. When she leaned forward to kiss him one more time, her heart almost stopped.

Did his chest move?

Was he breathing?

Please let him be breathing.

Oh, God. She slapped at his face. "Cole, baby. Wake up. Wake up, love. I need you."

Cole's eyes fluttered, and her hands shook. A crash sounded in the hallway and she froze.

"Wake up, Cole." She growled low. "It's time to get up, lazy cat. Don't make me pull your tail."

"Not. Lazy." Cole's voice was a low growl, and she almost wept.

"Cole!" Lucas called out quietly, dancing at Anya's feet. He and Owen had on scrub tops that were too large, but at least they weren't naked. Owen tugged at her arm, and she looked down to see her little boy holding another top.

"For Cole."

Hell, her boys were smarter than she was sometimes.

She pulled at Cole's shoulders and forced him to sit up. "I know you're hurting, but the humans are coming and we need to go. *Now*."

Cole blinked at her, but she didn't see the human part of him. His eyes were *all* cat.

That could be a good thing. He growled again, his chest bloody but rumbling.

"Put this on," she ordered, handing over the scrub top. When we're out of the building, we can't have a naked, bloody man walking around."

He growled low.

"Okay, then we can put it on when we get out of here. But come on. We *need* to go."

He reached out, his fingertips claws. Oh, yes, he was all cat right then, not a hint of the man.

"Mine," he growled.

She kissed his cheek, knowing they didn't have time for this. The boys pressed against Cole's legs, their little bodies shaking.

"We need to go. Now."

"Hold. Boys." Cole bit out. "I. Kill. Humans."

"Okay, baby. I can do that." She picked up her sons and

winced as her wrists almost gave out. She and Cole were in bad shape, but damn it, this was the best they could do for now.

Cole hissed as he stood. "Keep the boys safe," he growled out. He might only be mostly cat at this point, but she knew he was the most dangerous thing in the building. "*Our* cubs need to be safe."

Well, she didn't quite know what to think about that.

After that display of claiming, the door burst open and four men stumbled inside. Cole roared like the cat he was and pounced. Anya pressed her boys close, grabbed the stack of gauze and bandages on the counter, and followed as Cole laid waste to anyone in their path. He killed each and every single one of them in swift precision, his body shaking with adrenaline, rage, and most likely, agony.

Soon they were outside the building and on their way to the car. Cole pulled the shirt over his wounds and took Owen from her.

"You're hurt," she whispered.

"So are you," he said, as Owen laid his head on Cole's shoulder. As soon as they were in the car, Cole started the engine and they were on their way home. It took everything within her not to pile in the back with the boys and hold them close, but they needed to look as normal as possible for any humans that might look their way.

As they pulled away, she thought she saw the white-gold of Tucker's hair out of the corner of her eye, but she couldn't be sure.

She didn't understand that polar bear and his motives. But hell, she didn't care right then.

She had her babies. Cole was alive. And they were on their way home.

Other things could matter later.

They had to.

9

A branch cracked under the soft pad of a paw, but Cole didn't twitch his ears at the sound. He kept perfectly still on his perch in the tree beside his home. Unlike the last time these two had hunted him, they weren't stomping around the forest and were slightly quieter. It seemed they'd been learning about tracking since their last voyage to his tree.

He'd gladly be the one to teach them how to track and hunt.

He tried not to smile and kept his eyes firmly closed as the two little bear cubs tugged at his tail. Their claws were sheathed so it didn't hurt him. However, he might just pass out from the cuteness.

Lucas growled while Owen batted playfully. Cole couldn't help himself and grinned. He stood up, keeping his tail high so the boys would have to jump for him, and stretched. When he yawned, he let out a little purr then jumped from his branch. The boys rolled onto their little tummies and tried to growl at him.

He lowered his head, flicking his tail in the air. The boys pounced on his back, play fighting. He rolled around with them, letting their little paws swipe at him. They kicked his kidneys a bit, but it was worth it. His body didn't ache as much as it had. He'd had four days to heal from his torture. The boys seemed to have bounced back from their ordeal, as well.

Their collars were on and they smiled when in their human form.

He couldn't ask for much more.

The scent of honey and crisp apples hit him and he licked his lips. Okay, maybe he could ask for something more.

"Are these little cubs too much for you, lazy cat?" Anya teased.

He rolled on this stomach, gently nudging the boys to their feet. He shifted back and pulled on sweats as the boys shifted back to human form, as well. Owen and Lucas took out their spare pants from the same spot Cole had placed his. He grinned at the thought that they felt comfortable enough to share his space so freely.

"I have cakes for everyone," she said softly, her heart in her eyes. He was honestly surprised she'd been able to smile as much as she had since the kidnapping. But he supposed now that she had her boys with her, she could relax, if only for a moment.

Owen and Lucas reached for their dessert, murmuring their thanks as they stuffed their faces. Cole prowled toward Anya, wanting something much sweeter than a cake.

"Thank you," he whispered as he slid the treat from her fingertips. He brought her hand up to his lips and licked the excess frosting. "Delicious."

She blushed but rolled her eyes. In the four days since they'd returned to the den in secret, they hadn't spoken about what had occurred between them. They'd told their Alphas and most of the Pack about their ordeal, but that was it. They'd healed and tried to find balance within their lives. Only he wasn't sure he wanted to go back to the way things were.

Actually, he was really fucking sure he didn't want it.

"Boys," she reprimanded. "What did I say about coming out here without someone watching you?"

Lucas lowered his head, but Owen pressed his body into Cole's leg. He ran his hand over the boy's head.

"We were with Cole," Owen said. "We were safe."

Anya smiled softly. "I guess you were." She bent and kissed each boy on the cheek then rose and kissed Cole gently on the lips. He froze, not sure what to do. She gave him a secret smile then winked.

"Okay, boys, come hang out with me for a bit," Oliver said as he lumbered toward them. "We'll head to the den bonfire, and your mom and Cole can join us later."

Cole blinked a few times, unsure what was happening. From the way Oliver winked at Anya, the siblings had a plan in place. It would have been nice if he'd been let in on the secret, though.

They said goodbye to the twins, and suddenly, he was alone near his favorite tree with the one woman he wanted to call his own.

"Show me your place?" she asked, her voice low.

He took her hand and led her to his home, his heart racing. He'd been staying away to give her time to heal. He hadn't wanted to jump her the first chance he had and scare her away. Jesus, he was acting like some cub getting laid for the first time. He wasn't usually this clueless.

As soon as he closed the door behind them, Anya had her hands on his chest and his back pressed to the door.

"Four days is long enough to heal, don't you think?" she asked, her voice a purr. Damn, she sounded almost feline when she did that.

He ran his hands along her side and up to her face. "Fuck, yeah. It's way too long. But tell me what you're thinking, Anya. I thought you hated me."

She shook her head, kissing his palms. "No, I love you, you lazy cat. I want you, and I want us to be a family. I know you're my mate."

He grinned then leaned forward and nipped at her lip. "Don't call me lazy."

She rocked her body along his and he purred. "Since I'm still dressed and you haven't said anything about mating to me, maybe you *are* lazy." The quick shot of uncertainty in her eyes made him feel like a heel for teasing her.

"I love you, Anya. You're my mate and you know it. My cat claimed you long before you first tried to push me out of my tree."

"It wasn't a push. More like a tiny nudge."

He smiled then ran one hand down her back to cup her ass. "It was a push, but it's okay. You can push at me any time you want. Especially against doors and walls while you go down on me." He wiggled his eyebrows, and she snorted.

"Cole..."

"Baby, I love you. You know that. I know we're still learning each other, but we have the rest of our lives to do that. I want those cubs as mine. I want us to make babies of our own and see if they turn cat or bear. Either way, they'll be *ours*. *All* of them."

Tears filled her eyes and she leaned closer, brushing her lips along his. "Mate."

"Mate," he whispered back.

When she ground against him, he shifted their positions so she was against the door and he stood between her legs.

"Thank God you wore a dress today," he muttered then undid his pants. He slid his hand between them, found her wet, ready, and bare, then pushed into her with one thrust. They both moaned as soon as he was fully inside.

"No foreplay?" she asked, her voice breathless.

He slowly slid in and out of her, his hands on her thighs,

keeping her spread. "We've been having our own form of foreplay for weeks."

She smiled and rolled her hips. His eyes crossed and he pumped faster. Anya clung to his shoulders, and he rested his forehead on hers, needing her as close to him as possible. When he slid his hand between them and brushed his thumb over her clit, she stiffened before coming on his cock, her cunt clenching around him. The tight vice brought him over the edge and he roared her name. She tilted her head to the side, and he sunk his teeth into her shoulder, claiming her as his for all to see. His body still thrumming, he licked the wounds then turned his head for her to mark him.

When her teeth bit down, he almost came again, his body shaking at the sheer force of her claim.

"Mine," he whispered.

"Yours, though you're mine as well, lazy cat."

He grinned, licking up her neck to behind her ear. He was already hard again, slowly working his way in and out of her.

"Of course."

He had his bear, his mate, and no matter what happened next, he knew that he had found the path he'd never thought he needed. They'd complete their mating tattoos and show the Packs that it didn't matter that he was cat and she was bear. They were *one*. He would claim the boys as his own and raise them to be the men he knew they could be.

He'd found his future, his mate, his family.

The world and his den were changing with each passing moment, but he knew he would be able to face it. He wasn't alone anymore, no longer abandoned to the fate he thought he faced.

He was branded, but not forgotten.

He was Pack.

He was *hers*.

UNSEEN

10

Despite the sharp nip in the air, a large crowd was gathered in the center of the compound to share the evening meal.

It truly was an amazing sight. Wolf, cat, and bear all mingling together, despite the fact that they were all forced to share a cramped compound.

They weren't celebrating the death of Dr. Talbot. Not really. They were all sensitive to the fact that he was the biological father of two bear cubs. But there was an unmistakable sense of satisfaction in the knowledge that the bastard was no longer around to do his sick experiments on shifters.

Nicole Bradley, however, wasn't there to appreciate the sight of history being made. No. She was standing at the edge of the thick trees that circled the clearing to make sure that she could slip away undetected.

Slowly, her gaze skimmed over the familiar—and not so familiar—faces that were standing near the large bonfire where Soren's mate, Cora, was passing out sticks loaded with hot dogs to roast. The two had devoted endless hours to creating a sense of harmony among the shifters. Not an easy task when they were all short-tempered predators who'd been caged, branded, and collared.

Just for a minute, she felt a wistful regret that she couldn't join in the communal spirit.

Once upon a time, she would have been the first to offer to help Cora serve dinner. Or lead the game of volleyball that was starting up in the sandpit.

But her heart had died seven years ago with the brutal murder of her young pup. Now she felt nothing but a driving need to punish those responsible.

With a sad shake of her head, she turned away and melted into the darkness of the trees.

Only a few weeks ago she could have taken a direct route to the hidden tunnel she'd dug beneath the fence that surrounded the compound. With only the wolves in the area, they'd had a small measure of privacy to run through the forest. Now, however, she had to stay on constant guard; making sure not to cross paths with a bear or cat who was out for an evening stroll.

Twice she'd had to circle out of her way when she caught the scent of shifters, the delay only intensifying her pulsing need to be on the hunt.

Tonight, more than any other night, she had to be out of

the compound. She had to ease the choking sense of pain that was as raw and real as the day her son had died.

Which was why she ignored the sound of footsteps behind her.

She had to get out. Now.

Unfortunately, her pursuer had other ideas. Just a few feet from the towering fence, a male form abruptly darted past her to block the narrow path.

Forced to a halt, Nicole glared at the wolf shifter with dark tousled curls and eyes the color of cognac. Soren, the Beta of the River Pack. She might have known.

In truth, Nicole considered him her surrogate older brother. And over the past years, they'd been drawn even closer together by their mutual grief.

Which had been a wonderful thing, until he decided to poke his nose into her business.

Folding his arms across his chest, Soren allowed his gaze to slowly wander down her too-slender body. Wearing a pair of black spandex pants and a black turtleneck, with her tawny hair pulled into a ponytail, she knew that she looked like a teenager. An image that was only emphasized by her fragile features and the wide hazel eyes that were heavily fringed by black lashes.

She ruthlessly used her harmless appearance to her advantage. Being underestimated was a weapon as potent as her claws and fangs.

"Going somewhere, Nikki?" Soren drawled.

She scowled. She no longer used that name. Nikki had died with her son. Now she was Nicole.

"Soren." She struggled to contain her frustration. Usually, she could reason with her friend. But he was a male. Which meant that he could be annoyingly stubborn at the most inconvenient times. "Why aren't you with the others?"

"Why aren't you?" he countered.

She shrugged. "I wasn't in the mood for a party."

"It's not a party," he corrected her. "It's an opportunity for the shifter community to learn to work together."

She gave another shrug. "I'm not in the mood to..." she lifted her hands to give air quotes, "work together."

His features softened with sympathy. "No, you're angry and hurt and drowning in the past," he said softly. "A toxic combination."

Nicole instantly flinched at his pity. She refused to think of herself as a victim. She was a warrior.

"You're our Beta, not an Omega," she snapped.

"It's a shame we don't have one," he growled. They all felt the hole in the center of the Pack that came from the lack of an Omega. "They might have helped to heal you."

She gave a sad shake of her head. "There's no cure for mourning."

Soren grimaced. "Look, Nikki-"

"Don't call me that," she interrupted in sharp tones.

"Holden ordered us to keep a low profile for a few days," Soren continued.

"That's exactly what I intend to do," Nicole said with absolute honesty. She made it her life's goal to fly beneath the human's radar.

He rolled his eyes. "That means staying in the compound and not deliberately provoking the SAU."

She wrapped her arms around her waist. "I can't."

His brows snapped together. "Nikki. I'm not saying to stop your vendetta, just give it a rest for a few days."

"I'm going tonight, Soren." She tilted her chin. "One way or another."

"Why? What's so special about tonight..." Soren's breath caught and his eyes widened as he realized the date. Her son had been murdered precisely seven years ago. "Oh, shit."

"I'm not going to do anything stupid," she said.

He looked anything but convinced by her assurance.

"Just suicidal," he muttered.

She shook her head. She may be reckless at times, but she wasn't trying to get herself killed. No way in hell. She still had a mission to complete.

Stepping forward, she placed a hand on her friend's arm, not too proud to beg.

"Let me go, Soren."

There was a tense moment when the Beta struggled against his loyalty to his Alpha. After all, he was a male who understood what it was like to lose someone he loved.

"Dammit." He deliberately stepped to the side. "I hope you know that Holden's going to put my balls in a vice?"

"Cora is a lucky cat," she said with a small smile.

"Yeah, yeah." He studied her with a somber expression, reaching out to lightly touch her cheek. "Come home to us, Nikki. We need you."

Waiting until the male had grudgingly turned to disappear into the shadows of the trees, Nicole reached up to adjust the high neck of her sweater that hid her collar. The piece of metal marked her as a shifter, along with the brand that marred her forearm.

To be caught without the collar was a death sentence.

She shuddered, forcing herself to focus her thoughts on the future, not the past. And that included getting out of the compound without being seen.

Moving forward, she knelt next to the fence, closing her eyes as she concentrated on her heightened sense of smell. She caught the sharp tang of pines, and the musky scent of the fallen leaves that carpeted the ground. More distant was the acrid odor of smoke, and the meat that was sizzling over the fire.

There were no humans near.

Nicole didn't hesitate. It wouldn't be long before one of the human guards passed by during their regular sweep of the area. She wanted to be miles away from the compound before they arrived. Once she was in Denver, she should be able to pass as a human.

Shoving aside the rock that hid her exit, she entered the tunnel and shimmied through the narrow passageway that ran beneath the fence. She came out behind a line of

Dumpsters that the guards had shoved close enough to the compound to make sure the shifters would be continually assaulted by the stench of rotting garbage.

Bastards.

Cautiously crawling out of the narrow opening, Nicole quickly ran through the darkness, her soft boots barely making a sound. It was nearly an hour later when she arrived at the long metal shed where the SAU kept their vehicles—as well as their weapons. It was a new building that they'd built to replace the one Nicole had set fire to the year before. She had planned to blow this one up tonight, to mark the anniversary of her son's death.

Instead, she had a new mission.

Easily avoiding the cameras they had placed around the open yard surrounding the building, she headed toward the extra cars that were left in the back. Less than five minutes later, she had a Jeep hotwired and was heading along the outskirts of Boulder.

When she'd heard that Soren and Cora had actually discovered the headquarters of the SAU, she'd barely been able to contain her excitement.

For years, she'd tried to track down the secret lab. The covert government agency had a dozen different buildings spread throughout the country. Hell, they had at least three in Denver alone. That's where most of the staff had offices, and where the mundane work was accomplished.

But she'd always known there was more they kept hidden.

And now she had the opportunity to find out for herself.

Sticking to the side streets in case the Jeep got turned in as a stolen vehicle, she at last parked at Chautauqua Park. It was several miles from the headquarters, but it would allow her to approach the place without being noticed.

With a quick glance to make sure no one was watching, she hopped out of the Jeep and headed up the trail. Instantly, she was surrounded by the smells and sounds of the forest.

The tight ball in the pit of her stomach eased a fraction at the soothing peace of her surroundings. Inside, her wolf pressed against her skin, demanding to be released. This wide- open space with plenty of room to run was exactly what a shifter craved.

With effort, she resisted the temptation.

She needed to pass as human.

At least for now.

Moving at a swift pace, Nicole traveled in a wide arc that would lead her to the deepest part of the park before she was angling back toward Boulder. She didn't have the exact coordinates, but she'd overheard Soren talking to Holden. She had a general idea of where she was going.

She was just at the point of turning back towards civilization when there was the rustle of pine needles, and a form was suddenly blocking her path.

A very large, very male form.

God almighty. She skidded to a halt. How had he managed to sneak up on her? She hadn't heard a sound.

And she could still barely catch his warm, slightly tangy scent.

Had he appeared out of thin air?

Unnerved, Nicole took a step back; her head tilting as her heart slammed against her ribs. Yow. Somehow, she'd expected such a large man to look like a Neanderthal.

Instead, he was...beautiful.

Extravagantly, breathtakingly beautiful.

His hair was long enough to brush his broad shoulders and shimmered like white-gold in the moonlight. His features looked as if the hands of an artist had sculpted them. He had a wide brow over eyes that were as dark as a midnight sky. His nose was narrow, and his cheeks were chiseled, almost as if he had Asian blood in his distant ancestry. Even his lips were perfect. Full and sculpted with a sensuous curve.

Feeling as if she'd been struck by lightning, she allowed her gaze to skim down to the big body that rippled with muscles beneath the faded jeans and gray hoodie he wore.

Heat sizzled through her, making her toes curl in her soft boots. What was it about this guy? She'd never felt such an intense reaction before.

Okay. He was gorgeous. And fiercely male. But still...

Her awareness of him was completely over the top. She'd clearly gone too long without a lover.

Nicole abruptly shook herself out of her inane thoughts. Dammit. She was here with a purpose. And this man, no matter how delectable, wasn't part of her plan.

"Excuse me," she said politely, waiting for him to step aside. Seconds passed as he simply stood there, staring at her. "If you don't mind." She gave a shooing motion with her hand. "You're blocking the path."

The stranger slowly lifted his brows as if wondering whether she had a screw loose.

"Obviously, that was the point," he said, his voice husky with the faintest hint of an accent.

Yum.

No. She gave a shake of her head. Not yum. He was an oversized hurdle in her plans for the night.

She planted her fists on her hips. "Is there a problem?"

He remained silent as he did his own visual tour of her body, blatantly allowing his gaze to linger on the soft swells of her breasts before returning to meet her glare.

"What are you doing out here?"

Nicole forced herself to take a deep breath. She was supposed to be a normal human out for a stroll. Which meant she couldn't shift into a wolf and bite him on the ass.

"Just hiking through the woods."

"At this hour?"

She shrugged. "Is that a crime?"

He nodded toward a sign that was sticking out of a bush beside the path.

CLOSED UNTIL FURTHER NOTICE

"This area is off-limits to the public."

She narrowed her eyes. The sign had a weathered look that told her it'd been there for months. Maybe even years.

"Why?"

He arched a brow as if surprised that she wasn't scuttling away like a good little girl.

"The trails were damaged during the last rainstorm."

Nicole leaned to the side, peeking around his large body. "They look fine to me."

The air seemed to vibrate with the force of his growing annoyance. Good. She'd hate to be the only one irritated.

"Until they're repaired, they're too unstable to use," he said, his jaw clenched. "If you want to hike, you need to head north or west."

No doubt the wise thing to do would be to walk away. She was wasting precious time. And, of course, there was always the danger that he was a part of the SAU.

But the inexplicable sense of awareness that pulsed between them also made her wolf protest at backing down. Almost as if her animal didn't want to appear weak before this man.

"If this area is closed, what are you doing here?" she'd demanded before she could halt the words.

He gave a lift of his shoulder. "I'm a Park Ranger. I'm here to make sure little girls don't get hurt by going where they don't belong."

"Really?" Nicole arched a brow.

She didn't know much about the world outside the

compound, but she was certain that anyone in authority would be wearing a uniform. Or at least have a vehicle.

"Really."

"Shouldn't you have a badge or something?"

His eyes had seemed to glow in the dark a moment before he leaned forward.

"Let me escort you back to your car."

She took another instinctive step backward. She might be a predator, but there was something about this man that warned her to be careful.

"No need."

"Are you sure?" His husky voice was laced with an unmistakable warning. "I wouldn't want you to get lost."

Okay. Enough was enough. The man didn't appear to work for the SAU. Otherwise, he would be dressed in their uniform and flashing his badge to run her off. But he might very well be protecting a marijuana crop that he'd illegally planted on public land.

Or be finding a place to bury a body.

Either way, he may very well become violent if she didn't do as he asked. And as much as she loved a good fight, she couldn't risk being injured. Not tonight.

"I think I can find my way," she drawled.

"Good. You need to head home." He sent her a dark glare. Did he sense she was plotting to circle around him and continue on her way? "Now."

"Fine." She held up her hands in faux surrender. "Have a super awesome night."

He narrowed his eyes, his arms folded across his massive chest, as she turned to stroll away.

"Park Ranger, my ass," she muttered, loud enough for him to overhear.

"Don't come back," he called out.

She didn't bother to glance around. Instead, she lifted her hand and flipped him off.

Childish? Yeah, maybe.

But the man disturbed her on a cellular level.

Fiercely scrubbing all thoughts of the stranger from her mind, she headed down the trail, waiting until she was certain he wasn't following before she darted into the thick forest. Then, stripping off her clothing, she tucked them under a pile of leaves before shifting into her wolf form.

Agony, along with a thrilling euphoria, shivered through her. Her bones popped and her tendons ripped as the magic pulsed through her veins, altering her form in blast of fur and fangs.

Standing on four legs, she took a second to gain control of her balance before she was loping through the trees. She'd hoped to wait until she was closer to the SAU to change. A stray woman hiking through the park didn't attract nearly as much attention as a tawny female wolf.

But she wasn't going to be stopped again.

Her senses were much more acute in her wolf form. And even better, she had long, sharp teeth to deal with any aggravating men who tried to stand in her way.

꙳

TUCKER CONTINUED to stare at the pathway long after the female had disappeared.

He told himself that the urgent need to follow her was nothing more than concern for his Pack. They'd managed to remain hidden for years. Not only from the humans, but also the shifters living in the compounds.

It wasn't that they didn't feel compassion for those who'd been branded and collared by the SAU. Hell, they were doing everything in their power to bring an end to the prejudices against their people. But things were reaching a critical point. The last thing they needed was some nosey shifter blowing their cover.

Yep. It was all very logical that he was anxious about the female wolf making a sudden appearance where she didn't belong. But that didn't actually explain why his heart was thundering or why his cock was hard as a fucking rock.

Sucking in a slow breath, he allowed the warm scent of woman and wolf to seep through him. Delectable. And dangerous. Very, very dangerous.

His bear stirred, restlessly urging him to track the female down so he could continue to smell her.

And maybe have a little taste...

"Trouble?" A male voice floated from behind him.

Tucker gave a sharp laugh as Sinclair, the current Alpha of the Unseen Pack, moved to stand at his side. The wolf shifter was three inches shorter than Tucker with long, dark hair, a lean face that was always three days past the need for a shave, and ice-blue eyes.

He looked like a biker who'd just rolled out of bed, but anyone stupid enough to underestimate him was soon taught a painful lesson.

"Trouble on two legs," Tucker told his friend.

Sinclair tilted back his head, sniffing the air. "A wolf shifter," he growled. "What the hell was she doing out here?"

"She claimed she was hiking."

Sinclair's dark brows snapped together. "In the middle of the night?"

"Yep."

Tucker could sense Sinclair turning to study him, but his focus remained on the trail. Almost as if his bear were willing the female to return.

"What do you think?" Sinclair demanded.

"She sure as hell wasn't here to hike," he said.

"Damn." Sinclair abruptly began to pace from one side of the path to the other, his nervous energy prickling in the chilled air. "We're too close to finding the proof we need to show that it was the humans—not the shifters—who were responsible for the Verona Virus. We can't let anyone fuck up our plans now."

Tucker forced himself to turn and face his friend. He needed a distraction before his bear managed to overcome his logic and he gave in to his male impulse to track the female down and drag her back to his cave.

"What's the word from Mira?" he asked.

"I'm supposed to meet with her tonight," Sinclair grudgingly admitted.

Tucker arched a brow. Mira Reese was a computer nerd who worked at the regional CDC in Fort Collins. This was the second—or maybe third—time this week she and Sinclair were meeting.

That seemed a little...excessive, considering it was an hour drive for the young human woman.

"Has she managed to get any files decoded?"

Sinclair shrugged, his expression impossible to read. "She wouldn't have asked for a meeting if she didn't have any new intel."

Tucker snorted. "Yeah, right."

Sinclair halted his pacing long enough to meet Tucker's amused gaze. "What's that supposed to mean?"

Tucker blinked. Was the older male joking? Sinclair couldn't actually believe that the Pack hadn't noticed Mira's growing fascination with their Alpha.

"That woman would make up any excuse to spend time with you," he said.

Sinclair gave a low snarl of warning. "You don't know anything about her."

Tucker stilled. Well, well. He hadn't seen that coming.

"I know when a woman wants in a man's pants," he deliberately taunted. "Why else would she risk everything for you?"

Sinclair turned away, staring into the shadows of the

nearby trees. He rarely spoke of how he'd met the human, or the risks she was taking for all of them.

"She believes in our cause."

"Bullshit." Tucker kept his tone pitched low. They tried to keep the area protected, but it wasn't nearly as secluded as their usual campsite. It was only because the SAU head-quarters was nearby that they'd chosen the area. "She's in lust with you. Which is exactly why you chose her to help us."

Genuine anger flared in Sinclair's eyes, his wolf prowling close to the surface.

"I asked her to help because she's a fucking genius."

Tucker smiled. He had to accept Sinclair's assurance that the woman was a genius. After all, the Alpha rarely let anyone near her.

He'd always assumed Sinclair kept Mira isolated because he didn't want to frighten the human. Although they did their best to avoid attracting unwanted attention, the Unseen Pack was made up of a group of predators.

Cats, wolves, and bears.

There were times when their animal natures could frighten off the natives.

"And she wants you," he mocked.

"Enough," Sinclair snapped. "I'll deal with Mira."

Tucker lifted his hands in surrender. "Hey, I'm just glad you found her. If she's even half as good as you claim, then she should have some actual proof of who started the Verona Virus."

Sinclair made a visible effort to ease the tension in his shoulders.

"That's the plan."

Tucker leashed his impulse to press the older male about his relationship with Mira. It was clearly a sensitive subject.

Instead, he turned his attention to the question that'd been nagging at him since he'd heard the story of how Jonah Wilder managed to force the SAU to back down from their determination to capture an Alpha so they could create their own shifter.

"Did you ask her how Wilder managed to get his hands on those old reports?"

Sinclair gave a decisive shake of his head. "No. And I don't intend to."

Tucker was genuinely caught off guard. "Why not?"

"Because she's putting herself in enough danger. I'm not going to have her asking awkward questions that might attract the attention of our enemies."

"What the hell is the point of having a mole on the inside if we can't have her ask awkward questions?"

Sinclair bared his fangs, and Tucker instantly regretted the impulsive question. Not because he feared that his Alpha would attack. Sinclair might be the leader of the Unseen, but no one was stupid enough to take on a bear shifter. Not unless they had a death wish.

But he'd clearly rubbed against a raw nerve.

Something that Sinclair didn't need, especially when

there was so much riding on what happened over the next few months.

"Screw you," the older man snapped, clearly done with the entire conversation.

"Fine. You do your thing with the human, and I'll do a sweep of the border."

"No, I'll get Sonny to replace you on guard duty," Sinclair surprisingly offered. "I want you to follow the shifter."

It was Tucker's turn to stiffen. His bear was once again stirred into awareness at Sinclair's command.

With an inner growl, his animal pressed toward the surface. Hunt down the little she-wolf with the sweet scent and tart mouth? Oh, yeah. His bear was ready and willing. In fact, he was so willing, it was starting to scare the shit out of him.

Which meant that it was the last thing he should do.

"Why?"

Sinclair's hard features tightened, revealing the frustration that smoldered just below his brittle composure.

"I sent word to Holden, asking him not to interfere with our plans, but he's an arrogant bastard," he growled. "He might decide to ignore my request."

The Unseen had deliberately remained hidden from the world, but that didn't mean they hadn't kept careful watch on both the humans and their fellow shifters.

Especially the various Alphas. Which was how they'd

known that Holden was a fair but tough wolf leader who didn't lack for confidence in his ability to rule his wolves.

Now that Holden knew about the Unseen, he'd been trying to contact Sinclair, clearly feeling the need for a face-to-face meeting. Sinclair, however, wasn't about to run the risk of exposing their position to the SAU. Not after they'd spent the past ten years plotting and sacrificing to get to this point.

"What do you want me to do with the female?" Tucker forced himself to ask.

A sly glint entered the Alpha's icy blue eyes. "Anything you want. Just don't let her near the camp." Sinclair jerked his head toward the distant lights that glowed over the tops of the trees. "Or the SAU headquarters."

Shit. Tucker's cock was once again hard and aching. He scowled, trying to pretend that he wasn't itching with the need to charge down the path in pursuit of the female.

"Holden may not be happy if we detain one of his people," he pointed out.

"Too damned bad," Sinclair said, his eyes glowing in the moonlight. "This is my territory."

11

D irector George Markham, a large man with short, iron-gray hair, sat behind his heavy walnut desk. As head of the Denver division of the SAU, he was responsible for the most recent clusterfuck.

Not that it was his fault that the two shifters had been allowed to escape from this building. Or that his lead scientist had gone AWOL with their most sensitive research. Or that the damned shifters had threatened him with information they shouldn't have.

Still, he'd been in the military before joining the SAU. When he took the job of Director, he understood that it meant he would take the blame for any screw-ups. Period.

Which was why he was in his office at this hour, instead of home with a good bottle of bourbon and his dogs.

He tapped an impatient finger on the top of his desk,

watching as Richard Grant entered the room. The head of security came to a halt just inside the door.

Dressed in camo, the man had a square face that was emphasized by his buzz haircut. He had a handgun in a holster strapped around his waist, and no doubt several more weapons hidden on various parts of his body.

"Have you located Talbot?" Markham demanded, not bothering to offer the man a seat.

His office was like the Director himself. Large. Meticulous. Without any unwelcome clutter.

It was designed to be functional, not inviting to guests.

"No." Grant grimaced. "It's like he fell off the grid. No cell phone calls, no texts, no bank transactions, no activity on his computer."

"Damn."

When Markham had fired Dr. Frank Talbot, his head of research, he hadn't anticipated that the bastard would be able to use the chaos during the prisoners' escape to sneak away. Like the damned coward he was.

And, in truth, Markham wouldn't give a shit what happened to the traitor if it weren't for the fact that he'd taken information that could potentially destroy the SAU if it fell into the wrong hands.

"I think we should work under the assumption that the shifters have him and that he's been compromised," Grant said, clasping his hands behind his back and standing at attention as he waited for Markham's orders.

A perfect soldier.

Markham gave a sharp nod. He'd held out hope that they would be able to track Talbot down and quietly dispose of him. Now, time was running out.

They had to take action before disaster hit.

"Have all the locks on the building changed and back up all the computers to a secure location. Once you're sure we have the files copied, I want the computers in this building wiped clean," he said in decisive tones. "I don't want a damned government oversight committee coming in here to try and claim animal abuse or some other bullshit."

Grant nodded. Everyone who worked at the SAU knew that they weren't universally loved. In fact, there were several congressmen who hoped to earn the votes of the bleeding hearts by shutting the SAU down.

They'd use any excuse to nail his ass to the wall.

"You got it," Grant said.

"Oh, and tell the nerd herd to scale back on our testing until we can be sure we aren't being watched," he continued.

Grant made a sound of frustration. "We're going to lose weeks of research."

Markham narrowed his gaze. "Do you want to be hauled before Congress and interrogated?"

"Hell, no." The man shuddered in horror. "What I want is to know how the hell those shifters got their hands on those files."

Grant wasn't the only one who wanted answers. Markham, however, wasn't going to share the fact that he'd been contacted by someone who might be able to provide the information he needed.

"You just worry about-" Markham's words were cut short by a shrill beeping sound that abruptly reverberated through the room. "What the hell?"

Grant pulled out his cell phone to glance at the screen that was flashing.

"Our perimeter alarm has been triggered."

"Shit." Markham shoved himself to his feet. What now? "Get a team and check it out."

Grant pulled out his gun, turning toward the open door. "I'll report back when we locate the intruder."

"Grant." Markham halted the man's exit. "If it's one of the animals, make sure you take them alive," he commanded. "I have questions I want answered."

Grant offered a grim nod then headed out of the office and jogged down the hall.

Left alone, Markham dropped back into his chair. Then, yanking open his bottom drawer, he pulled out a bottle of bourbon and a small glass.

It was going to be another long night.

NICOLE HUNKERED in the thick brush, watching the humans as they scurried toward the back gate where she'd deliberately tripped the alarm.

Silently, she counted each guard and noted which exit

they used to leave the building. At the same time, she kept a close eye on the spots that were left unattended as they rushed to the unseen threat.

A narrow side gate was the most obvious hole in their security, but she couldn't be sure there weren't cameras keeping watch on it. There was also a small shed built outside the grounds that was close enough for a wolf to use to leap over the barbed wire that protected the top of the high fence.

Intent on determining the best means of entering the headquarters, she once again failed to catch the scent of the man who she'd encountered just an hour ago. Not until he was squatting directly in front of her.

"What the fuck?" he snarled in low tones, his beautiful face tight with fury.

Nicole froze. For a horrified moment, she thought she'd made a terrible mistake. Obviously this man was a part of the SAU. A strange, painful regret sliced through her heart. As if she were somehow...disappointed he was her enemy.

But when he made no effort to reveal her presence to the guards who were searching through the woods just to the south, her fear began to fade. Instead, a surge of annoyance raced through her.

Digging her claws in the soft ground, she gave a warning growl, her lips peeling back to reveal her lethal fangs.

The man should have run in terror. Instead, he leaned forward until their noses were nearly touching.

"Don't flash those teeth at me. My bite is much worse."

Nicole froze. Was he insane? Had all that testosterone rotted his brain?

That could be the only reasonable excuse for his lack of fear.

Dammit. Nicole might have fantasized about giving him a nip on the ass, but she didn't actually want to hurt the gorgeous, aggravating man.

Still, she needed to get rid of him before he revealed her presence to the guards. Darting forward, she snapped her teeth directly at his face.

"Shit," he jerked back, his eyes narrowed. "You wanna play, baby?" Without warning, he reached out to wrap his fingers around her muzzle, forcing her teeth together. "You're coming with me."

In disbelief, Nicole felt an arm being wrapped around her torso, and with a massive display of strength, he was tossing her over his shoulder.

Her shock lasted long enough for him to push himself upright and jog deeper into the thick woods. Then, realizing her best opportunity to sneak into the SAU headquarters was quickly slipping away, she dug her claws into his back and gave a sharp jerk.

"Stop fighting me," he snapped, his arm tightening around her until she feared he might crack a rib. "You're going to hurt yourself."

Nicole gave a last, frustrated growl, grudgingly accepting that she wasn't going to able to escape. At least not by force. Which meant there was no point in staying a wolf.

With a burst of magic that was more agony than ecstasy at shifting again so soon, Nicole changed back to her human form. For a few minutes, he continued to hold her over his shoulder, heading up a steep hill. But when she began to kick her feet dangerously close to his most vulnerable spot, he gave a low grunt and turned her so she was cradled against his broad chest.

Nicole felt her breath lodge in her lungs. This was better than being carried like a sack of potatoes, but...damn.

She'd never been so aware of her nudity. No doubt because she'd never before felt the intense excitement that was currently dancing over her bare skin like lightning.

Not that he seemed to be paying attention to her body that was shivering with excitement. Hell, he didn't even give a furtive glance at her breasts that were pressed against his hoodie.

Instead, he moved through the trees with strength and grace that proved he was no ordinary human. As if the heat pumping off his hard body weren't enough to give him away.

"Who are you?"

"Tucker Stone," he said, his gaze scanning the darkness as if searching for potential enemies.

"You're a shifter. But-" She bit off her words. Soren had told her that a shifter had helped him escape with Cora. He'd said that the wolf shifter wasn't wearing a collar and he hadn't been branded. He'd also said that the wolf was capable of disguising his scent. "You're an Unseen," she breathed, angered that he hadn't been honest from the start.

"I am."

"Wolf?"

"Bear."

Tucker the bear. Shit. She should have known. He was as big as a house.

"Put me down."

At last, he allowed his gaze to lower, his expression one of disbelief.

"Do I look stupid?"

"You don't want me to answer that," she snapped.

He gave a slow shake of his head. "I don't know whether to spank you or tie you to my bed."

She widened her eyes, squashing the vivid image of being tied to this male's bed with him posed above her. Dammit. She was supposed to be pissed. Not aroused.

"Try either and I'll rip out your throat."

His lips twitched. Could he read her thoughts?

"You don't lack for courage, female," he drawled, angling toward a narrow path. "Only brains."

"My name is Nicole, not female," she informed him with as much dignity as possible considering she was butt-naked and he was carrying her in his arms.

Then she sucked in a shocked breath as he stepped through the tree line and directly onto a narrow ledge that protruded from a sheer rock face. Until this moment, she hadn't realized how high they'd climbed. Now her stomach dropped to her toes as she gazed down the long, long distance to the bottom of the ravine.

"Dammit, where are you taking me?" she croaked.

He arched a mocking brow, moving with a speed that assured her that he'd traveled the narrow ledge several times.

"Worried?"

"Angry," she corrected, squeezing her eyes shut as he hopped from the ledge toward a flat rock just below them. "You just ruined everything."

"Ruined?" he protested in disbelief. "In case you hadn't noticed, I just saved your ass."

Turning to the side, he inched his way through a narrow crevice, at last stepping into a small valley that was protected by a circle of towering hills. She had a brief glimpse of several cabins and a long, wooden building that she assumed must be the community center for the Unseen before Tucker was carrying her into one of the cabins that were nearly hidden in a copse of pine trees.

Opening the door, he stepped inside. Then, slowly lowering her to her feet, he flicked on the lights.

Surprise raced through her. How were they getting electricity? A generator? Solar? Bootlegging it from the SAU?

With a shake of her head, she took in the comfortable space. There was an open living room filled with large, overstuffed furniture and an attached kitchen with the bare necessities. Across the wooden floor was a dining table with two chairs set next to a large window, and a cabinet filled with dishes. At the back, there were two doors leading into separate rooms. She assumed that one was where Tucker slept, and the other was potentially a bathroom.

It was basic but nicer than most of the homes the shifters were forced to live in at the compounds.

"You might as well make yourself at home," he told her in his low, husky voice.

She stiffened, turning to meet his stubborn expression. "Don't be an idiot."

The gorgeous black eyes narrowed. "Babe, you're wearing on my last nerve."

She blinked, unable to believe his arrogance. "Are you kidding me? I was just fine until you stuck your ugly nose in my business."

His hand lifted to touch his nose. "Ugly?"

"And now you bitch at me?" she continued, in full fury. "I should-"

Her words were cut off as a loud chirp sliced through the air.

"Don't move," Tucker commanded, pulling a phone from his pocket and pressing it to his ear as he stepped out of the cabin.

Nicole glanced toward the kitchen window, trying to judge if she could sneak out without him seeing. Unfortunately, she'd barely managed to take more than a couple of steps to the center of the room before Tucker was stepping back into the cabin and locking the door behind him.

Still holding the phone in his hand, he moved to stand directly in front of her.

Nicole's mouth went dry.

In the moonlight, he was stunning. Now, he was...

Spectacular.

The white-gold hair that looked as soft as satin. The sculpted features. The midnight dark eyes.

A dangerous thrill inched down her spine.

Thankfully unaware of her sizzling arousal, the bear folded his arms across his chest and glared down at her pale face.

"Start talking."

She met him glare for glare. "Am I your prisoner?"

"Yes."

Well, hell.

"When my Alpha discovers what you've done..." Her words trailed away as he held out the phone.

"You want to call and tell him?" His smile was one of pure challenge. "Go ahead."

For a crazed minute, she actually considered calling Holden and telling him exactly where she was and how the Unseen had treated her, then she came to her senses. Her Alpha would probably tell Tucker to lock her up and throw away the key.

She shrugged a shoulder. "Why are you doing this?"

He tossed the phone on a nearby chair, his eyes smoldering with an emotion she couldn't read.

Anger? Frustration?

"I'm asking the questions," he snarled.

She jerked at his tone, her hands clenching at her sides. "You know what?" She pointed a finger in his face. "Fuck you."

"Okay." Without warning, he reached out to grab her shoulders and yanked her against his hard body. "We can do that."

Her mouth parted in shock, but before she could protest, he was leaning down to seal her lips in a kiss that jolted her to the tips of her toes.

ON SOME LEVEL, Tucker knew he was acting badly. He hadn't intended to virtually kidnap the woman. Or haul her into his arms so he could at last taste the sharp sweetness of her lips.

But he couldn't stop himself. When he'd come through the trees to see her crouched within sight of the searching guards, something had exploded inside of him.

She'd scared the hell out of him, and he'd simply reacted.

Okay, maybe he'd done more than react. He'd gone a little ape-shit crazy.

But now that he actually had her warm, fragile body pressed against him, and her lips were parting in silent invitation, he was no longer thinking about the terrifying risk she'd taken. Or the reason he'd brought her to his private lair.

All he could do was drown in the tidal wave of intoxicating pleasure that was crashing through him.

From the second he'd caught sight of this female, he'd been consumed with a relentless hunger. As if some need he hadn't known he possessed was suddenly sparked to life. And now that he'd actually tasted her...

Nothing was ever going to be the same again.

With a restless movement, he unzipped his hoodie and tossed it aside. He wanted to feel her against his skin. Hell, he wanted to rub against her until she was saturated in his male musk.

Perhaps even more alarming, his bear wanted to maul her. In the best possible way.

Wrapping his arms around her slender waist, he pressed her against his body, a shudder shaking through him as their combined heat threatened to combust into a raging inferno.

Perhaps as staggered as he was by the sheer force of their attraction, Nicole tilted back her head, her pale blue eyes dazed with desire.

"What are you doing?"

"We can talk, or I can get naked," he growled. "Your choice."

Her hands lifted to press against his chest. "Are you threatening me with sex?"

"We both know it's not a threat." Lowering his head, he

pressed an open-mouthed kiss to the base of her throat. Her pulse thundered beneath his lips, and he allowed his fangs to lengthen to press against her tender flesh. Instantly, the air was scented with the tantalizing musk of her wolf. "I can smell your arousal," he murmured, his voice thick with passion.

She shivered, her tongue reaching out to touch her lips that were swollen from his kisses.

"This is crazy."

His hands rubbed up and down her back, savoring the satiny softness of her skin. At the same time, he nibbled a path of kisses along the top of her shoulder. His bear rumbled in approval, deciding this female was the one he'd been waiting to discover.

Christ.

"How can you taste so sweet when you're such a pain in the ass?" He spoke his confusion out loud.

A low whine was wrenched from her throat as she arched her neck, silently pleading for more.

Tucker didn't hesitate. If she wanted more, then by God, he was going to give her more.

Cupping her ass in his big hands, he hoisted her against the potent length of his arousal, his mouth moving over the upper curve of her breast before sucking her nipple between his lips.

Her claws dug into the flesh of his chest, her eyes squeezing shut in blatant pleasure.

Tucker gave a low rumble of satisfaction, his body

clenching with the mounting need to toss this woman over his shoulder and head into his bedroom. *Or maybe I'll take her here first*, his addled brain decided, easily visualizing her across the kitchen table while he stood between her legs.

Before he could put his thoughts into action, however, Nicole was abruptly jerking away, panic darkening her eyes.

"Wait," she rasped, a flush staining her cheeks. "I'll tell you."

Tucker moved forward, wrapping her in his arms again. "I changed my mind," he informed her, his hand moving to tug away the scrunchie thing that was holding her hair in a ponytail. Instantly, her locks fell to her shoulders in a mass of rich, tawny curls. Beautiful. Lowering his head, he buried his face in the glorious mass. "I don't want to talk."

He could feel her heart give a leap of excitement. "Tucker."

"Nicole."

For a timeless moment, they remained locked in the intimate embrace, both absorbing the new, unnervingly powerful bonds forming between them. Then, he could sense another wave of panic shaking through Nicole.

"I'm looking for the man who killed my son," she abruptly announced.

"Shit." Tucker froze. Her words were like a bucket of icy water, instantly destroying his desire.

Releasing his hold on her, Tucker silently moved through the cabin, entering his bedroom to collect a sweatshirt before returning to gently pull it over Nicole's head.

Even when she'd threaded her arms into the sleeves, it fell below her knees. But it would do.

Then, steering her toward the sofa, he pressed her onto the cushions and headed into the kitchen to grab a chilled bottle of wine and two glasses.

By the time he'd filled the glasses and settled on the sofa next to Nicole, he'd managed to regain control of his shaken nerves.

"Tell me what happened," he urged, pressing one of the glasses into Nicole's hand.

Absently she took a sip, her fingers unsteady and her expression brittle.

"Seven years ago, my son, Bowe, was playing near the fence of our compound." Her voice was a deliberate monotone. As if the words were so big and painful she had to strip them of all emotion. "We'd had an early snowstorm, and I was helping to clear a path to our greenhouses."

A dark sense of dread clenched his stomach. "How old was he?"

"Almost five." She hunched her shoulders, looking ridiculously young in the oversized sweatshirt with her hair tumbled around her tiny face. Not nearly old enough to have buried a child. "I was distracted and didn't pay attention when Bowe took off his collar. He was always scratching at it and complaining that it bothered him, but he'd never been able to undo the latch."

His gaze lowered to the collar that circled her neck. He'd done his best to ignore the visible sign that she was treated as an animal by the SAU. Just the sight of it tightened something in his chest that made his bear want to go on a rampage.

"You couldn't have known," he said softly.

She flinched, a tear rolling down her cheek. "I should have paid more attention."

He didn't bother to say she shouldn't beat herself up. She was clearly still working through her guilt.

Instead, he grimaced. "You don't have to say any more, Nicole."

"No." She took a large gulp of her wine. "I want to finish so you'll stop interfering," she said in fierce tones.

He studied her tense profile, wise enough not to share the fact that her confession had made him even more determined to stop her from doing anything crazy.

"Go ahead," he murmured.

"When I turned around, he was already tossing the collar on the ground. A second later, there was the sound of a gun firing and..." Her words faltered, her entire body trembling with pain.

His breath hissed between his teeth. God. What this woman had endured.

It was unbearable.

"Nicole, please don't."

"And he was falling to the ground," she grimly continued.

Grabbing her glass, he set it aside along with his own before gently tugging her into his arms.

"I'm sorry, Nicole."

Her head fell against his chest as if she couldn't hold it up any longer.

"There was so much blood." She trembled, her hands clenching and unclenching in an effort to contain the horror. "It just kept spreading across the snow, no matter what I did to try and stop it."

He pressed her closer, hoping to use the heat of his body to ease her knotted muscles.

"The shooter was a part of the SAU?" he demanded.

"Yes." She nodded, and Tucker caught the scent of her wolf's fury. It wasn't the sharp tang of a recent injury, but a seasoned, festering wound that no doubt shadowed her entire life. "There were three guards on gate duty. Each of them blamed the other, so no one actually explained why they'd murdered a helpless child."

His jaw clenched. He knew the SAU were ruthless bastards who would do anything to maintain their control over the shifters, but to murder a baby...someone had to pay.

"The government didn't do anything?"

"They claimed that Bowe had taken off his collar, so technically, the guards had every right to shoot him."

"Bastards," he snarled.

Lifting her head, she arched back to meet his smoldering gaze. "That's why you have to let me go."

He ignored her plea, and instead asked the question that still nagged at him.

"What do you want at the headquarters?"

She bit back a curse. "I managed to track down two of the guards."

His blood ran cold. Shit. Had she been sneaking out of her compound every night to play vigilante for the past seven years?

"Should I ask what happened to them?" he asked.

Her eyes went wolf, revealing the lethal predator beneath her air of fragile femininity.

"No."

Tucker battled back the male instinct that was telling him to cuff this female to his bed for her own protection.

"And the third?" he pressed.

Her lips flattened. "Both of the other guards claimed he was the one who pulled the trigger, but he disappeared after the shooting."

She didn't have to spell it out; he knew that she'd tortured the guards for answers before killing them.

"You believe them?"

"Yes."

Tucker wasn't so sure. Torture was always an unreliable way to get information. Still, now wasn't the time to debate the issue.

"And you assume that he's hiding at the headquarters?"

"If he isn't there, then at least there will be the files that they keep on their employees. I can get his name, and maybe an address." She jutted her chin at a stubborn angle. "That's all I want."

He frowned. It wasn't a bad plan, but it all depended on her being able to shuffle through hundreds—maybe even thousands—of files to find one employee.

"How will you recognize that it's him?"

"I'll never forget his face," she growled. "Now. Are you going to let me finish what I came here to do?"

He held her gaze, well aware that he was about to cause his she-wolf even more pain.

"No."

12

Sinclair paced the cramped hotel room, trying to ignore the disgusting green carpet that hadn't seen a vacuum for months, and the double bed that was covered by a mustard yellow blanket.

He always chose a random spot to meet with Mira, changing the location each time to make sure no one could predict where they would be. Unfortunately, that meant he hadn't had a chance to make sure the place wasn't a dump.

It shouldn't matter. This wasn't a date. And he sure the hell wasn't trying to impress the woman.

After all, Tucker had been right when he accused Sinclair of using the young woman's vulnerable emotions to manipulate her into helping them. Sinclair had spent years trying to find a way to collect proof that the humans had used shifter blood to create the vaccine that helped to contain the Verona Virus. Then, six months ago, his contact in the CDC had given him the name Mira Reese.

Deliberately, he'd sought her out, pretending to be a human so he could not only judge for himself whether or not she had the skills they needed, but if she could be convinced to help them. For weeks, he'd flirted and seduced Mira until she'd been ripe for the plucking.

But as he glanced around the cramped room, he discovered an unexpected pang of regret that he hadn't chosen someplace nicer. He didn't like the thought of Mira being exposed to the sleazy vibe that clung to the hotel like a film of slime.

And even worse, was his nagging concern that she was ten minutes late.

Mira was never late.

Ever.

Scowling at his strange mood, Sinclair forced himself to remain standing in the center of the room when the door was at last pushed open and Mira stepped inside. What he wanted to do was charge forward and...

And what?

Grab her by the shoulders and shake her for not calling to tell him that she was going to be late? Or wrap her in his arms so he could reassure himself that she wasn't hurt?

Neither was acceptable.

Instead, he folded his arms across his chest and watched as she placed her large purse on the bed so she could shrug out of her coat.

"Sorry I'm late," she muttered, pushing back the dark, corkscrew curls that were already escaping the tight braid that fell down her back. She had a pale, heart-shaped face and hazel eyes that were unremarkable at first glance, but Sinclair had slowly developed a fascination for the rapid-fire emotions that flickered over her features. He was closed off and aloof. Mira was open and dangerously vulnerable. "I circled around a few times to make sure I wasn't being followed."

The concern he'd been trying to dismiss exploded into full-fledged alarm.

"Why would you think you were being followed?" With three long steps, he was at the window, peering around the edge of the curtain at the dark parking lot. The hotel was miles away from the nearest town, which meant it was easy to track any approaching cars. "Did you see someone?"

"No." She tried to smile even as her arms wrapped around her waist in an unconsciously protective motion. "I'm just feeling jumpy."

This time, Sinclair couldn't resist his instinctive need to move to the young woman and gently smooth his hands over her shoulders and down her rigid arms.

"Mira." His brows snapped together as he felt her tiny shivers. Christ. She was terrified. "Take a breath."

"Sorry."

He pressed a finger to her lips, halting her ridiculous apology.

"Relax and tell me what has you so upset," he commanded.

She hesitated, almost as if she were thinking about denying her obvious unease. Then no doubt seeing the grim determination etched on his face, she heaved a small sigh.

"It isn't one thing, but a bunch of little stuff," she grudgingly admitted.

"Like what?"

She shrugged. "Monday, I thought I'd lost my phone, but when I searched for it, I found it in the seat of my car. I assumed it must have fallen out of my purse, but I always keep it in a side pocket that zips."

Sinclair had to consciously prevent himself from tightening his grip on her shoulders. He rarely touched human females, so he constantly feared that he might bruise Mira's pale skin.

"What else?" he prompted.

She wrinkled her nose. "Wednesday at work, I noticed that someone had tried to access my private information."

Sinclair bit back a curse. It was one thing for Mira to misplace her phone. It was another to have someone snooping on her computer.

Suddenly, he wished to hell he'd never asked Mira to help.

It'd been one thing to charm a sweet, innocent female into using her talent with computers, combined with her access to the CDC's private files to search for the original research on the vaccination. The information that would prove the shifters were the saviors of the human race instead of the monsters responsible for the virus. What was more important than freeing his people from the brutality of the SAU?

But now that he actually knew Mira, even liked her, he was acutely aware of the danger he'd placed her in.

"How do you know?" he demanded.

"We all have sensitive projects that we're supposed to keep protected with passwords," she said. "I've added extra layers of security to my computer. I can tell if anyone has used my computer when I'm away from my desk. I also keep track each time my name and password is used to log onto the CDC. If someone pretends to be me, it leaves a digital trail."

"Could you tell what they were trying to search for?"

She gave a firm shake of her head, her curls bouncing. Sinclair had a sharp, unreasonable urge to tug her braid loose so he could see the glorious ringlets tumbled around her face.

Or maybe across the pillows...

Shit. He stiffened, slamming the door on the renegade image.

"No. They couldn't break through my encryption." She paused, forcing herself to take a deep, steadying breath. "It could have been one of my supervisors checking on my work. Or a random hacker who hoped to piggyback my computer to steal private info from our payroll files."

Sinclair's wolf snarled. At the beginning, his animal had been wary of this female, unable to trust a human. But now that it suspected she was in danger, it was eager to hunt down the threat and destroy it.

"I don't believe in coincidences," he told her. "Now that the SAU knows the shifters have found the link between the Verona Virus and the human clinic, they're going to do everything in their power to destroy any actual proof."

She instinctively took a step closer, unconsciously seeking the comfort of his hard body.

"But how could they possibly know I'm searching for the same information?"

"I don't know," he admitted, his hands smoothing up and down her arms.

She grimaced. "Like I said, I could be overreacting."

Sinclair hardened his jaw. His role as Alpha meant he possessed a fierce need to protect his Pack. And, somehow, Mira had become a part of that Pack.

"I'm not willing to take the risk."

She blinked. "What?"

"It's too dangerous."

"But I'm so close." Without warning, she pulled away and turned to open her large leather bag. Reaching in, she pulled out a sheet of paper. "Look what I brought."

Sinclair unfolded the paper, his lips twisting at the letters and numbers that were dotted in random spots.

"I'm looking, but you're going to have to decipher this."

She moved to stand close to his side, her light floral scent teasing his senses.

"It's fragmented," she said. "I pulled it off an old CDC hard drive."

Sinclair sent her a startled glance. The outbreak had happened so quickly and with such virulence that there hadn't been time for anything but survival. And even after the vaccine was created, there'd still been years of turmoil. The last thing anyone cared about was keeping records. So when the SAU had started their crusade to destroy all evidence of the human's culpability in manufacturing the virus, or the shifter's assistance in saving their asses, no one did anything to stop them.

"How did you get your hands on it?" he breathed in shock. "I thought the computers had all been destroyed in the fire?"

The shadows were momentarily banished from her hazel eyes as they shimmered with excitement. Once Mira had committed herself to helping the shifters discover the truth, she'd jumped into her task with a passion that had both amused and intrigued Sinclair.

"I told you the last time we spoke that I'd had an idea of how to resurrect the dead," she reminded him.

Unable to resist temptation, he reached up to tug on one of her satiny curls.

"I thought you meant zombies."

She looked startled before giving a soft laugh. His humor was so rare it always caught people off guard.

"Not zombies," she corrected. "Novo-Auction."

Sinclair had heard of the online website where you could buy and sell items from pre-virus days.

"I don't understand."

"I developed a program that would run a search for the recycling service that was contracted by the CDC."

Sinclair shook his head. "What kind of recycling?"

"The old CDC electronics before the fire. I figured there had to be a few computers that were sent to the recycling center that had research about the virus still on the hard drives." She flashed a shy smile. "It took a long time. In fact, I'd given up hope. But I finally got a hit."

"Fuck." He studied her with a renewed sense of wonder. Sometimes he forgot just how smart she was. "That was brilliant."

She blushed. "I was lucky."

"No. There was no luck involved," he murmured. "Only skill."

Her blush deepened. He'd never met a woman who was so uncomfortable with compliments. "There were two old computers listed for sale, and I bought both of them," she hastily continued. "In one, the hard drive had been replaced, but the second one was original." She pointed toward the sheet of paper in his hand. "That's how I managed to retrieve that small bit of the original files that hadn't been fully overwritten."

Sinclair didn't even glance at the paper. He'd just realized the sheer depths of the risk she'd taken. She might as well have put a target on her back.

"Shit," he snarled, glaring at her pale face. "You didn't have the computers sent to your house, did you?"

"Of course not." She made a sound of impatience. "I'm not stupid. I used a false identity to buy them and had them delivered to a temporary mailbox."

"Hmm." Sinclair swallowed his cutting words.

She'd only been trying to help him. Even though she had to know that she was putting her life in danger.

"Do you want to discuss what I discovered or not?" she demanded.

He forced himself to nod. She would learn soon enough that she'd taken her last risk.

"Tell me."

She pointed to the top line that was printed on the paper.

"This is an email that's dated one year before the virus hit. It's addressed to a Dr. Lowman. I can't tell whom it's from, but it mentions the words 'unstable' and 'pandemic.'"

Sinclair studied the garbled note, trying not to jump to conclusions. The CDC, after all, had worked with dozens—maybe even hundreds—of pandemics over the years. Still, if this Dr. Lowman had known anything at all about the Verona Virus before it started to spread, they needed to see if they could track him or her down.

"Did you do a search on Dr. Lowman?"

"Of course."

"And?"

"He was a doctor at the CDC," Mira said. "He died of an unexpected heart attack just six months before the virus started to spread."

Sinclair sucked in a sharp breath. He didn't want to leap to conclusions, but then again, he didn't believe in coincidences.

Had someone tried to warn the doctor about the dangers of the research going on at the Verona clinic? And had the doctor tried to stop it? Or had he known too much?

"Any family?"

"He had a wife and two sons." She paused, tilting back her head to meet his gaze. "One of the sons worked for a private research lab."

A prickle of premonition inched down his spine. "In Verona?"

She gave a slow nod. "Yes."

Okay. This was no longer a leap, but a genuine clue. The room was suddenly filled with the scent of wolf as his animal strained to be released.

"Can we find him?"

"He disappeared during the chaos after the virus," she said, gently taking the paper from his hand and carefully folding it before returning it to her bag. "I couldn't find any trace of whether he's alive or dead."

Frustration exploded through him. It was always one minuscule step forward and two huge leaps back.

"Damn," he growled.

"I've pulled off a few more fragments, but it's a slow process," she said, clearly trying to soothe his irritation. "I'm also trying to find out who sent the original email."

He gave a shake of his head. If Doctor Lowman's son were still alive, Sinclair would find a way to track him down.

"Where are the hard drives?"

She arched a brow at his abrupt question. "At my home."

"I want you to gather them and any equipment you need to finish downloading the information and move into my lair."

She stilled, clearly caught off guard by his command. "Excuse me?"

"Fort Collins is no longer safe for you," he said, too anxious for her safety to consider his words. "We can protect you."

"Oh." She turned away, but not before he glimpsed the disappointment in her eyes. Shit. She'd thought he was inviting a more intimate relationship between them. Now she was hurt and eager to push him away. Exactly what he didn't need. "I can't just leave."

"Of course, you can."

"No." She kept her rigid back turned toward him. "I can't."

Sinclair knew he'd screwed up. What he didn't know was how to fix it.

"Why not?"

She gave a short, humorless laugh. "I realize you think my life is as boring as I am, but it's important to me."

He reached out to grab her shoulders, gently tugging her and turning her around to meet his frown.

"Mira."

"I have a job and a house that I love," she continued, standing stiffly in his grasp. "I have a cat."

Dammit. The woman had a genius IQ. She had to know that she was in danger.

"You already suspect that someone searched your computer." He leaned down, allowing his wolf to glow in his eyes. "What happens when they realize what you have in your precious home?"

She pressed her lips together, but she couldn't hide her sudden shiver.

"I told you that I wasn't sure if it had anything to do with my work with you," she ridiculously muttered. "And it's going to be a lot more suspicious if I simply disappear."

"You'll be alive."

"And then what?" she demanded with an unexpected burst of independence. "I can't hide forever. I promise I'll be careful."

He stepped back, folding his arms across his chest. She'd just challenged him. His wolf accepted.

"I'll give you two weeks."

Her eyes widened. "What?"

For the first time, he allowed her to experience the full force of his Alpha nature.

"Give your notice at work," he said, his voice slow and crisp. He didn't want any misunderstandings. "Tell them that you have a sick relative you have to take care of. Then pack whatever you can't live without, including your damned cat, and I'll pick you up."

"But-"

"Final offer, Mira."

13

Nicole was furious. No. She was *beyond* furious. Whatever that was.

How dare the damned bear encourage her to spill her guts, pretend as if he sympathized with her, and then refuse to let her go?

It was...torture.

Plain and simple.

Lost in her fury, she launched herself the short distance between them to pound her fists against his chest.

"Damn you," she rasped, indifferent to the fact that she was hurting herself more than she could possibly be hurting him.

With a grimace of regret, he reached to grasp her wrists, easily halting her attack.

"Hold on," he murmured softly.

It only pissed her off more that he took such care to ensure that his fingers didn't dig into her flesh.

"No." She bared her fangs. "You have no right to keep me here."

He held on to her, his expression difficult to read. "Would you please listen to me?"

"Why should I?"

"Because I can help you."

She froze, studying him with a wary gaze. "How?"

"There are a few of us who have managed to infiltrate the SAU."

Her heart leaped with excitement. She knew that there was an Unseen wolf who was working as a guard at the facility. He'd helped Soren and Cora escape. And it only made sense that the Pack had managed to sneak more than one spy into the enemy camp.

But she'd never dreamed that one of them might actually help her penetrate the heavy security.

"You can get me into the building?" she breathed in excitement.

His gaze went flat. As if startled she would even suggest such a thing.

"No."

She muttered a curse, glaring into his handsome face. "Are you just trying to be a dick?"

Without warning, he tugged her clenched fist to his mouth and pressed a gentle kiss to her knuckles.

"There's no need to go to the building," he assured her.

"We've hacked into their computer network. We can tap into the employment files tomorrow."

Her anger faltered, swiftly replaced by a fragile sense of hope.

Was it possible that she could actually find the identity of the guard without running the risk of being captured by the SAU? It sounded too good to be true.

"Why not now?" she demanded, the pounding need to hunt her prey refusing to leave her in peace.

"Because it's late," Tucker pointed out. "And Rios is temperamental, even for a jaguar." He pretended to give a shudder of horror. "You don't want to wake him and ask for a favor."

She leaned forward, forcing herself to say the words. "Tucker, please."

He stilled, clearly sensing her desperation.

"It's been seven years, Nicole," he said, his thumbs rubbing the pulse that thundered beneath the delicate skin of her inner wrists. "A few hours aren't going to make a difference, are they?"

She bit her lower lip. She didn't want to reveal any more. Not after she'd already stripped herself bare. But if that was what it took to get Tucker moving, then she'd do what she had to do.

"Today's the day," she abruptly announced.

He arched a brow. "What?"

"Today is the anniversary of Bowe's murder." She shivered. It hurt to say the words.

Tucker made a strangled sound, looking as if she'd just sucker-punched him.

"Christ."

Nicole surged to her feet. She'd never traded on sympathy for the death of Bowe to manipulate others; that would have been an insult to her son. But tonight, she needed Tucker to help her get into the employee files. She didn't care how or why.

"Let's go," she urged.

Tucker lifted himself off the sofa, but instead of heading toward the door, he reached out to grasp her hands.

"Wait."

She scowled. "Wait for what?"

He studied her upturned face for a long moment. "Where's the father?"

She shook her head. "I don't understand."

"The father of your child," he pressed. "Where is he?"

"Oh." Nicole gave a lift of her shoulder. She'd met Randall when they were both just pups, and they'd been best friends for years. Slowly, they'd developed an intimate relationship, but it'd never been more than a mutual desire for affection. When Nicole had realized she was pregnant, she was overjoyed, but she'd never expected Randall to take on the role of parent. "We were childhood sweethearts, but our animals never mated. After I realized that I was pregnant, he was transferred to a compound on the west coast," she explained in impatient tones.

Tucker studied her with a strange intensity. "He isn't a part of your life?"

"No." She tried—and failed—to remember the last time she'd even had any contact with her friend. "He found his true mate and started a new family. No bitterness." She frowned. "Why?"

He squeezed her fingers, heat smoldering in his eyes. "You know why."

She felt her mouth go dry. She *did* know why. Her wolf had been trying to tell her from the minute she'd caught sight of the male that they had a connection that went way beyond lust. Even when she'd been focused on trying to break into the SAU facility, her wolf had been anxious to return to where she'd crossed paths with the stranger.

But the mother in her refused to accept the primitive urges.

She still had a mission to complete. Until then, she couldn't focus on anything but tracking down the guard who'd shot her son.

"Tucker-"

"Later," he interrupted, as if he'd sensed that she wasn't prepared to think about the future. Not until the past was laid to rest. Pressing another kiss to her knuckles, he led her toward the door. "Come on."

She rolled her eyes, a dangerous tenderness squeezing her heart.

"Impossible bear," she muttered.

Stepping out of the cabin, they circled the edge of the

camp; Tucker maintaining a firm grip on her hand. Not that Nicole minded. She might be consumed with her thirst for revenge, but his warm touch was soothing her wolf in a way she'd never dreamed possible.

It was odd.

She'd always assumed that if she were fortunate enough to find her mate, it would be all about the passion. After all, when she'd seen mated pairs, they could barely keep their hands off each other. But while her whole body tingled with an intoxicating desire that was both thrilling and terrifying, it was the feeling of...connection that astonished her.

In just a few hours, she'd gone from a wolf who always stood alone—even when surrounded by her Pack—to a female who had an intelligent, ruthless, dazzlingly beautiful bear who was eager to offer his strength.

It was going to take time to adjust.

Together they moved through the shadows, skirting around a surprisingly large array of solar panels, as well as several small windmills that clearly powered the electrical grid. There were also bunkers that were dug deep into the base of the hill. She assumed they were filled with extra supplies, and maybe even hidden tunnels in case of a siege.

Smart.

They at last reached a cabin that was twice the size of Tucker's, with more solar panels on the roof, as well as a large generator at the back. At the moment, the building was ablaze with lights.

Tucker frowned, seemingly puzzled by the fact that his friend was still awake at the late hour. But without hesitation, he tugged her onto the porch and rapped on the front door.

TUCKER HADN'T WANTED to approach Rios this late.

Not only because he had plans to spend the night with Nicole, but also because he'd fully expected to find his friend busy with one of his various females. Or watching a soccer match. The male jaguar's two favorite activities. At least when he wasn't destroying some pathetic opponent on his favorite online computer game.

But even as the door was pulled open to reveal a tall, slender male with short, dark hair, black eyes, and rich golden-brown skin, Tucker could smell his friend's adrenaline.

"Tucker." Rios looked surprised, then disappointed. "Shit. I was hoping you were Sinclair."

"Good to see you, too, Rios," Tucker drawled, stepping into the cabin as the Feline shifter turned to hurry back toward the bank of computers that were lined against a paneled wall.

There were more computers and various monitors, and stacks of servers that were humming across the room. There was also a large screen TV that was currently tuned in to a soccer match.

Nicole stayed close to Tucker's side as he watched his friend dart from one computer to another.

"What's going on?"

"A disaster," Rios muttered, not bothering to turn around. "That's what's going on."

Tucker wrapped a protective arm around Nicole's shoulders as he studied his friend with a small frown.

"That's a little vague, amigo."

"The SAU are purging their computers," Rios said.

Tucker stiffened, sending Nicole a troubled glance before returning his attention to his friend.

"Shit. Have our files been compromised?"

"I hope not." Rios leaned forward, tapping on one of the keyboards before moving to the next computer. "I severed our connection as soon as I realized what was happening, but I can't be sure whether there was any damage until I reboot and do a thorough system check."

Tucker could sense Nicole's agitation as she realized that she might not get the answers she wanted. At least not as soon as she wanted them.

"How long will that take?" he demanded.

"Hours."

Tucker grimaced. "Damn."

"Yeah." Abruptly whirling around, Rios stabbed him with an impatient frown. "Have you seen Sinclair?"

"He's meeting with his CDC contact," Tucker shared. The Alpha had called just minutes before he took off for the secret rendezvous. "What do you need?"

His dark eyes glowed gold as Rios's animal reacted to his agitation.

"We need to find out why the bastards suddenly decided on the purge."

Tucker gave a slow nod. He was a healer, not a computer expert, but he knew there was no way the agency would have risked a complete purge unless it were an emergency.

Unless…

He wrinkled his brow. "They've had a lot of unwelcome attention focused on them over the past few weeks. They might just be getting rid of their nasty secrets before someone comes snooping."

"True." Rios continued to look worried. "Or maybe they realized someone hacked into their system."

Tucker glanced toward the door that he'd left open. This particular Unseen Pack wasn't large. Less than a hundred total. But it would still take time to efficiently evacuate them to a new location if this location were no longer secure.

"Could they use our computers to trace us?"

Rios gave a sharp shake of his head. "No, I've covered my tracks through a dozen different locations. But I want Sinclair to go in and figure out what the hell is going on before I try to reestablish a connection."

Tucker nodded. Sinclair was the only one with a security badge that would get him into the building at this hour.

"I'll send him a message," Tucker promised, abruptly distracted when Nicole tugged away from his protective grasp.

"What about the files I need?" she rasped, her face flushed.

As if noticing the female for the first time, Rios sent her a suspicious glare.

"Who's this?"

"Get back to your disaster," Tucker commanded, wrapping a firm arm around Nicole's waist to hurry her toward the door. "We'll come back in the morning."

"Tucker." She tried to dig in her heels, but despite her shifter strength, she was no match for a full-grown polar bear. With one smooth motion, he had her swept off her feet and cradled against his chest.

"You heard Rios," he said, leaping off the porch and swiftly jogging through the trees.

He preferred to have this argument in the privacy of his cabin. Shifters were nosy, interfering busybodies. He didn't need their input.

"Then we can sneak into the SAU headquarters," she stubbornly insisted. "Your friend Sinclair can use his badge to get us in."

"Sinclair isn't here." He never slowed his pace. As a bear, he didn't have the same fluid grace as some of his fellow shifters, but he could move with a speed that surprised most people. "And even if he were, he wouldn't agree to take you in."

"Why not?"

He glanced down, meeting her fierce glare. "Sinclair has already jeopardized his cover, his ability to not only spy on the SAU, but to also release those helpless shifters who are forced into the fighting pits and help your Pack members escape. There's no way he'll allow you to further endanger his cover." Tucker clenched his jaw. "In fact, if he finds out that I'm asking Rios to help you, he'll probably have me skinned and made into a rug."

"Then release me, and I'll do it on my own."

"Never." It was a promise, not a threat.

Tears pooled in her eyes as they reached his cabin. "Please."

"Tomorrow we'll find the man who murdered your son." He used his foot to nudge open the door, and once they were inside, he kicked it shut behind them. Then, lowering his head, he brushed a gentle kiss against her mouth. "Can you trust me?"

Her lips parted, almost as if she were going to pretend that her wolf wasn't already fully committed. Then she heaved a rueful sigh.

"Yes, I trust you, but "

He claimed another kiss. This one longer...more demanding.

"There is no 'but,'" he growled. "We'll deal with the guard tomorrow."

Easily sensing he wasn't going to budge, she visibly struggled to contain her burst of frustration.

"So what do you expect me to do tonight?" she snapped. "Sit around twiddling my thumbs?"

A slow, wicked smile curved his lips as he headed across the floor and into his bedroom.

"I think we can find something to do to pass the time."

He left the lights off as he crossed directly to the bed. Then, holding her gaze, he lowered her onto the center of the mattress.

For a timeless moment, they gazed at one another, the newness of their bond so fragile that they barely dared to breathe. But when he caught the unmistakable scent of her arousal, his bear was done playing the gentleman.

He wanted to sensually maul his mate.

And he wanted to do it now.

Still holding her gaze, he leaned down to tug off his boots before unfastening his jeans and allowing them to drop to the floor. Her eyes briefly widened at the sight of his fully erect cock that was standing at proud attention. He was a large man, and everything was proportional. He could be...intimidating to some females.

Ah. But not his courageous, reckless Nicole. Her gaze lifted to reveal the glow of her wolf, along with a hunger that pulsed through the air.

Planting his knee on the edge of the mattress, he leaned forward, his hands placed on either side of her shoulders as he dipped his head.

His lips touched her forehead and he paused. Inside, his bear rumbled in approval, savoring the intoxicating, womanly scent that he'd been craving since this female had walked up the trail. At the same time, he needed to mark her with his musk. To make sure that the world knew she belonged to him.

Rubbing his cheek over her tawny hair, he allowed his hands to drift down her soft curves. He shivered at the feel of her silken curls brushing against his skin. Nicole made a sound of pleasure, the wolf in her clearly enjoying the sensation of being petted.

Careful to keep his touch light and teasing, he nuzzled a path of kisses down the side of her neck. He hesitated as his mouth reached the top of her collar, a strange tightness wrapping around his chest.

Christ. He hated the damned thing. But for now, there wasn't a damned thing he could do about it.

Anxious not to spoil the mood, he forced himself to squash his impulse to rip off the tangible sign of her imprisonment, and concentrated on offering her a night of sheer bliss instead.

For the next three hours, there would be no thoughts of the past or the tenuous future.

They would live in the moment.

Focused on the soft stroke of his lips, Nicole made no protest when he grasped the bottom of the sweatshirt she wore and pulled it over her head. He tossed it aside with a flick of his hand.

"I like to see you wearing my clothes," he murmured, his gaze searing over her slender body revealed by the silver shaft of moonlight that slid through the window. She was exquisite. Her slender curves. The soft mounds of her breasts that were tipped with rosy nipples. The small patch of tawny curls that marked the entrance to her body. "But I prefer you without any at all."

He heard her breath catch, as his fingers skimmed the narrow curve of her waist, her hands lifting to press her nails into his chest. A beautiful blush stained her cheeks.

"I left my clothes in the woods."

"Don't worry." He allowed his hands to cup the soft swell of her breasts, his mouth watering as the nipples tightened to hard tips of temptation. "You're not going to need them."

With a roll of her eyes, she smacked her hand against his chest. "I have to get them before the sun comes up. I'm not going to walk around in just your sweatshirt."

He chuckled, using the tip of his tongue to trace the prominent line of her collarbone.

"One of the guards on duty will have already found them and disposed of them," he murmured.

She stiffened. "Why would they destroy them?"

He kissed a path over the upper curve of her breast, barely capable of concentrating on her question. Not surprising. The taste of her on his tongue made his gut clench with savage lust.

He'd enjoyed lovers before. He might be a loner, but he was also a male who needed the enticing diversion of spending time with a female. None of them, however, had ever made him so desperate to have them in his arms that he was willing to kidnap them and hold them virtual hostages in his lair.

"The members of this Pack were specifically chosen because they're capable of masking their scent," he husked, his fingers reaching the silken skin of her inner thigh. He groaned, his arousal heavy with painful need. "It was the only way we could live close enough to the SAU headquarters and avoid detection by the dogs they use to sweep the area. Your clothing would have the musk of your wolf all over it."

Her eyes darkened with the hunger of her wolf, her fingers exploring the tense muscles of his chest. Excitement slammed into him with a potent force.

"You could have warned me earlier," she murmured. "Now I'm stuck wearing clothes from a bear twice my size."

Beyond reasonable thought, Tucker continued to stroke his fingers up and down the tender skin of her thigh. He was lost in the beauty of her slender, perfect body and the glorious sense of fate that settled deeply inside his animal.

"I have a pair of sweats that will fit you," he managed to rasp.

"If they belonged to your lover, then forget it," she warned, her tone distracted as Tucker slowly lowered himself to the mattress beside her. "I don't wear hand-me-downs."

He framed her face with his hands, his lips skimming over her flushed face.

"Feeling a little possessive, my sweet Nicole?"

"Yes."

His heart missed a beat at her ready response, before melting in utter devotion.

Oh...hell. He was lost. Well and truly lost.

"Good," he growled, slowly lowering his head. "Because from this night on, I belong to you, and you belong to me."

Her body arched toward him in unmistakable invitation. "You're kind of bossy for a bear."

He chuckled. "Get used to it."

"I..." Her words broke off with a shuddering sigh as his mouth traveled down the curve of her throat and feathered light kisses ever lower. "Tucker."

His tongue circled the straining bud of her nipple. "Tell me what you want."

She cried out, her fingers shoving into his hair as she shifted restlessly beneath him.

"You," she breathed. "I want you."

"You admit that you belong to me?"

"Yes."

Raw relief surged through his body. He might very well have rammed his head into the nearest wall if she'd denied him.

With a driven groan, he suckled her nipple, releasing the last of his restraint. She tasted of soap and sweet temptation, and Tucker wanted to nibble her from head to toe. He was a bear. Which meant he had the patience and skill as a lover to devote hours to a woman's pleasure.

Wrapping his arms around her, he slid his hands down Nicole's back, easing her toward his aching body. She readily arched forward, groaning softly at the feel of his erection pressed against her lower stomach. At the same time, she speared her fingers through his hair and urged his mouth toward the tight buds of her breasts.

Never one to miss an opportunity, Tucker tugged her nipple between his lips, using his teeth and tongue until she was squirming against him with pleasure. His hands slid over the curve of her ass and down the back of her thigh. With a small tug, he had her leg draped over his hip, allowing his cock to press against her damp heat.

Raw lust slammed into him as the friction of their skin brushing together created a combustible heat. Restlessly, he turned his attention to her other breast.

Desire sizzled through him, his cock painfully hard, even as he reminded himself that she might be a wolf, but she was still much smaller than him, and more fragile. He had to take care not to be too rough.

"Sweet Nicole," he groaned, "I need you."

"Then take me."

He chuckled at her stark command, his hand softly brushing the back of her leg, edging slowly upward.

"And you call *me* bossy?"

"I'm supposed to be," she breathed, hissing in pleasure as his fingers slid between her legs.

Tucker clenched his teeth, staggered by his need to be inside this woman. She was so soft, so delicate, so utterly his...

His.

His gut twisted. The powerful emotions that were tangling themselves around his heart should have been terrifying. Instead, he'd never felt more smugly happy.

Stroking a finger through her tender flesh, he found her clitoris, teasing it softly while he captured her lips in a deep, demanding kiss.

Nicole arched against him, her claws scraping down his back. Her wolf was eager to play.

His bear gave a chuff of laughter, fully on board.

With a smooth motion, he rolled Nicole onto her back, settling between her parted legs and continuing his relentless caresses. He heard her choked moan as he released her lips to trail a path of fevered kisses down her throat, forcing himself to ignore the collar.

Tonight was all about mutual bliss.

His muscles trembled with the effort to not simply plunge into her and ease his craving. He wanted to prolong this precious moment. To capture it in his mind so he would never forget.

His heart was pounding, his breath coming in sharp rasps as his animal prowled beneath his skin.

Pulling back, he studied her face surrounded by the tumble of tawny curls. The pale, creamy skin. The fan of dark lashes that lay against her flushed cheeks. The soft lips that were parted in invitation.

So beautiful. A flare of raw male possession gripped his heart as he positioned himself at her entrance, and with a slow, steady thrust, sank into her heat. For a brief moment,

Nicole tensed, and Tucker forced himself to halt as her body adjusted to his large size. Continuing to pet and tease her, he waited for her muscles to ease around his cock before he at last pushed in until his balls were pressed against her ass.

His breath hissed through his teeth at the electric sensations that jolted through his body. She was magnificent. An alluring, courageous woman who'd suffered for far too long.

"Nicole," he husked, his hips pulling gently back before sinking back into her welcoming body. "My sweet Nicole."

"Yes," she rasped, her claws raking down his back.

The tiny shock of pain was like a spark to his very short fuse. With a groan of surrender, he lost himself in the pagan rhythm that was as ancient and powerful as the magic that ran through their veins.

14

Nicole slowly woke to discover herself wrapped in a pair of massive arms with her face pressed against a chest that was rough with hair.

Instantly, she blinked in confusion.

Not just at the fact that she wasn't in her bed at her lair, but at the realization that she'd actually slept for hours without being tortured by the nightmares that always lurked in her subconscious.

Pushing her tangled hair out of her face, she took a minute to allow the memories to seep through the fog in her mind. She remembered traveling through the woods and being halted by a large man...no, not a man. An Unseen. And then, when she'd tried to slip into the SAU headquarters, that same aggravating male had once again interfered, hauling her back to his lair. And into his bed.

After that...

Well, it'd been hours of supreme, white-knuckled bliss as Tucker taught her just how skilled a bear could be when he set his mind to pleasing his mate.

Mate.

A tiny shiver shook her, her entire body trembling with sated satisfaction.

But even as she felt Tucker's large hand skimming up the curve of her back, she gave a small gasp at the sunlight that dappled through the trees just outside the window.

"What time is it?" she breathed.

Tucker continued to stroke her back as he glanced toward the nightstand on the other side of her.

"Almost nine."

"Shit." She tried to sit up, only to be held in place when his arms tightened around her. "I can't believe I slept so long."

His lips brushed the curve of her ear. "It wasn't long," he teased. "In case you've forgotten, you spent most of the night seducing me."

Excitement fluttered in her stomach, her toes curling as heat flowed through her veins.

It had been so terribly long since she had allowed herself to enjoy the pleasure of a male's touch. Not since the death of her son.

Now she found it impossible to resist the melting pleasure as Tucker kissed a path of fire down the side of her neck.

"Yeah, right," she muttered. "Is your bear always so insatiable?" she accused.

"No." Lifting his head, he gazed down at her with fierce emotion that made her breath catch in her throat. "Only with you."

"Tucker, I...I have to return to the compound before I'm missed." The words tumbled from her lips as a jolt of panic raced through her.

Tucker tensed, then, with a deliberate motion, he lowered his head to allow his warm breath to tease the delicate skin of her neck. Jolts of pleasure shivered down her spine.

"Do they do a count each day?"

Unnerved by her reaction, she arched away from the potent heat of his caressing lips.

"No, it's always random so we can't anticipate when it will be done." She wrinkled her nose. It always infuriated the Pack when the guards entered the compound and forced them to line up to be checked against the photo IDs the SAU kept on each shifter. It was not only a tedious waste of time, but also a painful reminder that they were prisoners. "But they usually do it at least once a month."

"When was the last count?"

She shivered. The compound was so crowded, that the last lineup had been one of chaos and pain. The guards had herded them together like animals with cattle prods that had enough voltage to send a grown man to his knees.

"Just after the bears were forced into the compound."

His grip tightened, and with relentless determination, he turned her in his arms to meet the blazing darkness of his eyes.

"Then you surely have a few days before they return," he rasped, his hands gripping her hips and pressing her against the swollen jut of his arousal.

Dangerous temptation whispered through her mind, urging her to toss caution to the wind.

"You don't have to deal with Holden," she forced herself to say. She didn't doubt for a second that the older wolf would be foaming at the mouth with fury when she finally returned. "Every hour that I'm gone is another hour where I'm pissing him off."

"You don't have to deal with him either."

She arched her brows, startled by the lethal edge to his husky voice.

"What do you mean?"

He placed a hand against her cheek, his expression hard. Deep in his dark eyes, his bear watched her with patience that was different from a wolf. He wasn't all fang and fury. He was slow and methodical and as relentless as an avalanche.

"Holden is no longer your Alpha," he said.

"Tucker..."

"Your home is with the Unseen." He leaned down until they were nose to nose. "You belong to me."

Her heart faltered at the sheer certainty in his voice. "Tucker, I have to go back or they'll punish everyone in the compound." She had to halt to clear the lump from her throat. "Even the children."

His black gaze blazed over her face. "We'll figure something out."

She lifted her hands to press them against his chest. It was so tempting to give in to his urgings. To simply believe that they could somehow be together.

But she'd spent a lifetime learning that fate was rarely kind.

Nicole shook her head in denial. "It's not possible."

"Anything is possible." He bent his head and covered her mouth with a tempestuous kiss that stole her breath. He tasted of bear and male desire. A heady combination that made her entire body clench with an aching hunger. "Believe in me."

She was far from convinced that he could perform a miracle, but he kissed her again, and she forgot to care. Instead, she lifted her arms to circle his neck, her lips parting in silent invitation.

Distantly, she was aware that Tucker's Pack mates were up and about as they started the day, but she ignored the sounds that filtered through the window.

She wanted Tucker.

Even after a night of passion, she still ached to be in his arms.

"I have waited for you, my sweet," he rasped against her lips. "Without even knowing what was missing from my life."

Treacherous warmth flooded her heart. Dear Lord, how many nights had she cried herself to sleep because of the aching hollowness that haunted her? It'd been more than the loss of Bowe, although that was deep and seemingly bottomless. It was also the knowledge that the bed beside her was empty.

To the world, she had offered the fierce image of a mother consumed by her need for revenge. But inside...

Inside she had hidden the wounds that never healed.

Not until Tucker, a tiny voice whispered.

He was an unexpected gift that she intended to treasure. Even after she was forced to walk away.

She thrust aside the pain that sliced through her heart.

She wasn't going to think about the loneliness of her future or the unbearable loss in her past. For now, she would accept the pleasure Tucker offered.

Nicole's heart raced as his tongue slipped into her mouth. Arching against the hardness of his chest, she shoved her fingers into the thick satin of his hair.

She loved the feel of the white-gold strands.

Rolling on top of her, he groaned. Her wolf should have been outraged by the sense of being pinned. Tucker was not only twice her size, but he was a lethal predator who could rip out her throat before she could blink. Instead, she relished the feeling of being pressed into the mattress and the rough scrape of his hair against her skin.

Last night had been a gentle seduction. Today there was a raw craving that refused to be denied.

"Nicole..." He spread heated kisses over her face, his hands outlining the curve of her hips. "Tell me if I'm too rough."

"You won't hurt me," she assured him in a voice thick with need. "I'm tougher than I look."

A growl rumbled in his chest, his mouth trailing down her throat and over the upper curve of her breasts. Nicole's toes curled, her wolf thoroughly approving of the ferocious hunger.

In response, his hands moved to cup her breasts so he could ravage them with his lips and tongue and just a hint of fang.

Nicole cried out in pleasure, her legs parting so he could settle between them. The blunt tip of his arousal pressed against her inner thigh. She trembled, craving the feeling of him deep inside of her.

"Now, Tucker," she ordered.

He gave a chuffing laugh. "Patience," he admonished, his mouth trailing over the soft swell of her stomach. His hands slipped beneath her hips so he could lift her to an easier angle for his seeking mouth.

"Yes," she breathed, trembling beneath the onslaught of sensations.

He was wicked, skilled, and decadently beautiful.

And all hers.

How was she supposed to resist?

A soft moan was ripped from her throat as Tucker

nibbled on the flesh of her inner thigh, his hands holding her still as she squirmed in pleasure.

His lips stroked ever higher, at last finding the very heart of her desire. She closed her eyes in appreciation, her fingers threading through his hair as he stroked his tongue across her clit.

Her pulse pounded and her soft pants filled the air. Her orgasm loomed as he continued his sensual attack. Over and over he teased the tiny nub, obviously enjoying her muffled groans.

At last she tugged at his hair, hovering perilously close to the edge of pure bliss.

"Now, Tucker," she begged, her voice barely recognizable.

His head lifted to meet her dazed gaze, his bear close to the surface.

"I could become addicted to your taste, my sweet."

"I need you," she whispered.

"Yes."

Surging upward, he entered her with one smooth thrust.

Nicole sucked in a sharp breath, her hands sliding down the rigid muscles of his back as he set a swift, relentless pace that had them both soaring toward a shattering climax.

TUCKER STEPPED into Rios's cabin, impatiently raking back his still-damp hair.

He hadn't wanted to leave the warm shower he'd been sharing with Nicole, but she'd made it clear that her patience was at an end. Either she got the list of employees from Rios, or she was headed back to the SAU facility.

It'd taken nearly a half hour of fast-talking to convince her to finish her shower while he went in search of the information. And even then he understood the clock was ticking.

If he didn't return soon, she'd take off on her own.

But it wasn't just her impatience that was driving his urgency to complete his self-imposed task.

Nicole had offered him her fragile trust by allowing him to go without her. A trust that he was determined to be worthy of, even if it meant infuriating his Pack mate.

Stretched on the leather sofa in front of the TV that was showing a replay of the soccer game, Rios surged to his feet. His dark hair was tousled, and his jaw shadowed with unshaven whiskers, proving he hadn't been to bed yet.

"Hey, bear." Wearing nothing but a loose pair of sweatpants, Rios stretched his arms over his head, his muscles rippling beneath his bronzed skin. "I expected you back before now."

"I was busy."

Dark eyes flared with feline amusement as Rios deliberately glanced toward the bite marks still visible on Tucker's throat.

"Yeah, I can tell," he taunted, no doubt hoping to embarrass his friend. Unfortunately for him, Tucker had deliberately chosen the cream, cable-knit sweater because the neckline was loose enough show the visible signs of Nicole's possession. "Do you want to tell me about your little wolf?"

Tucker stepped forward, a hint of warning in his tone. "She's not up for discussion. Not ever."

Rios gave a low whistle. "Like that, is it?"

Tucker held his gaze. "It's exactly like that."

The jaguar moved forward to slap him on the back. "Congrats." He gave a sudden burst of laughter. "At least, I think."

Tucker ignored the sly dig. Rios might be a male who enjoyed spreading his affection far and wide, but eventually, he would meet his match and find himself longing to settle down.

It happened to all of them sooner or later.

"Tell me what's happening here," Tucker commanded.

Instantly, Rios was all business. "I managed to salvage the files we had downloaded, but I'm waiting for the green light from Sinclair before I try to tap into their system."

Tucker arched a brow. "He's at headquarters?"

"Yeah, got back a few hours ago from his meeting with his CDC contact, and as soon as I told him what was going on, he headed down to HQ."

It didn't surprise Tucker that the Alpha had taken off the second he learned there might be trouble. Even if Sinclair were exhausted from his trip to meet Mira, he would have demanded that he be the one to take the risk.

But, he didn't like the fact that Sinclair hadn't returned.

How long did it take to find out what was going on with the computers?

"He's still with them?" he asked.

Rios nodded. "He texted to say the purging was in response to Dr. Talbot's disappearance." The jaguar gave a humorless laugh. "They have to prepare for the potential investigation if word of their unsanctioned research reaches the ears of D.C."

Tucker grimaced. The doctor was more than "disappeared." The last he'd heard, the scientist had been suitably punished for his decision to use his own children in his sick experiments.

Of course, the SAU couldn't know what the doctor had or had not shared with the shifters. And not everyone in Congress was pleased with the shadowy government agency. They had to worry that someone in authority might come nosing around.

"That makes sense." Tucker folded his arms over his chest, not entirely reassured. "If he knows why there was a purge, then why isn't he back?"

Rios shrugged. "He said a stranger arrived not long after he did, demanding to see Director Markham."

Tucker felt a pang of surprise. The location of the headquarters was a tightly guarded secret. In fact, Tucker still didn't know how Sinclair had managed to locate it. So any unexpected visitor would stir a lot of attention.

"Someone from the government?"

Rios gave a lift of his hands. "He didn't know, but he had a feeling it was important."

"Hmm." Tucker briefly considered trying to call his friend, only to dismiss the urge. If Sinclair was in touch with Rios, then he had to be okay. And he wouldn't thank Tucker for interrupting his investigation. Instead, Tucker turned his attention to the reason he'd sought out the jaguar. "I need a favor."

"Does this have something to do with your pretty wolf?" Rios easily guessed.

"Yes."

A wicked smile curved his lips. "Then ask."

"SAU guards murdered her young son seven years ago," he said bluntly. It wasn't like there was any easy way to share the information.

All humor leeched from Rios's face and his eyes flashed gold. Like most Unseen, the jaguar had lost several family members to the SAU.

"Fuck."

Tucker nodded. "My thoughts exactly."

"How can I help?"

Tucker felt a flare of warmth at Rios's immediate offer of assistance. *This* was why he'd joined a Pack despite his loner nature. They were a true family, who supported one another while they worked to create a world where shifters could live without fear.

"Nicole managed to track down and dispose of two of the guards," he said, his lips twisting at the enormous task it must have been for a female who was not only grieving, but locked in a compound to accomplish. "But she hasn't been able to locate the actual shooter. She's hoping she can use the employee database to identify him."

"We can give it a try, but the bastards are smart enough to keep many of their employees off the main payroll. I assume they get paid in cash," Rios said, heading toward one of the computers that were lined up on a long table. Once seated, he glanced over his shoulder as Tucker moved to stand directly behind him. "Where is she?"

Tucker sent his friend a tight smile. "I convinced her there would be an easier way."

Rios arched a brow. "What's that?"

Tucker's smile widened. "You're the computer expert. You tell me."

"Christ. You don't ask much."

"That's what friends are for, right?"

Rios turned back to the computers with a shake of his head.

"Friends are a pain in the ass," he muttered, tapping on the keyboard to pull up the files they'd stolen from the SAU. "There should be some internal reports about the incident."

"Murder," Tucker corrected.

Rios continued to skim through the files. "What?"

"It wasn't an incident, it was murder."

"Got it," Rios agreed.

There was a long silence, broken only by the soft hum of the electronics and Rios's occasional click of the mouse.

Tucker was impatiently glancing toward the window, futilely wishing he had a view of his cabin. How long would Nicole wait? An hour? Fifteen minutes?

"Here." Leaning forward, Rios studied the monitor with his brow furrowed. "It looks like they tried to keep all record of the guards involved from any news media. Even during the investigation they were referred to by initials."

Tucker released a low growl. "There has to be something to identify them."

"If it's here, I'll find it," Rios swore in distracted tones. There were a few more clicks, then the jaguar abruptly stiffened. "Shit."

"What is it?" Tucker grasped the back of Rios's chair as he leaned over his friend's shoulder.

"Those bastards." Rios turned the monitor so Tucker had a clear view.

There was the sound of wood splintering as Tucker crushed the chair beneath his hands. In that second, he knew that the sight of the dead child lying in the snow stained with his blood would be forever seared into his mind.

The raw, aching regret he felt could be nothing compared to what Nicole lived with day after day, but it was enough to make his gut twist and bile rise to his throat.

"Tell me you have a name," he said, his voice thick with fury.

Rios leaned to the side as the printer began to spit out sheets of paper.

"I not only have a name, I have an address." The jaguar neatly placed the papers in a folder. "And get this..." He shoved the folder in Tucker's hand. "It's local."

Opening the folder, Tucker studied the information that Rios had managed to pull out of the archives. Not only the guards involved, but those who had assisted in the cover-up.

A devious idea slowly began to form in the back of his mind.

It wouldn't be easy to convince Nicole. In fact, he feared that he might cause her even more pain. But he had to try.

Turning, Tucker headed toward the door of the cabin, glancing over his shoulder to give his friend a small bow of his head.

"I owe you."

"No, you don't." Rios rose to his feet, his expression somber. "Take care of your wolf."

"Count on it."

15

Nicole was pacing the floor, wearing an oversized robe that threatened to trip her with every step.

How had she allowed Tucker to talk her into waiting here? Okay, he'd had her naked in the shower. And he'd been doing all sorts of delicious things with his tongue, but still...

The sound of approaching footsteps intruded into her frustrated thoughts. Hiking up the folds of Tucker's robes, she rushed out of the bedroom.

"Tucker?"

The front door was pushed open and her gorgeous bear stepped into the room. Instantly, the air was filled with his warm, spicy scent along with the prickling power of his animal.

A tingle of excitement raced through her. How the hell

had she ever missed the fact that he was a shifter? His presence was a tangible force.

"I come with gifts," he murmured, tossing her a canvas bag.

Instinctively she caught it, opening the zipper to pull out a pair of jeans and a peach turtleneck sweater, along with some silky underwear. Her lips twisted at the sight of the tags that were still attached.

He'd clearly remembered her fierce refusal to wear anything that might have belonged to one of his lovers.

A bear who could be trained, she wryly acknowledged.

Dangerous.

"Thanks," she muttered, shrugging out of the robe to pull on the clothing. They were loose, but they were better than drowning in Tucker's clothes. She reached back into the bag to pull out the tennis shoes and slid them onto her feet. Once she had them tied, she straightened to meet Tucker's watchful gaze. "Did you find the name of the guard?"

He gave a slow nod. "I did. Ian Viker."

Ian Viker. She committed the name to memory. She wanted to see it etched on a gravestone.

"Did you get an address?"

Another slow nod. "Just a few miles away."

Disbelief jolted through her. After all these years. After all the dead ends and disappointments.

Could she dare to hope that her prey was within her grasp?

"Then what are we waiting for?" she demanded in thick tones.

His expression was unreadable. "We need to talk."

"No." She planted her fists on her hips. She knew what those words meant. She'd endured them a thousand times over the past seven years. "I don't want to hear any sermons on turning the other cheek or bullshit about the emptiness of revenge."

He stepped forward, his eyes dark with understanding. "I'm not going to say any of those things."

"Then what?"

He paused before saying the words he clearly sensed she wasn't going to like.

"Have you considered the possibility that your greatest revenge might come from leaving the guard alive?"

Nicole flinched. As if she'd been slapped in the face.

Leave the monster who'd shot down her child alive?

"No."

He stepped forward. "Hear me out. Please."

She huffed out an impatient sigh. It was the 'please' that did it.

"Fine."

He grimaced, easily hearing the pain in her voice. "The bastard deserves to die. Hell, I want to rip out his heart and stuff it down his throat," he rasped, his eyes abruptly glowing with the power of his bear. "But he's just a small part of the evil. We have to cut off the head of the snake if we want it to die."

Nicole wrapped her arms around her waist. She didn't want to accept that he might have a point. Who cared if he could help the shifters? She wanted to destroy the man who'd ruined her life.

She'd waited so long.

Too long.

But he continued to stare at her, clearly needing her to hear him out.

"So what are you suggesting?" she grudgingly asked.

"The SAU managed to cover up the crime five years ago, but the political climate isn't the same," he said in a gentle voice. "If we could capture the guard and force him to confess to a room full of reporters that he murdered an innocent child, they might start to see just how corrupt the SAU has become."

She immediately shook his head. "They would never believe him."

"They would if we had proof." He lifted his hand, revealing a file folder.

Nicole reached out, only to yank back her hand. She'd had enough nightmares, thank you very much. She didn't need to add to her sleepless nights.

She grimaced. "The SAU would crush the story before it could ever get out."

"We have contacts with media outlets that aren't intimidated by the SAU," he revealed. "In fact, they relish the opportunity to expose the bastards."

Nicole shrugged. She found it hard to believe that

anyone had the ability to fight against the subversive agency. They'd been the boogiemen who'd intimidated and imprisoned and brutalized her people for so long, they didn't even remember what it was like to be free.

But even if there were a few brave journalists willing to spread the story, it didn't mean that it would change anything.

"You don't know what you're asking," she hissed.

"You're right. I don't," he admitted, reaching out to brush the back of his fingers down her cheek. "I can't even imagine the pain you've had to suffer day after day. But I do understand your need for blood. I felt the same way after my father's death, even though I was just a young child."

Nicole's simmering frustration faltered. She knew Tucker's heart and soul.

He was loyal, kind, fiercely protective, and unexpectedly playful.

But there were large parts of his life that remained a mystery.

"He was killed?" she asked.

"Yes." A bone-deep pain tightened his beautiful features. "When they started rounding up shifters, my father sent my mother and me into hiding but he stayed behind to try and stand with those who refused to be caged." His eyes were unfocused as if he were lost in his memories. "He was shot in the back."

Nicole reached out to lay her fingers on his forearm. Her own parents had died during the roundup of shifters. She'd been raised by an aunt, although it'd been Soren's mother who'd truly taken on the role of parent.

"I'm sorry," she husked.

He dipped his head in acknowledgment of her sympathy. "I can barely recall his face, but I have a vivid memory of learning he was dead. I was overwhelmed with the primitive urge to hunt down and destroy those responsible." He paused before giving a sharp shake of his head. Perhaps dismissing the painful memories. "Instead, I can only use my powers as a healer to try and save as many of my people as possible. I hope in some small way I'm honoring his sacrifice."

Nicole dropped her hand and took a step back. Logically, she realized he was making sense, but her heart still ached for revenge.

"I need to see him dead," she said in a harsh voice.

"Then he's dead," Tucker announced with a shocking swiftness. Placing the file on a nearby table, he held out his hand. "Let's go."

She frowned. Tucker had many fine qualities, but he was stubborn as a mule.

"That's it?" she asked with blatant suspicion. "You aren't going to argue?"

He held her gaze as if willing her to accept the sincerity of his words.

"Only you can decide how this is going to play out," he told her. "I'm just going along to provide the muscle."

Another layer of the ice that had coated her heart since

Bowe's death melted. This male possessed a unique ability to strip away the defenses that she'd built with such painstaking care.

Still, she ignored the hand he continued to hold out.

She wasn't losing another person she loved.

"No."

He blinked in confusion. "No?"

She folded her arms over her chest, preparing for a fight. "You're not going."

Tucker moved forward. He didn't have the smooth prowl of a feline. Or even the grace of a wolf. Instead, he plowed straight toward her, his bear glowing in his eyes.

"I'm fairly certain that I didn't hear you right."

She wasn't a submissive, but it took every ounce of her willpower not to cringe beneath the force of his over-whelming presence.

"You're a part of the Unseen," she managed to mutter between stiff lips.

His nose flared. "That's not a newsflash."

"You can't be caught with a shifter," she continued. Did she really have to spell it out? It seemed she did, as he simply glared at her with smoldering anger. "You'll put your entire Pack at risk."

"It's my decision."

She rolled her eyes. She didn't have much experience with bears, but she didn't think they were all so aggravating.

Were they?

"You're not thinking clearly," she informed him.

A humorless smile stretched his lips. "I'm freshly mated. I'm not supposed to be thinking clearly."

"Tucker-"

He pressed a finger to her lips, halting her protest. "We both go. Or neither of us." He leaned down, his expression hard with an unmistakable warning. "Decide."

Shit. He was serious.

If she didn't agree to let him go with her, then he wasn't going to give her the information she so desperately craved. Hell. She didn't doubt he would lock her in this cabin if she didn't give in.

She made a sound of annoyance. "Bossy bear."

TUCKER PULLED the nondescript mid-size car to a halt on the corner of the quiet street. Broomfield was a suburb close to Boulder, with streets that were lined with brick homes, neatly trimmed yards, and family cars parked in the driveways.

Not the sort of place he would expect to find a ruthless killer. But then again, that could be the point. If the SAU wanted to keep the guard from being found, then what better place to hide him?

However, the info that'd been put in the file may have been a deliberate trick for anyone searching for information on the ruthless murderer. He and Nicole could easily be walking into a trap.

Seated beside him, Nicole sent him a frown. "Why are you stopping?"

He nodded to the small house that was nearly hidden behind a wooden fence.

"Viker's home is at the end of the street," he murmured, muttering a curse as she shoved her car door open. Reaching out, he grasped her arm. "Nicole."

She scowled, her teeth gritted. Nothing unusual. She'd been scowling and gritting her teeth since he refused to allow her to run off without him.

"Do you sense something?" she demanded.

"Not yet," he admitted, his gaze moving over the neighborhood that was drenched in the late morning sunlight. "But I'm not going to charge in until we know exactly what we're getting into."

She gave a grudging nod. She might be frustrated with him, but she wasn't stupid.

"You want me to do a search?" she asked.

"Yes, but first we watch," he decided.

He could feel her studying his profile. "Watch for what?"

His gaze continued to skim from one house to another. "Security cameras. Local cops. Suspicious traffic. Every neighborhood has its own pulse."

He settled back in the seat that wasn't created for a man his size. Of course, he'd spent enough time on stakeouts to know that even the most comfortable seat became cramped and lumpy over time.

The only plus this time was the sweet scent of Nicole

that teased at his senses, reminding him of the long hours of pleasure they'd shared in his bed.

They settled in to watch the humans go about their business. Most houses were empty since the occupants had already left for work, but there were a few mothers with younger kids at home. There were also delivery trucks, a postal carrier, and a construction crew that was replacing the roof on a garage.

"What happened after your father died?" Nicole abruptly broke the silence.

"My mother raised me near the North Pole."

She gave a startled laugh. "Like Santa Claus?"

"Yep." He turned his head to witness her rare smile, his bear savoring the knowledge that he'd earned such an elusive gift. "It was brutally cold, so I spent most of my time as a bear until Sinclair traveled through the area and recruited me to join his Pack."

"Why did you join him?"

He considered for a long moment. It was a question he'd asked himself. After all, he'd been perfectly satisfied spending his life roaming the Arctic as a bear. The sheer simplicity of it was addictive, and there were times when he went weeks without recalling that he had a human side. But once Sinclair had intruded into his solitary existence, he'd found the urge to be a part of a Pack stirred to life.

"I believed in his cause," he said.

"And what's that?"

He shrugged. "Destroying the SAU from the inside out."

She nodded, thankfully not demanding a thorough explanation of the Unseen's plans to topple the SAU. He trusted her with his very life, but Sinclair would skin him if he shared sensitive information before they were formally mated.

Something he intended to complete as soon as she was done with Ian Viker.

Unlike the shifters that were collared and branded, the Unseen didn't use tattoos to display their commitment to one another. Instead, when they mated, he and Nicole would exchange amulets that they would place around each other's necks as a symbol of the bonds that had already pulled them together.

"What about your mother?" she asked.

A wave of fond exasperation raced through Tucker. He'd tried a hundred times to get his stubborn mother to join him in his cabin. Or at least move somewhere that he could easily get to her if she needed him.

And every time, she'd gently claim that she loved roaming free too much to every become fully civilized.

Tucker thought it had more to do with her grief at the loss of her mate. When she was in her bear form, she didn't have to deal with human emotions.

"She still lives in a remote village," he told Nicole. "I travel to see her several times a year."

"She must be lonely."

"No." He gave a firm shake of his head. "She likes the isolation. We'll go see her in a few weeks."

Her eyes widened as if caught off guard by his words, which was ridiculous. She had to know that his mother would be anxious to meet the female who'd stolen the heart of her only cub?

"Tucker," she breathed.

"Don't worry." He flashed a teasing grin. "She's going to love you."

Her lips parted as if she intended to remind him of all the obstacles that stood between the two of them mating, only to heave a resigned sigh at the stubborn jut of his jaw.

"We're going to have to discuss your habit of thinking you can toss out orders and simply have them obeyed," she muttered.

"No doubt we're going to have a lot of those discussions," he assured her.

"No doubt."

Another silence filled the car as they returned their attention to their surroundings. An hour had passed before Tucker accepted that there was nothing suspicious to be seen from their place on the street.

"Okay," he murmured. "I'm going to do a sweep of the block."

Nicole gave a swift nod. "You go around the front, I'll meet you in the back."

Tucker stiffened, his primitive male mind instantly rebelling at the thought of allowing his female to be in danger.

"Nicole."

There was a low growl of warning as Nicole leaned forward, her wolf visible in her eyes.

"Don't."

He grimaced. As much as he wanted to forbid her, he couldn't. This was her fight. She should be the one to hunt her prey.

"Be careful."

Before she could say anything, he moved forward to capture her lips in a fierce kiss that revealed all the worry and wonderment and love that filled his heart. Then, pulling away, he shoved open his door and climbed out of the car.

He casually strolled down the street, using his heightened sense of smell. His eyesight wasn't as good as other shifters', but it was good enough to make sure there were no humans lingering near the house at the end of the road.

Rounding the block, he waited until he was sure no one was watching to vault over the back fence. Nicole was already waiting for him near the French doors.

"Anything?" he demanded, knowing she would have done a thorough search despite her urgency to confront the guard.

"Humans. A few dogs and cats." She wrinkled her nose, looking more like a teenager than a female intent on bloody vengeance. "And a ferret. What about you?"

"Nothing that stood out as suspicious," he said, resisting the urge to invent some reason for them to leave.

"Good," she said on a low growl. "I'm done waiting."

Reaching out, she grasped the handle of the French door and gave it a yank. The flimsy lock snapped, allowing her to slide it open. Then they moved with shifter-silence through the kitchen that had dishes piled in the sink and a linoleum floor that was sticky with...hell, Tucker didn't want to know. They paused and silently listened for any sounds that would indicate that their entrance had been noticed. Finally, they stepped through an arched opening into the front living room.

Tucker shuddered. The drapes were closed against the afternoon light, but he could still make out the worn furniture that looked as if it'd been found in the local dump, and the rug that was littered with empty beer cans, pizza boxes, and bags of chips.

And on the sofa was a small, wiry man with thinning brown hair and a narrow face. He was dressed in creased khakis and a white tee that was in dire need of a washing machine.

At first glance, he looked like he was asleep, but as Nicole stepped forward, he abruptly lifted his head to glance at them in astonishment.

"What the hell?" he muttered, his gaze moving to Tucker, who towered in the background before returning to Nicole. "If you're here to rob me, then you're fucking idiots. I don't have jack shit..." His words trailed away as his eyes widened with a sudden recognition. "You," he breathed.

16

Nicole allowed a cold smile to curve her lips. She was pleased that the guard recognized her. She wanted him to know exactly why he was about to die.

"Yes, me." She watched as he shakily shoved himself off the couch, his face a pasty shade of ash. "Hello, Ian."

The man inched to the side. Was he hoping he could somehow sneak his way to the front door?

Idiot.

"How did you find me?"

She released a short laugh that echoed through the room. "Did you think you could avoid justice forever?"

He held up his hands in an unspoken plea for mercy. "Listen, what happened-"

"You mean the cold-blooded murder of my son?" she interrupted, ice coating each word.

He licked his lips, a trickle of sweat inching from his

forehead down his unshaven cheek. He didn't look the same as the guard who'd shot Bowe.

Although she'd only gotten a brief glance, the man's face had been seared into her mind.

Now she realized that he'd lost at least twenty pounds. His clothes hung on his gaunt frame as if he couldn't be bothered to buy anything that fit. And his hair had thinned. There were also new lines on his face, giving him the appearance of having aged at least twenty years instead of seven.

But the biggest change was the lack of swagger.

Even after shooting a mere child, he'd strutted around as if he'd done something amazing. Today, he looked as if he'd spent the past years on a drunken binge.

"It wasn't my fault," he whined.

"Lies." She stepped forward as the coward continued to inch to the side. Tucker followed closely behind her, his heat wrapping around her with unspoken support. "Your fellow guards already told me that you pulled the trigger."

"I was ordered to do it," Ian told her.

Continuing to prowl forward, she made a sound of disgust. "Convenient."

"No, please." He bumped into the tall entertainment center behind him, more sweat trickling down his face. "You have to believe me."

"Nicole." Tucker covertly brushed his hand down her rigid back. The warmth of his touch was an anchor that allowed her to find her way through the red mist that clouded her mind.

"Talk," she snapped.

The man's gaze briefly flickered toward Tucker before returning to Nicole. Clearly he didn't realize that Tucker was an even greater threat than she was. No surprise. Without a collar or a brand, it was impossible for humans to determine who was or was not a shifter.

That was one of the reasons many people were so anxious to keep them locked behind walls.

"The SAU recruited me to become a guard at the River Pack compound," he said.

She frowned, not missing the key word. "Recruited from where?"

"The military."

She studied the wiry form that she could break in two. He didn't look like a person anyone would choose as a guard.

"Why would they recruit you?"

"Because I was a sharp-shooter."

She regarded him with growing suspicion. She didn't give a shit why he'd become a guard. All that mattered was the fact that he'd pulled the trigger. He'd murdered her son.

But the certainty that he was hiding something nagged at the edge of her mind.

Dammit.

Now she had to know.

"There's a lot of sharp-shooters," she pointed out, the

wolf in her fighting to be released so she could taste his blood on her tongue. "Why you?"

He gave a lift of his shoulder. "I'm the best."

Her lips curled back, revealing her elongated fangs. "He isn't going to tell the truth," she told Tucker with a flare of satisfaction. "I may as well rip out his throat."

Tucker moved to stand at her side, his arms folded over his massive chest.

"Go for it."

The man gave a desperate shake of his head. "Hold on."

Nicole tried to step forward, only to be halted when Tucker grasped the back of her sweater, firmly keeping her in place.

Ignoring her companion, she glared at the face that still haunted her dreams.

"Say it," she snarled.

His hands gripped the shelves behind him as if his knees were weak with fear. Like most bullies, he turned into a groveling chicken when confronted by someone stronger than him.

"I'd been accused of shooting a fellow solider in the back."

She heard Tucker hiss a breath through his clenched teeth. He had an ingrained sense of integrity, and would be deeply offended by the man's confession.

"Why did you shoot him?" she demanded.

Pale eyes flickered. A sure sign that he was about to tell a lie. "It was an accident," he said. "I was cleaning my gun and it fired."

"And the real reason?" Nicole insisted.

There was a short hesitation before Ian revealed the truth. "I wanted his bunk."

Heat blasted from Tucker's big body. "Shit."

Nicole grimaced. "You're truly sick," she muttered.

The human hunched his shoulders. "You wanted the truth."

Suddenly, Nicole understood why the secret agency would decide this man was suitable to wear their uniform.

Not every human would be willing to shoot an innocent man in the back just because he wanted his bed.

"So the SAU wanted a sharp-shooter without morals," she said.

Ian didn't look offended. Either he'd accepted that he was a depraved bastard, or he was a straight up psychopath, unable to comprehend the depths of his evil.

The knowledge twisted Nicole's stomach with aching sadness. This empty shell of a man had stolen a bright, beautiful light from this world.

"Yeah, I guess so," he muttered.

As if sensing her distress, Tucker ran his hand up and down her back, glaring at the unfeeling monster.

"Why?" he demanded.

"Director Markham had just taken control of the Denver Division, and he wanted to crack down on the wolves."

Nicole scowled. She'd seen the Director from a distance, but he rarely came to the compound.

"Why would he want to crack down?"

Ian shrugged. "He felt like the Alpha of the wolves hadn't given him the proper respect during their first meeting. He wanted to send a message."

"He ordered the death of a child because he didn't get the *respect* he thought he deserved?" Nicole breathed in disbelief.

The man continued to grip the shelf behind his back, his eyes averted as if he were considering how much to reveal before Nicole snapped and ripped out his throat.

Smart man. Nicole could already feel her claws slicing through the tips of her fingers and her fangs throbbing with the need to sink into his flesh.

"Those weren't his exact words," he slowly confessed.

"What did he say?"

Ian nervously transferred his weight from one foot to the other.

"He wanted us to keep an eye out for any infractions, and publically punish the offenders so the animals would know that the new Director wasn't going to take any shit."

Nicole stared at him in pained disbelief. "And you decided to kill my son?"

"It was an impulsive decision." His gaze flickered around the dark, filthy room. "And trust me, I've paid for it."

Paid for it? Nicole hissed as the red mist of fury once again clogged her brain.

"No, you haven't," she snarled. His face turned a paler shade of ash, as her wolf flashed in her eyes. "But you will."

"I swear I've suffered," he desperately pleaded for his life. "I was sacked from my job, and threatened with being fed to the wolves if I ever spoke about this to anyone. What else do you want from me?"

"Your blood."

His gaze locked on her exposed fangs, his entire body shaking with fear.

"Killing me won't bring your son back."

"It'll allow him to rest in peace."

"Fine, if you want to punish someone, then it should be Markham." Ian readily tossed his boss under the bus. Clearly the old saying was true. There was no honor among thieves. "He's the one who sought me out and put me in an SAU uniform."

The truth of his words slammed into Nicole with unexpected force. Shit. Her animal wanted a simple, clean death. It's what she'd been dreaming about for seven years. But she couldn't shake the nagging voice in the back of her mind.

Was Tucker right? Was it possible to actually use this pathetic excuse of a human to bring down the SAU?

"Would you swear to that?" she abruptly demanded, the words barely making it past her stiff lips.

Ian studied her in wary confusion. "What?"

"Would you stand before the world and reveal your crimes?" she pressed.

"Markham would never allow me to speak."

It was Tucker who responded. "You'll be protected from the SAU."

"Yeah, right." The man gave a sharp laugh. "And what about the shifters?"

"What about them?" Tucker asked.

Ian deliberately stared at Nicole's fangs that were visibly bared.

"Would I be protected from them?"

Tucker shrugged. "As long as you...no!"

With head-dizzying speed, Tucker was shoving Nicole to the side. Caught off guard, she stumbled to her knees, stunned by the unexpected sound of a handgun being fired.

Shit, shit, shit.

While she'd thought Ian Viker was cowering in fear against the shelves, he'd clearly been placing himself in the perfect position to get his hands on a hidden weapon.

And Tucker had placed himself between her and the gun to save her.

In horror, Nicole watched as Tucker hit the floor with a loud thud. His eyes were closed, and his face was dangerously pale. But it was the blood that gushed from the bullet hole in the center of his chest that made her heart squeeze with terror.

One bullet shouldn't be able to take down a bear shifter. But Tucker had obviously been shot at point-blank range.

Who the hell knew how much internal damage had been done?

"Tucker." Still on her knees, she reached out to touch his

outstretched arm, relief shuddering through her at the feel of his steady pulse.

He was alive. But for how long?

"No." She heard Ian snap. "Don't move."

Fury exploded through her. She'd tried to temper her thirst for revenge and think about the bigger picture. But she was done.

This man needed to die.

Now.

But even as she prepared to shift into her wolf, she felt the pinprick of prongs biting into her back. For a second she assumed that the bastard had shot her. Instead, she felt a massive volt of electricity sizzling through her body.

A Taser that'd been modified to take down a shifter. One of the SAU's little toys.

Terrifyingly helpless, Nicole crumpled forward, her muscles refusing to obey her command to shift. She gagged at the stench of the filthy carpet and the smell of Tucker's blood that filled the air.

A shadow fell over her as Ian stood above her head, staring down at her with a smug smile.

"If you're going to kill me, then kill me," she rasped, her body twitching in pain.

He gave a slow shake of his head, a hectic glitter of excitement glowing in his pale eyes.

"Ironically, you're worth much more to me alive than dead."

A ball of dread lodged in the pit of her stomach. She

didn't fear death. Or even pain. That was nothing compared to the grief she'd endured.

But she couldn't bear the thought of being used by the SAU to further their evil agenda against the shifters.

She struggled to form the words. "What are you going to do with me?"

An ugly expression settled on his narrow face. "I was condemned to suburb purgatory because Markham said I'd created a PR nightmare." He allowed his gaze to roam over her. "Perhaps if I bring him a PR showpiece, I'll be reinstated."

PR showpiece? She tried to think through the panic that was threatening to overwhelm her. It still didn't make any sense.

"I don't know what you're talking about."

He leaned over her, smart enough to stay just out of reach. Not that she could actually do any damage. She felt as weak as a kitten.

"Then let me spell it out. When I tell people what happened, it's going to go something like this..." His tone was condescending. As if he were convinced that he now had the upper hand. "I was quietly watching TV with my old friend." He nodded toward the unconscious Tucker. "When a crazed shifter broke into my house and killed my pal."

A flare of relief raced through her at the knowledge Ian assumed that Tucker was dead. At the same time, she tried to clear her mind enough to find a way to keep Ian distracted. She could already feel her muscles easing. In a few minutes, she'd be able to call on her wolf.

Then the man was dead.

"Why would a shifter shoot a human?" she challenged.

He waved aside her logic. "By the time Markham is done setting the scene, I can assure you the whole world will believe the body was mauled."

A low growl rumbled in her throat. After she killed Ian, she was going to hunt down Markham. Tucker was right. They had to cut off the head of the snake.

"You consider that good PR?" she taunted.

Ian shrugged. "The SAU can prove exactly why the shifters should be kept locked away. And why the agency should be better funded." A slow smile curved his lips. "Hell. I'll be a hero."

Nicole gave a pained shake of her head. "You really are crazy."

Obviously the word 'crazy' hit a nerve. Probably because he'd heard it a thousand times before.

Whatever the cause, the thin lips pressed together, and before Nicole could try to protect herself, he lifted his foot and slammed it into the side of her head.

Starbursts of pain exploded behind her eyes, the colors dazzling her before everything went black.

17

S inclair was exhausted. Returning to his Pack after secretly following Mira to make sure she'd made it safely back to her house, he'd discovered that he had a dozen text messages from Rios. He'd immediately gone to speak with his computer expert before heading to the SAU headquarters to find out why they would be purging their computers.

It hadn't taken long to realize that they were all freaked out by the fear of the missing Dr. Talbot giving away secrets. Even after the question was answered, however, Sinclair lingered.

The stranger who'd arrived and demanded entrance to the facility had intrigued him. No one seemed to know whom he was, or why the Director had so readily agreed to meet with him. Then, just as surprisingly, Markham had left out the back door at the same time as the visitor.

It could be nothing. Hell, for all Sinclair knew, the man was a relation of Markham's. Or a lover. But the secretive departure was enough out of the norm to stir Sinclair's interest. If something had spooked the Director, then Sinclair wanted to know what it was.

Waiting until the upper floor was clear, he pressed open Markham's door and stepped into the man's office.

A swift glance proved it would be easy to search. There were no piles of paper or locked file cabinets. In fact, there was nothing beyond the heavy desk and the shelves on the wall—nowhere to hide anything.

Crossing to the desk, Sinclair came to an abrupt halt at the faint smell that clung to the air.

That didn't belong to Markham. Or the male stranger.

It was distinctly female. And oddly familiar.

Distracted by the elusive scent, Sinclair was caught off guard by the sudden sound of a male voice behind him.

"What are you doing in here?"

Smoothing his expression to an unreadable mask, he slowly turned to discover Grant regarding him with open suspicion. Of course, the head of security was always suspicious.

Thankfully, he wasn't very bright.

"I had a meeting scheduled with the Director," Sinclair said, lifting his arm to glance at his watch. "I was waiting for him to show up."

Grant scowled but readily accepted the excuse. "He's out of town."

Hmm. The only time that Markham was willing to leave his petty dictatorship in Boulder was when he was forced to travel to D.C.

"Really? That was sudden." Sinclair carefully studied Grant, monitoring every emotion that flickered over his square face. "An emergency?"

Grant was instantly bristling at the question. Which told Sinclair that the head of security didn't know where Markham had gone, or why. Which was obviously pissing the former soldier off.

"The Director doesn't have to share his schedule with his employees," he snapped.

Sinclair gave a nonchalant lift of his hands, resisting the urge to make up a reason to linger in the office. Grant might not be brilliant, but he wasn't completely stupid. And there was no reason to draw attention to himself. Right now they believed he was just another guard.

To stay effective, he had to keep his cover.

"Hey, that's fine with me," he said, strolling toward the door. "I'll go back home and wait for my shift."

Waiting until they were both in the hallway, Grant firmly pulled the door shut behind them with a warning glare in Sinclair's direction.

"Don't come in this office unless Markham is here. Got it?"

Sinclair shrugged. "Got it."

At the point of strolling away, both men froze when the

unmistakable sound of shouting was heard, followed by someone beeping a car horn over and over.

"Now what?" Grant bit out. "Come with me," he ordered Sinclair, jogging down the hallway to the steel door at the end.

He had to pause to use his keycard to trip the lock, and then they were hurrying down the emergency stairs and out the back exit.

The sound of beeping continued as they hurried toward the gate. Five minutes later, they were confronted with the sight of a uniformed guard with his weapon pointed at a man on the other side of the fence. The stranger was standing next to his car with his arm shoved through the open window so he could continue to lean on the horn.

Grant stormed up to the guard, his face flushed with anger. Clearly the morning hadn't been going well for the head of security.

"What's going on here?" he snarled.

The guard lowered his weapon, but his gaze remained trained on the stranger who'd thankfully stopped honking his horn. Sinclair breathed a sigh of relief.

There were times when super hearing sucked.

"This man is insisting he's an employee," the guard explained. "But he refuses to show his I.D."

The head of security sent an impatient glance toward the intruder and abruptly stiffened in shock.

"Viker," the man breathed.

"Grant."

The stranger slammed his car door shut and strolled forward. He looked like he'd just crawled out of the gutter with his hair matted and his face unshaven. Even more surprising, there was a feverish flush to his cheeks, and a glitter in his eyes that made Sinclair question whether or not he was entirely sane.

So how was he connected to the SAU?

Reaching the fence, the man flashed a smile at the rigid head of security.

"Good to see you."

With a small shake of his head, Grant turned to flick a hand in the guard's direction.

"I'll deal with this."

The guard nodded, turning to head toward the small building where the guards could keep watch with the security cameras. At the same time, Sinclair silently stepped into the shadows of the building, giving himself a perfect view of the men without drawing attention to himself.

"Have you lost your mind, Viker?" Grant snapped, stepping toward the fence. "You were warned that if you showed your face in public you would be signing your death warrant."

Sinclair arched a brow. Viker? The name wasn't familiar, but the two obviously knew one another. And they hadn't parted as friends.

"I need to see Markham," the intruder insisted.

"He's not here."

Viker scowled in frustration. "Shit."

Grant planted his hands on his hips, puffing out his chest.

"Consider yourself lucky. He has standing orders to have you shot on sight. If the guard had recognized you, you'd already be dead. And if Markham had been here..." An ugly smile stretched Grant's lips. "He would have pulled the trigger himself."

The intruder licked his lips, glancing over his shoulder at his car before returning his attention to Grant.

"Then he'd be a fool," he warned. "I have something he wants."

Sinclair grimaced. He half expected the creepy dude to rub his hands together and cackle like a madman.

Grant, on the other hand, simply looked annoyed. "Another supposed animal mauling you found posted on the Internet?"

"No, this time I have the real thing."

Opening the back door, he bent down so he could reach inside, nearly disappearing from sight before shuffling backward. Sinclair prowled forward, a bad feeling clenching his stomach.

Even before Viker was dragging the unconscious female from the back of the vehicle, Sinclair had caught the musk of a wolf shifter. Then, as the man dumped the female onto the dirt road, Sinclair's agitation became outright horror.

He recognized that particular shifter scent. It was the female who'd been sniffing around the park last night. The one that Rios had told him Tucker was not only intending to claim, but was also helping to track down the bastard responsible for killing her son.

Shit, shit, shit.

Where was Tucker?

Grant made a choked sound, his ruddy face paling at the sight of an unconscious woman with blood trickling from her forehead being dumped at his back gate.

"What have you done?" he rasped, his gaze moving to the unmistakable collar around her neck.

"She broke into my house and tried to attack me."

Muttering under his breath, Grant moved forward to pull open the gate. Then, yanking his handgun from his holster, he moved to stand next to the female, gingerly poking her with the toe of his boot. When she didn't move, he leaned down to shove up the sleeve of her sweater, revealing the brand that was nearly covered by the intricate tattoo on her forearm.

He gave a shake of his head. "A wolf? How did she get out of the compound? And what the hell would she be doing in your house?"

Viker hunched his shoulders. "She's the mother of the kid that died."

Grant took a hasty step backward. "Are you fucking kidding me? How did she find you?"

"The animals are smarter than you give them credit for," the man muttered. "I've tried to warn you."

Grant gave a shake of his head and stepped back to study Viker with open suspicion.

"If she truly attacked you, then why are you still alive?"

Viker's gaze flicked down to the unconscious female before returning to Grant. Sinclair didn't need to see the sly little smile to recognize that the man was about to play his ace in the hole.

"Because first she was trying to convince me to admit that I'd been hired by the SAU to murder her son," he said, deliberately pausing to give his next words extra weight. "It's clearly a political ploy by the shifters to destroy the agency."

Sinclair felt a flicker of admiration. Clever female. If Viker had truly been hired to kill an innocent child, then he would be priceless to the Unseen. If they could actually prove...

His distracted thoughts were sharply interrupted as Grant poked a finger in the center of Viker's chest.

"Why did you bring her here?" he demanded. "She has to be destroyed."

Sinclair tensed, ready to strike. Dammit. The last thing he wanted was to expose himself, not when they were so close. But he couldn't stand there and watch them murder Tucker's female.

"Wait." Viker stepped between Grant and the unconscious woman. "I have a better idea."

Sinclair remained poised to pounce if necessary.

Grant frowned with impatience. "What?"

"She wasn't alone," he admitted.

"There's another shifter on the loose?" Grant rasped in disbelief.

"No. A human," the man reassured him. "He probably helped her escape."

Tucker. It had to be. Sinclair struggled to keep his face devoid of emotion. He didn't think anyone had noticed him inching his way forward, but he hadn't managed to infiltrate the enemy camp by being careless.

Grant looked at his companion in disbelief. "Why didn't you bring him with you?"

Viker slowly smiled, that glitter even more pronounced. "He was...indisposed."

Sinclair's hands curled into fists. If the bastard had hurt Tucker, he was going kill him.

Straight up.

"Just answer the question, Viker," Grant snapped.

"I had to shoot him."

"He's dead?"

"Yeah."

Sinclair's low growl of fury was thankfully drowned out by Grant's loud, inventive string of curses.

"You're sure?" the head of security at last managed to regain enough of his composure to ask.

Indifferent to Grant's seething anger, Viker smiled with smug satisfaction.

"I shot him in the heart, and he fell to the ground bleeding like a stuck pig," he said. "What more proof do you need?"

Sinclair felt a sharp stab of relief. No one wanted to be shot. It hurt like a bitch. But a bullet was usually only lethal to the very young, or the very old. Even if Tucker had been hit in the heart.

There was a very good chance that he was swiftly healing.

Grant was far less pleased with his friend's explanation.

"And you just left his body in your house that's rented by the SAU?" he asked, his voice rising to a shrill pitch. "Are you a complete moron?"

Viker's brows snapped together, a dangerous flush staining his unshaven cheeks.

"I happen to have a brilliant plan if you'll just shut up and listen."

In the blink of an eye, the head of security had his gun pointed at the intruder.

Viker may be unstable, but Grant was a ruthless bully who enjoyed causing pain.

"Do you think I won't shoot you?" he asked.

Sane enough to realize he'd crossed a dangerous line, Viker lifted in hands in a gesture of peace.

"Sorry. Please, hear me out."

Grant slowly lowered his gun. "This had better be good."

Viker folded his arms over his chest, once again looking smugly pleased with himself.

"Markham is always searching for a way to prove that the shifters are rabid animals who will devour us all if we don't keep them penned in cages," he said.

Grant sent a hurried glance around as if making sure

there was no one loitering in the area. It was supposed to be a big secret that the SAU deliberately exaggerated—and sometimes outright lied—about the shifters and the danger they posed to civilization.

Reassured that no damage had been done, Grant returned his attention to Viker.

"So?"

"Take a couple of the dogs to my house and let them chew on the body," he ridiculously proposed. "Then we can take some photos and post them on the Internet. It won't be long until we have a full-fledged panic."

Sinclair swallowed a choked sound of disbelief. The man was either stupid or delusional. Grant appeared to share his opinion as he gave an irritated shake of his head.

"The authorities won't be fooled by a few dog bites on a dead body."

Sinclair abruptly stepped forward, knowing he had to take command of the situation.

Eventually, Tweedledee and Tweedledum would end their squabbling. Once that happened, there was a very real possibility that Grant would insist on killing the female shifter.

Sinclair had to make sure that there was a reason to keep her alive.

"Then do your own autopsy before they can get their hands on the corpse," he broke into the conversation, moving until he'd stepped through the gate to stand beside the female stretched across the road.

If worse came to worst, he was going to grab her and make a run for it.

Thankfully, both men were the type that preferred to be given orders they could carry out without having to use their brains.

They eagerly latched onto Sinclair's proposition to salvage the situation before Markham returned and had them both thrown in a cell.

"He's right," Viker said. "Once it's done, we can give out any results we want."

Grant scowled, but he gave a slow nod of his head. "Fine." He glanced at Sinclair. "Get the doctor."

Sinclair leaned down. "I'll take the female to the pens first."

"No." Grant reached out to grasp Sinclair's arm and yanked him backward. "I'll take her myself."

Sinclair's wolf snarled and snapped inside him, and he was forced to turn his head to keep the idiots from seeing the animal glowing in his eyes.

"Wait," Viker snapped, moving to block Grant from the female.

Sinclair turned back in time to see the head of security tighten his hand on his gun. No doubt he was fighting the urge to shoot the bastard.

"What?"

"I'm not handing her over until we negotiate my price," he warned.

"Name it," Grant snapped.

"I want to be reinstated."

"Impossible."

Viker narrowed his pale eyes, the stench of his desperation tainting the air.

"That's up to Markham," he told Grant. "He's the Director."

"I know who the hell the Director is," Grant snapped, "But I'm in charge of the guards."

Unable to argue the point, Viker tilted his chin to a stubborn angle.

"Then give me a job behind a desk."

Grant frowned as if confused by the man's insistence. "You get a paycheck each month, not to mention the fact that we pay for your rent. Why work?"

"I'm trapped in hell. You try being stuck in that house day after day with nothing to do and no one to talk to." Flecks of foam edged the corners of Viker's mouth. "I want out. One way or another."

Sinclair arched a brow. The warning was clear. Either Grant gave Viker what he wanted, or the man was going to tell his story to the authorities.

Shit. If only Sinclair could rescue the shifter and capture Viker...

"I'm sure a position can be arranged," Grant ground out between clenched teeth. "Maybe overseas."

"I was thinking Vegas." Viker pressed his luck, making Sinclair wonder how he'd managed to live for so long.

He was, quite simply, the sort of man that needed to be gagged for his own safety.

Grant hesitated, then with obvious reluctance, gave a stiff nod of his head.

"I'll see that it's taken care of."

Viker stepped back, spreading his arms wide. "Then she's all yours."

Sinclair parted his lips to once again suggest he take charge of the female, only to snap them shut when Grant gestured toward the guardhouse. Two uniformed soldiers came running.

Shit.

If he insisted that he be allowed to stay with the female, it would only put her at greater risk. For now, Grant seemed willing to leave her alive. He had to trust they could get her out before the head of security changed his mind.

And he had a crazy idea of how they were going to do that.

"You." Turning to Sinclair, Grant nodded toward a Jeep that was parked next to the gate. "Get the doctor."

Sinclair gave a nod and hurried to jump into the vehicle.

The first thing he had to do was track Tucker down.

A polar bear shifter on the hunt for his mate would be...catastrophic.

Tucker groaned as he slowly regained consciousness.

He felt sluggish, as if he'd spent the night drinking his way through a barrel of whiskey. It wouldn't be the first time. But he thought he'd outgrown his occasional need to join his friends in a night of drunken mayhem.

Forcing his eyes open, his puzzlement only deepened.

What the hell? He was in a house. A *human's* house.

Unnerved, he planted his hands on the nasty carpet and shoved himself into a seated position. It was only when he glanced down to see the blood staining his shirt that the memories came flooding back.

Nicole.

In one fluid movement, he was on his feet and racing through the house. Seconds later, he was back in the living room. She was gone. And worse, he could detect the faint scent of her blood.

Fury burned away the lingering lethargy that came with the intense amount of energy he'd used to heal his wound. Thankfully, however, it hadn't completely destroyed his ability to use his brain.

Which was the only reason he managed to contain himself long enough to leave the house and drive to the outskirts of town before he shifted into his animal form.

There was nothing that attracted attention like a massive polar bear running through the streets of Broomfield.

Once shifted, Tucker loped his way through the wildlife refuge before heading north.

He had no way of knowing exactly where Ian Viker

would take Nicole, but Tucker was betting that he would be headed to the SAU headquarters.

Otherwise...

No. He wasn't going to let himself even consider the possibility that the bastard may have disappeared with his female. Not if he wanted to stay sane.

Intent on reaching the headquarters, he ignored the wolf that was suddenly running at his side. He didn't have time to explain things to his Alpha.

Right now, nothing mattered but finding Nicole.

Sinclair bared his teeth in warning then nipped at Tucker's haunch. Still, Tucker refused to slow. It wasn't until Sinclair had actually rammed into his side to knock him into a shallow stream that he was forced to halt.

With a shimmer of power, Sinclair was shifting into his human form, glaring at Tucker, who was trying to shake the chilled water from his fur.

"Listen to me," the Alpha commanded, his brows drawing together as Tucker widened his jaws and prepared to attack. "Christ. Do you want to save Nicole or not?"

Those were the only words that saved Sinclair from being sliced to bloody ribbons.

With agonizing pain, Tucker forced himself to shift back to human. It was too soon to make the transition easy, but if Sinclair had information about Nicole, he had to be able to communicate.

Naked and wet, Tucker shivered as he climbed back

onto the road. Not that he gave a shit about the chill in the air.

"Where is she?" he demanded.

Sinclair surveyed Tucker, his piercing gaze moving down to the tender bullet wound that was still visible. Then he answered.

"The SAU headquarters," he said, swiftly moving to block the path as Tucker took a step forward. "Wait."

Tucker bared his fangs. Dammit. He would destroy anything and anyone who tried to get between him and his female. Including his friend.

"Get out of my way," he snarled.

Sinclair refused to budge. Typical Alpha.

"You're going to get her killed if you go charging in there."

Tucker growled in frustration.

He didn't want to acknowledge that Sinclair might have a point. Not if it meant he couldn't rampage his way through the building, killing the humans who'd stolen his future mate.

"What do you suggest?" he snapped, in no mood to be reasonable. "That I leave her there?"

Sinclair's expression hardened, but he refrained from shoving his fist in Tucker's face.

"Of course not. But I don't intend to let you put yourself or your female in danger."

With an effort, Tucker sucked in a deep breath. As much as his animal may want to create a bloodbath, he knew that it might very well endanger Nicole.

Clenching his hands at his side, he tried to clear his mind of his primitive fury.

"You've seen her?" he asked, his voice still edged with lethal anger.

Sinclair gave a slow dip of his head, no doubt preparing to physically try and stop Tucker if necessary.

"Yes."

"Has she been hurt?"

A nerve twitched in Sinclair's jaw. "She's fine."

Tucker quivered, barely capable of leashing his animal. "You're usually a better liar," he told his friend.

Sinclair grimaced before reaching out to place his hand on Tucker's shoulder.

"She'll be fine." His fingers tightened in a silent warning. "As long as you're smart about rescuing her."

Tucker gave a slow dip of his head, accepting that his friend was right. Only then did Sinclair release his grip and take a step back.

"You have a plan?"

"I'm assuming you were the companion who was shot?" Sinclair asked.

Tucker sent his companion a startled glance. How the hell had he known?

"Yeah." He grimaced. He was going to have nightmares for years about how close Viker had come to shooting Nicole. "I got careless."

Sinclair waved aside his pained confession. "They're sending dogs to gnaw on your corpse."

Tucker blinked. Was Sinclair joking? Or was that some sort of code?

"What are you talking about?"

"It doesn't matter," Sinclair muttered. "But when the SAU guards find you gone, they're going to panic."

Well, that made it all as clear as mud.

"You want me to go back so I can be mauled by dogs?" Tucker asked.

"No." Sinclair squared his shoulders. "I need you to be Dr. Tucker. I'll find another body to replace you in the house."

It was the last thing Tucker expected.

His role as a researcher in the SAU labs gave him the perfect opportunity to spy on their enemy, as well as screw with the various results to make sure they were compromised. Amazingly, no one had managed to figure out why they couldn't come up with accurate data on the shifters yet.

He didn't, however, understand how the hell his position was going to help rescue Nicole.

"Why?"

Sinclair's lips twisted. "You're going to do an autopsy on yourself."

Tucker leaned forward, holding his friend's gaze. "This isn't the time to screw with me."

"I wish I was screwing with you." Tucker gave an impatient shake of his head. "Come on. You need to get dressed so we can get to headquarters."

"And then what?"

Sinclair glanced in the direction of the SAU facility. "I think I know how we can get your female out."

18

Nicole swallowed a groan as she battled her way back to reality. A part of her wanted to stay floating in the peaceful darkness. She already knew that there was going to be a world of pain waiting for her.

But the one thing she'd never been was a coward, and with grim determination, she forced her eyes open.

She grimaced, not particularly surprised to discover she was lying on a hard, cement floor. Or even the fact that she seemed to be in some sort of cramped cell with a heavy, metal door.

Viker had made it clear even before he'd kicked her in the head that he intended to use her as some sort of 'get out of jail free' card. He wanted forgiveness from the SAU, and he stupidly assumed she could be his bargaining chip.

With a low groan at the pain that throbbed behind her right eye, she shoved herself to a sitting position. She was healing, but the kick had been vicious enough that it would have killed a human. She was lucky that her eyes weren't swollen shut.

Giving her head time to stop spinning, she scooted toward the front of the cell and grasped the handle of the door. She didn't think they would have been kind enough to leave it unlocked, but it gave her something to hold on to as she pulled herself to her feet.

Leaning against the cold steel, she pressed her face against the small window. She frowned as a shadow passed by. Someone was approaching.

"Hello?" she called out. "Is anyone there?"

There was a click as the lock was tumbled, and then the door was pressed open, knocking Nicole backward.

A tall, lean male with long, black hair stepped into the cell, his blue eyes cold with warning.

"Don't say a word," he commanded in low tones.

Nicole frowned, puzzled by the faintly familiar scent. "Who are you?"

He stepped toward her. "You're going to have to trust me."

Yeah, right. Her gaze dipped down to the uniform that belonged to the SAU. She'd rather trust a rattlesnake.

"Why should I?" she demanded, her back straight and her chin tilted to a proud angle.

His lips parted, but before he could speak, there was the unmistakable sound of footsteps. He had sent her a warning glance before he was stepping to the side to let a man with a broad face and buzzed head stroll through the open door.

Another guard. Only this one had an arrogant swagger that assured Nicole he was the one in charge.

"You again," he drawled, jaw tight with annoyance as he glanced at the man standing beside her.

"Hello, Grant."

"I'm getting tired of finding you in places you don't belong, Sinclair."

Nicole stiffened, barely suppressing her gasp of surprise.

Sinclair was the guard who'd helped Soren escape. And Tucker's Alpha.

He had to be here to help her.

Or at least that was the hope she was going to cling to.

Sinclair shrugged. "I'm just carrying out orders, sir."

Grant's brows snapped together, clearly not liking the answer. "Whose orders?"

"Dr. Tucker's."

Again Nicole struggled to hide her reaction. Was he talking about *her* Tucker? He'd told her that he was a healer, but she hadn't realized that he actually worked at the facility.

No doubt he hadn't told her because he knew she would be terrified. He was obviously placing himself in constant danger. After all, each time he entered the headquarters, the risk of being exposed and destroyed was high.

The older man tried to hide his flare of relief. "He's here?"

"Yep. In the lab."

"So why would he send you down to the pens?"

Sinclair didn't hesitate.

"He wasn't entirely convinced that we could fool the authorities if they demanded to see the body after the autopsy," he said smoothly.

Autopsy? Nicole frowned. Had someone died? Or...

Her distracted thoughts were brought to a sharp end as Grant released a string of curses.

"I knew it would never work. We need to get rid of the evidence." Reaching for his gun, he pulled it out of his holster, his gaze locking on Nicole. "Starting with her."

Oh, shit.

Her breath locked in her lungs. There was a flat coldness in the man's eyes. She didn't doubt for a second that he would kill her and dump her without an ounce of regret.

"No." Sinclair took a subtle step to the side, half blocking her from the man's icy glare. "Doc Tucker came up with a better suggestion."

There was a tense hesitation, as if Grant were debating whether to give in to his impulse to kill his prisoner, or listen to what Sinclair had to say.

At long last, his gaze moved to his fellow guard. "What's the suggestion?"

Sinclair took another step, making sure he was positioned so Grant would have to go through him to get to Nicole.

Any other time she might have been offended. She

wasn't a female who hid behind a male. But at the moment, she was still weak from the blow to her head, and not at all opposed to having a bit of shielding.

"Why use dogs to bite the dead body when we have the real thing right here?" Sinclair said.

Nicole grimaced. Okay. Now there was not only a dead body, but they also intended to have dogs bite it? Were they sick?

Her unease only deepened as both men studied her with unwavering interest.

"We've never been able to force them to shift into their animals," the older guard said at last, his gaze skimming up and down her tense body. "Hell, I've beaten more than one to death trying to force them."

Nicole felt a blast of heat from Sinclair, but clearly accustomed to hiding his hatred for his enemies, the Alpha managed to give a nonchalant lift of his shoulder.

"The Doc claims that he's found a drug that will force them to shift whether they want to or not," he said, reaching out to grasp Nicole's arm in what must have looked like a punishing grip.

Nicole, however, understood that it was meant as a caution for her to keep her mouth shut. Not that she needed the warning. If Sinclair and Tucker had a plan to get her out of the facility, she would keep her lips zipped and locked.

"Drug?" Grant looked as confused as Nicole felt. "I've never heard of any drug."

"It's still in the testing phase," Sinclair smoothly lied. And it was a lie. Nicole could smell it. "But it's worth a try."

Unable to sense that he was being manipulated, the guard frowned at Nicole.

"That still doesn't mean we can force it to bite."

Nicole clenched her teeth. *It*? She wasn't even a female? She was an it?

Sinclair gave another squeeze to her arm as he answered. "Get an animal mad enough, and it'll attack."

On cue, Nicole allowed her fangs to lengthen as she released a loud, dramatic growl.

Instantly, Grant backed away. "Shit," he breathed. "Fine, we'll give it a try," he muttered. "I'll call the guards who went to get the body-"

"I already took care of it," Sinclair interrupted. "Doc wanted me to have them bring the stiff straight to the lab."

Instantly, Grant was bristling with outrage.

"Who the fuck does he think he is?" he snapped. "I'm in charge of the division while Markham is gone."

"He's a nerd," Sinclair soothed. "They think they own the damned place."

"Yeah, well, I can teach him who's in charge," the guard muttered.

"Okay." Sinclair kept ahold of Nicole's arm with one hand while he reached into his front pocket with his other. "Do you want the body put back in the house?"

Grant's bluster abruptly collapsed at Sinclair's easy capitulation.

Clearly he was a man who wanted to pretend like he was in charge, without actually needing to make decisions.

"Christ, no." Shoving the gun back in its holster, he ran a shaky hand over his buzzed hair. "What a disaster."

"The Doc seems confident that this will work," Sinclair murmured, his voice soft and persuasive. Nicole felt a stab of admiration. No wonder this male was Alpha. He was capable of using the human's greatest weakness to his advantage. "And if it does, then Markham will have the ammunition he needs to keep D.C. off his back."

Hunger flickered in the man's eyes as if he craved his employer's approval.

"True." He squared his shoulders. "Take her to the lab."

Sinclair gave her a tug, leading her past Grant and out the door of the cell.

"What about Viker?" he asked as they crossed a large room that was lined with steel cells and several cages in the center of the cement floor.

Her wolf snarled in fury at the memory of the man who'd murdered her son and had then shot Tucker.

The bastard.

Hurrying to walk a step ahead of Sinclair, Grant sent him an impatient glance.

"What *about* Viker?" Grant demanded.

"I thought he might want to know about the change in plans," Sinclair drawled, firmly pulling Nicole closer to his side.

No doubt he could sense her wolf's restless fury.

Grant made a sound of disgust, pulling out a key card to wave it in front of an electronic reader. Instantly, the hidden elevator doors slid open.

They all stepped in, and Grant gave another wave of his card to close the doors. Then, leaning forward, he stabbed the button that would take them to the third floor.

"Viker is a mistake that should have been dealt with seven years ago," Grant admitted, his expression hard. "For now, he's in my office waiting for me to set up his transfer."

Nicole didn't know what the hell they were talking about, but she wasn't surprised that Viker had managed to make enemies of his own people. He was a nasty, spineless creep.

Sinclair released a short laugh. "I assume he isn't going to Vegas?"

"Hell, no." Grant's lips twisted. "As soon as we're sure we can pass off the body as a shifter attack, I'm going to make sure he heads straight to his well-deserved retirement."

Ah. So that was it. They intended to make it look like she'd attacked someone. But if it wasn't Viker, then who was she supposed to bite?

The doors of the elevators slid open, and Sinclair shoved her forward.

"I'll take the wolf to the lab," he told Grant, urging her down the corridor.

"Wait." Grant hurried to catch up with them, seeming to realize he was being dismissed. "I'll go with you."

Sinclair's fingers tightened on her arm, but his expression remained unconcerned.

"It could take awhile before the drug works," he said.

"I don't care. I won't have any more decisions made without me," Grant retorted in petulant tones. "It's my ass on the line."

"Whatever."

In silence, they walked down the corridor until they reached the end door. Sinclair leaned forward to open it, jerking her over the threshold and into the large lab.

Nicole had a brief impression of white tiles and shiny stainless steel equipment with lights bright enough to blind her. But her attention was consumed by the large, beautiful male who was standing next to a metal gurney.

Tucker. Thank God.

Something painful eased within her. She hadn't allowed herself to even consider the possibility that he might be dead. It was too unbearable. But there had been a nagging fear he may be seriously injured.

Now she eagerly allowed her gaze to run over his muscular body that was covered by a pair of scrubs and a white lab coat before moving to his beautiful face that had a healthy color.

There was nothing to indicate that he'd been shot in the chest just...hmm.

She frowned. She didn't know how much time had passed.

Stepping forward, Tucker pointed toward the gurney, his

face carefully devoid of emotion. Nicole, however, could catch the scent of his fury.

"Put her on the table."

Nicole pretended to struggle even as she held Tucker's gaze. He was hanging on to his composure by a thread. The last thing she wanted was to give him a reason to snap.

Sinclair easily lifted her onto the table, pressing her down as Tucker moved to attach a heavy chain to her collar. Just like an animal being manacled.

Then, leaning to the side, he grabbed a syringe that was filled with a clear liquid. He turned so that the watching Grant couldn't see his expression as he slid the needle into her arm, injecting her with what she hoped was some sort of placebo.

He didn't have to say anything out loud. He was telling her with his eyes to follow his lead.

Perhaps sensing that there was something going on between them, Grant moved forward to stand beside the gurney, his brow furrowed.

"So tell me about this drug," he commanded, "and why I wasn't informed that you were using it."

Tucker stepped back, tossing the syringe onto a tray next to him.

"It was Talbot's secret project," he told the guard. "None of us knew about it until we found it in his private files."

"Typical." Grant gave a shake of his head. "That traitor better hope he's dead. If I get my hands on him, I can guarantee he's going to wish the animals had gotten to him first."

Ignoring the man's tirade, Nicole kept her attention locked on Tucker. She had to go on faith that she was following the silent clues he was giving her.

So when he gave a small dip of his head, she didn't hesitate.

With a surge of power, she shifted into her wolf. Agonized pleasure exploded through her, but she barely waited until she was fully transformed before she was surging forward to snap her jaws directly in Grant's face.

The guard gave a loud squeal of terror, knocking over the table behind him as he leaped out of the way of her fangs.

"Holy shit," Grant breathed, his hand raised to his neck.

Tucker moved to stand at Grant's side, his expression concerned even as his eyes urged her to continue her frantic howls while her claws scratched loudly against the metal table.

"I was afraid of this," Tucker murmured.

Grant sent him a horrified glance. "Afraid of what?"

"The side effects of a drug-induced shift seem to make them more aggressive," he lied with the same ease as Sinclair, his expression suitably somber. "And much stronger," he added for good measure. "Like a human on PCP."

Grant shuddered, licking his lips as his gaze returned to Nicole, who strained at the chain holding her captive.

"Why the hell didn't you warn me?"

Tucker sent him a baffled glance as if astonished the

guard wasn't fascinated by Nicole's response to the supposed drug.

"You can leave if you want," he offered in condescending tones. "I can let you know when we're done."

Grant wavered. He obviously wanted to be far away from the crazed wolf. But on the other hand, he probably couldn't stand the thought of someone thinking he was a coward.

At last he managed to stiffen his spine, although Nicole didn't miss the way he took another step backward.

"I'm staying," he snapped. "Where the hell are those idiots with the body?"

Abruptly, Sinclair stepped forward, positioning himself next to the gurney.

"I'll give them a call," he offered, pulling his cell phone from his pocket and lifting it to his ear.

Not exactly sure what was coming, Nicole assumed that she was supposed to continue with her act of a crazed wolf. She gave another lunge, making the chain snap in protest.

Grant flinched, glancing toward Tucker. "Are you sure those restraints will hold?"

Tucker pretended to consider for a long moment. "Maybe I should just double check. Sometimes the latch can come loose," he at last murmured.

With hesitant steps, Tucker inched forward, approaching her from the opposite side of the gurney as Sinclair. Almost as if he wanted to make sure they were framing her. Then, reaching out his hand, he gave the chain a small tug.

Instantly, Nicole felt the latch release at the same time he gave a low command.

"Go for his throat," he breathed so softly only a shifter could catch the words. "Trust me."

Never doubting Tucker for one second, Nicole widened her jaws. The second she felt him drop the chain, she leaped off the gurney straight at the guard.

Grant screamed, holding his hands over his face as her fangs skimmed his throat.

"Fuck." He fell backward, pissing his pants as Nicole loomed above him. "Shoot the bitch. Shoot her."

Not entirely sure what to expect, Nicole didn't have to fake her loud yelp of pain as something small and hard was shot into her side. Not a bullet. Maybe birdshot? Whatever it was, it hurt like a bitch. Two more slammed into her side and she tumbled to the side, feeling blood trickle through her fur.

Instantly, Tucker was kneeling at her side, his fingers touching her neck even as he whispered in her ear.

"Play dead."

TUCKER BREATHED a sigh of relief as Nicole allowed her eyes to slide shut, her body going limp beneath his fingers.

He'd nearly had a heart attack when Grant entered the

lab. They'd depended on the ability to explain the plan to Nicole before calling for the head of security to join them.

Thankfully Tucker's chosen mate was as brilliant as she was beautiful.

She'd played her role to perfection.

Now he glanced up to watch as Sinclair holstered the gun he'd just fired and helped the guard to his feet. The Alpha's lips twisted at the sight of the human's flushed face and wet trousers.

"That dog almost killed me," Grant breathed in shock, struggling to stay upright.

"You don't have to worry," Tucker said, continuing to kneel at Nicole's side. "She's not going to be attacking anyone again."

"How bad?" Grant demanded.

"Dead."

"What?" Grant's brows snapped together. "Bullets can't kill a full-grown shifter."

Tucker was prepared for the argument. It was the same one that he'd made to Sinclair when his Alpha had first proposed the wild, dangerous plan.

"I think it might be a combination of the drugs mixed with the trauma of her injuries," he said, the pronouncement filled with authority. It was amazing how easy it was to convince people to believe him just by his tone of voice. "Her heart stopped."

As hoped, Grant turned away instead of trying to determine for himself whether or not Nicole was truly dead.

"What a clusterfuck," he muttered, the air thick with the stench of his fear. "Markham is going to go ballistic."

On cue, Sinclair moved to stand at his side. Not going so far as to put an arm around his shoulder, but sublimely letting him think that they were in this mess together.

"Not if we get this cleaned up before he gets back," he offered in sympathetic tones.

Grant stilled, a hopeful expression easing his tight expression. "You think I can keep this a secret?"

"Naw." Sinclair gave a shake of his head. "But you can blame it on Viker. He was the one who dumped the shifter on your doorstep and put the SAU in danger by killing a human."

Grant gave a hesitant nod. "I suppose that's true."

Sinclair swiftly tried to press his advantage. "Doc can dispose of the shifter while I make sure that Viker disappears."

Of course, Grant couldn't simply agree.

That would be too easy.

"No," the head of security abruptly muttered, digging in his heels. "Tucker can get rid of the wolf. You go find the guards and help them bury the human someplace it can't be found," he commanded Sinclair. "I'm putting Viker in the pens just in case someone in authority gets wind of this mess. We'll need a patsy to pay for this shit."

Sinclair frowned. "But-"

"Go," Grant snapped, his nerves clearly rubbed raw.

Tucker didn't hesitate. He understood the worth of

having Viker in their hands to reveal the truth of the SAU, but right now, all he cared about was getting his mate out of the facility.

Scooping Nicole into his arms, Tucker rose to his feet, careful to pretend to stagger beneath her weight. Then, making a straight path to the door, he headed toward the waiting elevator. Less than ten minutes later, they were in the underground parking lot.

Striding to where they'd left his SUV out of sight of the security cameras, he opened the passenger door and laid Nicole across the seat. Then, making sure his body blocked any curious passersby, he reached out to run his fingers through her tawny fur.

"Are you okay?" he demanded in low tones.

There was a swirl of magic as Nicole painfully changed back to her human form, her hair tangled and her eyes still haunted as she rubbed the large bruises that marred the side of her torso.

"Those bullets hurt," she groused, allowing him to wrap his lab coat around her naked body. "Couldn't you have found a less painful way to get me out?"

Neither of them jumped when Sinclair appeared to stand next to Tucker, his lean face unrepentant.

"Not if you want to be with your mate," he drawled.

Nicole stilled, a fragile flare of hope shimmering to life in her hazel eyes.

"What are you talking about?"

Sinclair leaned against the car door. "As of now, Nicole

Bradley is officially dead. At least as far as the SAU is concerned."

Her lips parted, her gaze moving to Tucker in dazed understanding.

"Dead," she breathed in wonderment.

Sinclair sent her a wicked smile. "Don't worry, I'll contact Holden to let him know you're now a part of the Unseen Pack."

19

Tucker reached out to gently smooth the hair from Nicole's flushed cheek, his heart squeezing with a love that threatened to overwhelm him.

"We'll need to keep a low profile. I think it would be best if we go visit my mother for a few weeks," he murmured, barely daring to breathe until she gave a slow nod of her head.

It was one thing to make plans that included this female as his mate; it was another to actually wait for her to accept that they belonged together.

"Yes," she agreed with a tentative smile.

"Okay." Sinclair slapped him on the back, knowing just how earth-shattering the moment had been. "I'll come up with a cover story for your absence with the SAU."

Leaning down to brush a tender kiss over her forehead, Tucker turned his head to glance at his friend.

"What about you?"

Sinclair wrinkled his nose. "First I need to contact the guards and tell them to return the body to the house."

"I've been wondering about that," Nicole abruptly said, her gaze ricocheting between the two males. "What body are you talking about?"

"You don't want to know," Tucker assured her.

He wasn't sure everyone would understand Sinclair's decision to steal an unclaimed body from the local morgue to leave in Viker's house.

"Hey, I'll have it taken back to the morgue," Sinclair said with a shrug. "No harm, no foul."

Tucker easily dismissed the iffy morality of their decision. As far as he was concerned, nothing mattered but rescuing Nicole.

"Then what?"

"I-"

Sinclair snapped off his words as all three of them caught the scent of a human sneaking through the gloom that had gathered at the end of the parking lot.

Viker.

Obviously the idiot had realized there wasn't going to be any free trips to Vegas.

Tucker stepped away from the vehicle, his ears ringing and his mind clouding with a red mist of fury.

Almost as if sensing that predators were watching him, Viker slowly turned, his face paling at the sight of Tucker prowling forward.

"You." Viker stumbled backward. "You're alive."

Tucker growled low in his throat, lunging forward.

"Shit," a male voice said from behind him. "Tucker, no."

Tucker was nearly on top of Viker when Sinclair leaped in front of him.

"Stop," he commanded, in full Alpha-mode.

Tucker skidded to a halt, his fangs elongated as he snarled in frustration.

Sinclair held up his hand. "Yeah, I get you want to taste his blood, but we can use him," he tried to soothe. "You can eat him later."

Viker was pressed against a cement pillar, his eyes wide with shock as his gaze flitted from Tucker's elongated fangs to Sinclair's eyes that glowed with the power of his wolf.

"You're shifters," he breathed in horror.

Sinclair slowly moved to stand at Tucker's side, staring at the cringing Viker with a critical eye.

"He's not very bright, is he?"

Tucker trembled with the effort to keep his bear leashed. "He works for the SAU, how smart could he be?"

Suddenly, Nicole was pressed close against his side, her arm wrapped around his waist. Instantly, the trembling halted. Just the warm scent of her musk was enough to ease the animal clawing inside him.

"If someone gets to eat him, it should be me," she said, glaring down at the man with searing hatred.

"She has a point," Tucker told his friend.

"Agreed," Sinclair said. "But first I intend to use him to

prove that the SAU is made up of a bunch of unscrupulous bastards who've lied to the public for years."

Viker shook his head in panic.

"I won't do it," he said in a shrill voice. "Not unless you swear I won't be harmed."

"Fine." Sinclair took a step forward. "Do you want to go back inside and be shot in the head by Grant? Or would you prefer to be eaten by the lovely Nicole."

"I..." Viker's words faded away. He was trapped between a rock and a hard place.

Sinclair grabbed him by the chin, squeezing hard enough to crack his jawbone.

"Choose."

"I'll talk. I swear," the man abruptly sobbed. "I'll tell you everything I know about Markham and the SAU."

Sinclair patted his cheek. "Good boy." Grabbing Viker by the front of his shirt, the Unseen Alpha sent Tucker a small smile. "Enjoy your honeymoon, but don't forget you belong with the Pack." He glanced toward Nicole. "Both of you."

With obvious enjoyment, Sinclair headed toward a nearby Jeep, hauling the crying Viker behind him.

Wrapping his arm around Nicole's shoulders, Tucker steered her back to the SAU, sensing her tension.

"Someday soon, babe," he murmured, knowing how hard it must be for her to allow Viker to slip from her grasp. She'd spent seven years plotting his death. "I promise."

Reaching the vehicle, she climbed into the passenger

seat. "If he can help expose the SAU, that's the best revenge I can imagine."

Tucker studied her in surprise. "You sound as if you mean that."

"I do." She lifted her hand to lay her palm against his cheek, her eyes soft with love. "I've lived in the past long enough. It's time to start living for my future."

Tucker was fairly certain that his heart was about to explode with happiness.

THREE DAYS LATER, Nicole stared in the mirror of the bathroom. It was the only mirror in the small cabin she shared with Tucker.

Built near Tucker's mother's home, it was a simple structure without many modern amenities, but Nicole had never been happier.

Not only was she free of the compound, but she also adored Tucker's mother, who'd been careful to give the newly mated couple plenty of time to be alone.

And, of course, there was Tucker.

Her beautiful, powerful, loyal bear.

Almost as if she'd conjured him with her thoughts, there was a sharp knock on the door.

"Nicole," he called through the thick wood.

"What?"

"Are you ever coming out?" Turning, she pulled open

the door. Warily, he stepped into the tiny room, his broad shoulders barely fitting. "You've been in here so long I was worried about you."

She grimaced. She'd lost track of time. But who could blame her?

When Tucker had insisted this morning that they get rid of the collar before they returned to civilization, she'd had no idea how emotional it would be for her.

"I've never been without my collar." She lifted her hand to touch her bare throat. "It feels..."

"Yes?" he prompted, as her words trailed away.

She allowed a slow smile to curve her lips. "Glorious."

Something that might have been relief, followed by a strange uncertainty, flashed through his dark eyes.

"I have something else glorious."

Her brows arched as she gave a short laugh. They were still in their bathrobes after yet another bout of hot, sweaty lovemaking.

"Good Lord. I didn't know bears were so insatiable," she teased.

He gave an unexpected burst of laughter. "Why, Nicole Bradley. Is sex the only thing on your mind?"

As always, she was dazzled by his beauty. How the hell had she ever managed to capture this sensational creature?

"Me?" she forced herself to protest. "You brought it up."

"I said I have something glorious," he reminded her with open amusement. "You were the one who assumed it meant having your wicked way with my body."

She lifted her hands to slide them in the loose opening of his robe, savoring the feel of his hard muscles beneath her palms.

"It is glorious," she murmured.

"True."

"Shameless." She gave him a light smack. "If you weren't trying to lure me back to bed, then what were you talking about?"

He reached into the pocket of his robe to pull out two silver necklaces.

"This."

Her eyes widened as he held them up so she could see that each chain had a tiny medallion. One was perfectly shaped to resemble a polar bear while the other was designed to look like a wolf.

"Oh, Tucker," she murmured. "They're exquisite."

"I had them custom made by a local artist," he said, his voice oddly gruff. "The Unseen don't share tattoos to celebrate a mating. We exchange amulets." He held up the necklace with the polar bear. "This one is for you. Will you accept this as a gift from me?"

"Yes," she whispered, pure joy flowing through her heart. "Yes, I will." With reverent care, Tucker slid the chain over her head, allowing the amulet to rest between her breasts. Then he handed the second necklace to her. "And this is to mark your claim on me."

Taking the chain, she waited for him to lean down, tugging it over his head until it settled around his thick neck.

Something warm spread through her. A sense of destiny being fulfilled.

"Mine," she said in solemn tones.

He wrapped her in his arms, kissing her with tenderness that made her toes curl.

"Always, and for all eternity," he pledged against her lips.

Nicole leaned her head against his chest, allowing the sound of his steady heartbeat to combine with the peace that settled deep inside her.

She would always mourn the loss of her son, but the pain was tolerable as long as she had this male to help her carry the load.

Pulling back, Tucker led her out of the tiny bathroom. Then, holding hands, they stepped out of the shadows of the house and into the bright sunshine.

Together.

Forever.

A NOTE FROM ALEXANDRA AND CARRIE ANN

We hoped you enjoyed reading **ABANDONED AND UNSEEN**. This is just the start of our dark and gritty Branded Packs series. With more to come, we can't wait to hear what you think. If you enjoyed it and have time, we'd so appreciate a review on Goodreads and where your digital retailer. Every review, no matter how long, helps authors and readers. You won't have to wait long for more in this series! Happy Reading!

The Branded Pack Series:
    Book 1: <u>Stolen and Forgiven</u>
    Book 2: Abandoned and Unseen
    Book 3: Buried and Shadowed

ABOUT CARRIE ANN AND HER BOOKS

Carrie Ann Ryan is the New York Times and USA Today bestselling author of contemporary and paranormal romance. Her works include the Montgomery Ink, Redwood Pack, Talon Pack, and Gallagher Brothers series, which have sold over 2.0 million books worldwide. She started writing while in graduate school for her advanced degree in chemistry and hasn't stopped since. Carrie Ann has written over fifty novels and novellas with more in the works. When she's not writing about bearded tattooed men or alpha wolves that need to find their mates, she's reading as much as she can and exploring the world of baking and gourmet cooking.

www.CarrieAnnRyan.com

Montgomery Ink: Colorado Springs

Book 1: Fallen Ink
Book 2: Restless Ink
Book 2.5: Ashes to Ink
Book 3: Jagged Ink
Book 3.5: Ink by Numbers

The Fractured Connections Series:
A Montgomery Ink Spin Off Series
Book 1: Breaking Without You
Book 2: Shouldn't Have You
Book 3: Falling With You

The Montgomery Ink: Boulder Series:
Book 1: Wrapped in Ink

The Less Than Series:
A Montgomery Ink Spin Off Series
Book 1: Breathless With Her
Book 2: Reckless With You

The Elements of Five Series:
Book 1: From Breath and Ruin
Book 2: From Flame and Ash

Montgomery Ink:
Book 0.5: Ink Inspired
Book 0.6: Ink Reunited
Book 1: Delicate Ink

Book 1.5: Forever Ink

Book 2: Tempting Boundaries

Book 3: Harder than Words

Book 4: Written in Ink

Book 4.5: Hidden Ink

Book 5: Ink Enduring

Book 6: Ink Exposed

Book 6.5: Adoring Ink

Book 6.6: Love, Honor, & Ink

Book 7: Inked Expressions

Book 7.3: Dropout

Book 7.5: Executive Ink

Book 8: Inked Memories

Book 8.5: Inked Nights

Book 8.7: Second Chance Ink

The Gallagher Brothers Series:

A Montgomery Ink Spin Off Series

Book 1: Love Restored

Book 2: Passion Restored

Book 3: Hope Restored

The Whiskey and Lies Series:

A Montgomery Ink Spin Off Series

Book 1: Whiskey Secrets

Book 2: Whiskey Reveals

Book 3: Whiskey Undone

The Talon Pack:

Book 1: Tattered Loyalties

Book 2: <u>An Alpha's Choice</u>

Book 3: Mated in Mist

Book 4: Wolf Betrayed

Book 5: Fractured Silence

Book 6: Destiny Disgraced

Book 7: Eternal Mourning

Book 8: Strength Enduring

Book 9: Forever Broken

Redwood Pack Series:

Book 1: An Alpha's Path

Book 2: A Taste for a Mate

Book 3: Trinity Bound

Redwood Pack Box Set (Contains Books 1-3)

Book 3.5: A Night Away

Book 4: Enforcer's Redemption

Book 4.5: Blurred Expectations

Book 4.7: Forgiveness

Book 5: Shattered Emotions

Book 6: Hidden Destiny

Book 6.5: A Beta's Haven

Book 7: Fighting Fate

Book 7.5: Loving the Omega

Book 7.7: The Hunted Heart

Book 8: Wicked Wolf

The Complete Redwood Pack Box Set (Contains Books

1-7.7)

The Branded Pack Series:
  (Written with Alexandra Ivy)
  Book 1: Stolen and Forgiven
  Book 2: Abandoned and Unseen
  Book 3: Buried and Shadowed

Dante's Circle Series:
  Book 1: Dust of My Wings
  Book 2: Her Warriors' Three Wishes
  Book 3: An Unlucky Moon
  The Dante's Circle Box Set (Contains Books 1-3)
  Book 3.5: His Choice
  Book 4: Tangled Innocence
  Book 5: Fierce Enchantment
  Book 6: An Immortal's Song
  Book 7: Prowled Darkness
  The Complete Dante's Circle Series (Contains Books
1-7)

Holiday, Montana Series:
  Book 1: Charmed Spirits
  Book 2: Santa's Executive
  Book 3: Finding Abigail
  The Holiday, Montana Box Set (Contains Books 1-3)
  Book 4: Her Lucky Love
  Book 5: Dreams of Ivory

The Complete Holiday, Montana Box Set (Contains Books 1-5)

The Happy Ever After Series:
Flame and Ink
Ink Ever After

Single Title:
Finally Found You

ABOUT ALEXANDRA AND HER BOOKS

Alexandra Ivy is a *New York Times* and *USA Today* best-selling author of the Guardians of Eternity, as well as the Sentinels, Dragons of Eternity and ARES series. After majoring in theatre she decided she prefers to bring her characters to life on paper rather than stage. She lives in Missouri with her family. Visit her website at alexandraivy.com.

Guardians Of Eternity
When Darkness Ends
Embrace the Darkness
Darkness Everlasting
Darkness Revealed
Darkness Unleashed
Beyond the Darkness
Devoured by Darkness

Yours for Eternity

Darkness Eternal

Supernatural

Bound by Darkness

The Real Housewives of Vampire County

Fear the Darkness

Levet

Darkness Avenged

Hunt the Darkness

A Very Levet Christmas

When Darkness Ends

Masters Of Seduction

Masters Of Seduction Volume One

Masters Of Seduction Two:

Ruthless: House of Zanthe

Reckless: House Of Furia

Ares Series

Kill Without Mercy

Bayou Heat Series

Bayou Heat Collection One

Bayou Heat Collection Two

Raphael/Parish

Bayon/Jean Baptiste

Talon/Xavior

Bayou Noel

Sebastian/Aristide
Lian/Roch
Hakan/Severin
Angel/Hiss
Michel/Striker

Branded Packs
Stolen And Forgiven
Abandoned And Unessn

Dragons Of Eternity
Burned By Darkness

Sentinels:
Out of Control
Born in Blood
Blood Assassin